"Delicious examples of the pulp genre, written by women and reissued by the Feminist Press. . . . When people think of pulp they generally conjure up male authors like Dashiell Hammett or Raymond Chandler. But in its heyday women were there alongside the men, sometimes subverting its conventions. . . . These stories moved fast, and they were a guilty pleasure, easy to hide under the mattress." —*New York Times*

"Femmes Fatales offers a window on another time and place. . . . It offers little details, daily dreams often overlooked by history books. . . . Pulp, after all, is about pushing limits, about revealing the edges of a culture we can't quite see. Especially at a moment when society seems to be turning backwards this series may help tell us who we are." —*Los Angeles Times*

"Fascinating pulp. . . . A lot of fun to read as well as illuminating sociologically." —**"Fresh Air," National Public Radio**

"Fun sells and these books are both historic and fun. To me, the Femmes Fatales series is genius. It's the kind of thing that's going to take the Feminist Press to the end of the century." —Susan Post, owner, BookWoman, in *Publishers Weekly*

"Each of these rediscovered gems boasts its original, gleefully provocative cover art, with dayglow titles, snappy-looking 'broads' and hilarious taglines. . . . Plus, they've got spiffy new commentaries putting each title into modern perspective. . . . This isn't pulp, it's got permanence." —Caroline Leavitt, *Boston Globe*

"The feminist perspective does give these works an undeniable extra dimension." —*Village Voice*

"When we think of the pulp era today, we tend mainly to think of crime novels and male authors. The folks at the Feminist Press are here to set us straight. Their new reprint series . . . celebrates a group of female authors [who] . . . deserve a second look. . . . Damn were they cool." —Bill Ott, *Booklist*

BEDELIA

FEMMES FATALES
WOMEN WRITE PULP

BEDELIA

VERA CASPARY

AFTERWORD BY A.B. EMRYS

THE FEMINIST PRESS
AT THE CITY UNIVERSITY OF NEW YORK
NEW YORK

Published by the Feminist Press at the City University of New York
The Graduate Center, 365 Fifth Avenue, Suite 5406
New York, NY 10016, www.feministpress.org

First Feminist Press Edition, 2005

10 09 08 07 06 05   5 4 3 2 1

Published in 1946 by Sun Dial Press Reprint Edition, by special arrangement with
Houghton Mifflin Company.

Library of Congress Cataloging-in-Publication Data

Caspary, Vera, 1904-1987
  Bedelia / by Vera Caspary ; afterword by A.B. Emrys.
      p. cm. — (Femmes fatales : women write pulp)
  ISBN-13: 978-1-55861-507-6 (pbk.)
  ISBN-10: 1-55861-507-5 (pbk.)
  ISBN-13: 978-1-55861-508-3 (cloth)
  ISBN-10: 1-55861-508-3 (cloth)
  1. Women murderers—Fiction. 2. Serial murderers—Fiction. 3. Husbands—
Crimes against—Fiction. I. Title. II. Series.
  PS3505.A842B43 2006
  813'.52—dc22

                                            2005029368

Text design by Dayna Navaro
Printed on acid-free paper by Transcontinental Printing
Printed in Canada

Women write pulp? In today's popular image of pulp fiction, it seems like a contradiction in terms. This image has been shaped by the noir revival of the past decade—by reprints of classics by Jim Thompson and best-sellers by neo-noir writer James Ellroy, the re-release of classic film noir on video, and the revisioning of the form by Quentin Tarantino. Fans of such works would be hard pressed to name a woman pulp author, or even a character who isn't a dangerous femme fatale.

But women did write pulp, in large numbers and in all the classic pulp fiction genres, from hard-boiled noirs to breathless romances to edgy science fiction and taboo lesbian pulps. And while employing the conventions of each genre, women brought a different, gendered perspective to these forms. These women writers of pulp were often ahead of their male counterparts in confronting received ideas about gender, race, and class, and exploring forbidden territories that were hidden from view off the typed page. They were an important part of a literary phenomenon, grounded in its particular time and place, that had a powerful impact on American popular culture in the middle of the twentieth century, and continue to exert their influence today.

Pulp fiction encompasses a broader array of works, and occupies a more complex place in the literary, social, and commercial culture of its era, than the handful of contemporary revivals and tributes to pulp suggest. Pulp emerged as an alternative format for books in the 1930s, building on the popularity of pulp magazines, which flourished from the 1920s to the 1940s, and drawing on traditions established by the dime novel of the nineteenth and early twentieth centuries. The dime novel had developed the Western, the romance, the sleuth story, and the adventure story as genres, with narratives geared largely to young readers. Pulp magazines, needing to compete with early motion pictures and connect with an urban audience, offered similar stories with an edge. Grouping fiction or believe-it-or-not fact under themes like crime, horror, and adventure, magazines such as *Black Mask*, *Weird Tales*, and *Dime Adventure* demonstrated the existence of a market for inexpensive and provocative teen and adult reading matter. The move to book-length narratives provided an expanded scope for a voracious literature rooted in American popular culture, reflective of American obsessions, and willing to explore American underworlds.

Printed on wood-grain, or pulp, paper, and cheaply bound, the books were markedly different from hardbound, cloth editions. These first modern paperbacks served different purposes—entertainment, thrill, or introduction to "serious culture"—and were presumably read differently. Books intended for the pulp lists were undoubtedly produced differently, with less time given to the writing, and less money and status accruing to the authors. As pulp publishers grew in number (Fawcett, Pocketbook, Bantam, Ace, Signet, Dell), economic patterns emerged in the treatment of authors and texts: pulp authors often received one-time payment (no royalties); editors focused on keeping books short, tight, and engrossing; and author identity was often submerged behind the publisher's pulp brand-name and the lurid cover art that sold the books. Some pulp authors used pseudonyms to conceal an everyday identity behind a more saleable one, often of the opposite gender. Georgina Ann Randolph Craig (1908-1957) wrote prolifically as Craig Rice. Some used several names, each evocative of a genre they wrote in: Velma Young (1913-1997) published lesbian pulp under the name Valerie Taylor, poetry as Nacella Young, and romances as Francine Davenport. Eventually some contemporary authors emerged as brands themselves: a Faith Baldwin romance was a predictable product.

At the same time, classics and contemporary best-sellers were reincarnated as pulp, as the format absorbed and repositioned literature that might otherwise have been inaccessible to working-class readers. Pulp publishers seem to have selected classic fiction with an eye to class politics, favoring, for example, the French Revolution and Dickens. They tended to present science as an arena where good old-fashioned ingenuity and stick-to-itiveness win the day. The life of Marie Curie was a pulp hit. When classics were reprinted as pulp—for example, *The Count of Monte Cristo* or *The Origin of Species*—author identity might move to the fore on covers and in descriptive copy, but in becoming pulp the works acquired a popular aura and gravitated into pulp genres such as adventure and romance. Again, when new titles like William Faulkner's *Sanctuary* or Mary McCarthy's *The Company She Keeps* were issued in pulp editions, the cover art planted the works firmly in pulp categories: ruined woman, Southern variety; the many adventures and many men of a fast city girl. The genre, more than the author's name, was the selling point.

As the stories in pulp magazines were marketed by themes, so book-length tales were distinctively packaged by genre—Dell used a red heart to mark its romance line, for instance. Over time there were Westerns, science fiction, romance, mystery, crime/noir, and various others to choose from. Genres were to a large extent gendered. Crime/noir, for instance, focused on a masculine world of detectives, crooks, femmes fatales (positioned as foils to men), corruption, and violence, all described in hardboiled prose. Romance focused on women's problems around courtship, virginity, marriage, motherhood, and careers, earnestly or coyly described. Since genres were gendered, the assumption has been that men wrote and read crime/noir and women wrote and read romances. In fact, this assumption proves largely false.

Because genre tended to rely on formulaic treatments, it was not difficult for writers to learn the ingredients that make up noir or, for that matter, how to write a lesbian love scene. The fact that authorial name and persona were rarely linked to real-life identity further permitted writers to explore transgender, or transgenre, writing. In so doing, they might self-consciously accentuate the gendered elements of a given genre, sometimes approximating parody, or they might attempt to regender a genre—for instance, writing a Western that foregrounds a romance. These freedoms, combined with the willingness of pulp publishers to buy work from anyone with the skill to write, meant that women had the chance to write in modes that were typically considered antithetical to them, and to explore gender across all genres. Leigh Brackett (1915-1978), a premier woman author of pulp, wrote hard-boiled crime books, science fiction, and Westerns, in addition to scripting sharp repartee for Bogart and Bacall in *The Big Sleep*. (Director Howard Hawks hired her on the basis of her novel *No Good from a Corpse*—assuming she was a man, as did many of her fans.) Other women authors wrote whodunnit mysteries with girl heroines, science fiction battles of the sexes, and romances which start with a Reno divorce. Women wrote from male perspectives, narrating from inside the head of a serial killer, a PI, or a small-town pharmacist who knows all the town dirt. They also wrote from places where women weren't supposed to go.

Notoriously, pulp explored U.S. subcultures, which generated their own pulp subgenres. Where 1930s and 1940s pulp depicted gangster life and small-town chicanery, 1950s and 1960s pulp turned its attention, often with a pseudo-anthropological lens, to juvenile delinquents, lesbians (far more than gay men), and beatniks, introducing its readers to such settings as reform schools, women's prisons, and "dangerous" places like Greenwich Village. These books exploited subcultures as suggestive settings for sexuality and nonconformism, often focusing on trangsressive women or "bad girls": consider *Farm Hussy* and *Shack Baby* (two of a surprisingly large group in the highly specific rural white trash slut subgenre), *Reefer Girl* (and its competitor, *Marijuana Girl*), *Women's Barracks*, *Reform School Girl*, and *Hippie Harlot*. Other books posited menaces present in the heart of middle-class life: *Suburbia: Jungle of Sex*, *Shadow on the Hearth*.

While a strengthened Hayes Code sanitized movies in 1934, and "legitimate" publishers fought legal battles in order to get *Ulysses* and *Lady Chatterley's Lover* past the censors, pulp fiction, selling at 25 cents a book at newsstands, gas stations, and bus terminals, explored the taboo without provoking public outcry, or even dialogue. (Notably, though, pulp avoided the four-letter words that marked works like *Ulysses*, deploying instead hip street lingo to refer to sex, drink and drugs, and guns.) As famed lesbian pulp author Anne Bannon has noted, this "benign neglect pro vided a much-needed veil behind which we writers could work in peace." Pulp offered readers interracial romances during the segregation era, and blacklisted leftists encoded class struggle between pulp covers. The neglect by censors and critics had to do with the transience of pulp.

Circulating in a manner that matched the increasing mobility of American culture, pulps rarely adorned libraries, private or public. Small, slim, and ultimately disposable, they were meant for the road, or for easy access at home. They could be read furtively, in between household chores or during a lunch break. When finished, they could be left in a train compartment or casually stashed in a work shed. Publishers increasingly emphasized ease of consumption in the packaging of pulp: Ace produced "Ace Doubles," two titles reverse-bound together, so that the reader had only to flip the book over to enjoy a second colorful cover and enticing story; Bantam produced "L.A.s," specially sized to be sold from vending machines, the product's name evoking the mecca of the automobile and interstate highway culture; Fawcett launched a book club for its Gold Medal line, promising home delivery of four new sensational Gold Medal titles a month. To join, one cut out a coupon at the back of a Gold Medal book – clearly the need to damage a pulp volume would not impede owners from acting on the special offer.

The mass appeal of pulp proved uncontainable by print. Characters and stories that originated in pulp soon found their way onto radio airwaves (e.g., *The Shadow*); onto the screen in the form of pre-Code sizzlers, noirs, and adventure films; and into comic books and newspaper comic strips. Through all these media, pulp penetrated to the heart of the American popular imagination (and the popular image of America beyond its borders), shaping as well as reflecting the culture that consumed it.

Far more frequently than has been acknowledged, the source of these American icons, story lines, and genres were women, and often working-class women who put bread on the table by creating imaginary worlds, or by exploring existing but risky or taboo worlds, to fulfill the appetites of readers of both genders. But these writers, and the rich variety of work they produced, are today nearly invisible, despite the pulp revival of the last decade.

This revival of interest in pulp fiction has repopularized the work of a number of male writers, especially of the hard-boiled variety. The best-remembered pulp authors tend to be not only male, but unapologetically misogynistic as well; pulp icon Jim Thompson's *A Hell of a Woman* and *A Swell-Looking Babe* are not untypical of the titles found on the noir classics recently restored to print.

In fact, it is interesting to note, even in a broader survey of the genres, how many male-authored, and presumably male-directed, pulps were focused on women (remember *Shack Baby* and *Reefer Girl*)—a phenomenon not found in the highbrow literature of the period. Men even wrote a fair number of lesbian pulps. But more often than not, the women in these books are dangerous and predatory as well as irresistible, exploiting men's desire for their own purposes. Or they are wayward women who either come to a bad end, or come to their senses with the help of a man who sets them straight (in the various senses of the word). Some critics have noted that such female characters proliferated in the immediate post-World War II period, when servicemen were returning to a world in which women had occupied, briefly, a powerful position in the workplace and other areas of the public sphere—a world in which the balance between the genders had been irrevocably altered.

In contrast with these bad girls and femmes fatales were the heroines of traditional romance pulps, most of them relentlessly pretty and spunky girls-next-door. They occupied the centers of their own stories, and navigated sometimes complicated social and emotional terrain, but in the end always seemed to get—or be gotten by—their man.

Given this background, and given the strict generic dictates to which all successful pulp writers were subject, did women writing in undeniably male-dominated pulp genres such as crime/noir write differently from their male counterparts? And did women writers of formulaic romances, both heterosexual and lesbian, reveal the genuine conflicts facing real women in their time, and explore the limits of female agency? They could hardly fail to do so.

Relatively little scholarship has been done on pulp fiction; less still on women writers of pulp. It is not possible to speculate on the intentions of women pulp authors, and few would suggest that they were undercover feminists seeking to subvert patriarchal culture by embedding radical messages in cheap popular novels. Yet from a contemporary vantage point, some of their work certainly does seem subversive, regardless of the intention behind it.

Women writers provided the first pulps with happy endings for lesbians: Valerie Taylor's *The Girls in 3-B* is a prime example of this surprisingly revolutionary phenomenon, and further intriguing for its contrast of the different options and obstacles faced by heterosexual and homosexual women in the 1950s (with little doubt as to which looked better to the author). The femme fatale of *In A Lonely Place*, the luscious Laurel Grey, has brains and integrity as well as curves—and in the end, she is not the one who turns out to be deadly. In fact, Dorothy B. Hughes's bold twist on the noir genre can be seen as addressing the crisis in postwar masculinity, with its backlash taken to the furthest extremes. The protagonist of Faith Baldwin's *Skyscraper* is typically pretty and plucky; she longs for domestic bliss and she loves her man. But she also loves the bustle and buzz of the office where she works, the rows of gleaming desks and file cabinets, the sense of being part of the larger, public world of business—and she epitomizes a new kind of heroine in a new kind of romance plot, a career girl with a wider set of choices to negotiate.

These premier books in the Feminist Press's Femmes Fatales series were selected for their bold and sometimes transgressive uses of genre forms, as well as the richness of their social and historical settings and their lively and skillful writing. We also chose books that seemed to have some impact on public consciousness in their time—in these cases, rather inexactly measured by the fact that they crossed over into different, and even more popular, media: Both *In a Lonely Place* and *Skyscraper* were made into films—and astonishingly, *The Girls in 3-B* (properly sanitized of lesbian love) was the basis for a comic strip of the same name that ran in daily newspapers across the country.

In the past three decades, feminist scholars have laid claim to women's popular fiction as a legitimate focus of attention and scholarship, and a rich source of information on women's lives and thought in various eras. (Some scholars have in fact questioned the use—and the uses—of the term *popular fiction*, which seems to have been disproportionately applied to the work of women writers, especially those who wrote "women's books.") The Feminist Press views the Femmes Fatales series as an important new initiative in this ongoing work of cultural reclamation. As such, it is also a natural expression of the Press's overall mission to ensure that women's voices are fully represented in the public discourse, in the literary "canon," and on bookstore and library shelves.

We leave it to scholars doing groundbreaking new work on women's pulp—including our own afterword writers—to help us fully appreciate all that these works have to offer, both as literary texts and as social documents. And we leave it to our readers to discover for themselves, as we have, all of the entertaining, disturbing, suggestive, and thoroughly fascinating work that can be found behind the juicy covers of women's pulp fiction.

Livia Tenzer, Editorial Director
Jean Casella, Publisher
New York City
May 2003

For I. G.

His wife came into the room and Charlie turned to watch her. She wore a dark-blue velvet dress whose sheath skirt was slit to show her pretty ankles and high-heeled bronze pumps.

The Yule log caught fire. Flames licked the crusty bark. This was a great moment for Charlie. He had cut the log himself and had had it drying in the shed for a whole year. Bedelia, perceiving his pleasure, flashed him a smile and skipped across the Orientals to the love-seat, perched beside him, and rested her head against his shoulder. He took her hand. The Yule log cast its ruddy glow upon them. At this moment, ten minutes after five on December twenty-fifth, 1913, Charlie Horst believed himself the luckiest man in the world.

This was to be his wife's first Christmas in Charlie's house. They had been married in August. She was a tiny creature, lovable as a kitten. Her eyes were lively, dark, and always slightly moist. In contrast with her brunette radiance, Charlie seemed all the more pallid, angular, and restrained.

In the bow window from which the love-seat had been removed stood a tree whose boughs were festooned with tinsel, hung with colored globes and spirals, flannel angels, *paper-maché* reindeer, gingerbread Santa Clauses, cardboard houses, and peppermint canes. Underneath it, instead of the usual glaring white cotton sheet, was an arrangement of fir boughs upon green paper, simulating the floor of the forest. On the dining-room table was another of Bedelia's clever arrangements. The centerpiece of white narcissus seemed actually to be growing out of a bank of holly and laurel leaves.

She had been working for days on the preparations for the party. Platters and trays were heaped with a variety of cakes, and Charlie's grandmother's silver shell dishes were simply loaded with home-made fondant, marzipan, and salted nuts. On the buffet a dozen eggnog cups waited in line, and for those who liked stronger drinks there were the pewter mugs to be filled with Charlie's special hot rum toddy. And besides there was a profusion of salted and spiced delicacies, canapés of *fois gras*, smoked oysters, sardellen butter, anchovies, and thin crackers spread with a delicious paste that Bedelia had made of a combination of cheeses.

Charlie's Christmas present to his wife had been an antique gold ring twisted into a bow knot and set with garnets. She wore it on the fourth finger of her right hand and at intervals held it at arm's length and cocked her head to study the effect. Her hands were plump and dimpled, the fingers tapered to the tips of pointed nails which were polished until they shone like pink gems.

'How my little jackdaw loves finery!' Charlie said. The metaphor was literary. Charlie had never seen a jackdaw. Brought up on English literature, he preferred such allusions to the commoner symbols of his own experience. When he was a small boy his mother had sung:

'Things are seldom what they seem,
Skim milk masquerades as cream,
Jackdaws strut in peacock feathers,
Highlows pass as patent leathers.'

His wife accepted the criticism with her usual grace, curving her red lips and showing her dimples.

'You do really like it?' he asked anxiously.

'Better than platinum and diamonds.'

'Or *pearls*?'

'That was your reason for giving me this, wasn't it?' Bedelia spoke shyly.

'Looks like snow,' Charlie said.

To the west of the house, below the terrace, the river tumbled over great rocks, chattering ceaselessly. Their house was only a little way out of a big manufacturing town, but the country around was too rocky to be worthy cultivating, and the woods and stone-strewn fields were as wild as when the first white settlers had come to Connecticut.

The doorbell rang. Straightening her new apron, Mary ran through the hall. At the door she stiffened, arranged her ruffles and, as she let the guests in, cried, 'Hello, Mr. Johnson. Merry Christmas, Mrs. Johnson.'

Bedelia hurried to greet them. As usual Wells Johnson became awkward in her presence, mumbled a greeting and shifted the gold-sealed, tissue-paper package from one mittened hand to the other. Lucy Johnson took the box from him and handed it to Bedelia.

'Merry Christmas.'

'Oh, you shouldn't have.'

'Wait till you see it before you say anything. You may think I'm crazy.'

'I love presents,' Bedelia said.

'How are you, Charlie-Horse?' said Wells Johnson.

'Never felt better in my life. Let me take your coat.'

Gravely Bedelia studied the size and shape of the package, the neat wrappings and elaborate seals. 'We're not opening anything until all the guests are here.' She placed the Johnsons' gift in a bare space under the tree.

The bell kept on ringing, guests pouring in: greetings and laughter growing louder, the air thickening with the smells of rice powder, toilet water, rum and spices. The heat of the house and the exertion of making and passing drinks made Charlie sweat. Bedelia's ivory-tinted skin continued to look as fresh and cool as the white rose she had pinned in her sash.

The rose had been one of a dozen brought by their new friend and neighbor, Ben Chaney.

'You're too kind,' Bedelia had said, offering Ben both hands and smiling to show her dimples. 'You'll spoil me with all your attentions.'

'Spoil you? Impossible!' Ben said.

Charlie and Ben shook hands.

'Merry Christmas.'

'Eggnog?'

'Oh, Charlie,' Bedelia said, 'you know about Ben and cider brandy.'

Both men laughed. Bedelia had made it sound as if Ben and cider brandy were immortal lovers. As Charlie poured Ben's drink, Bedelia offered a tray of canapés. He selected one spread with the cheese paste.

'You've got Gorgonzola in it,' he said with an air of smugness. 'Now I know you were thinking of me.'

'She thinks of everyone,' Charlie boasted.

At six o'clock the guests had had enough of everything, of food and drink, of greetings, gossip, and examination by the women of holiday garments. Bedelia proposed that they open the gifts. For her this was the party's climax, the moment she had been awaiting like a gay and nervous child.

'Everyone's here but Ellen, and if she can't manage to get here on time, I don't see why everyone else should wait.'

'She's probably been kept at the office.'

'On Christmas?'

'Newspapers are printed on Christmas, you know.'

Bedelia looked around the room anxiously, measuring the temper of her guests. 'All right, dear, we'll wait a little longer.'

Doctor Meyers had overheard. 'If there's a gift for me under the tree, I'd better collect it now. I'm due at the hospital in a little while and I'll have to take Mama home first.'

'Now, Papa,' his wife said, 'what makes you think anybody's giving Christmas presents to an old man like you?'

Bedelia sought Charlie's approval. He saw how much she

wanted to open the packages, and gave in like an indulgent father.

'Open yours first, Bedelia.'

'It wouldn't be fair. I'm the hostess, mine should come last.'

Judge Bennett suggested that they alternate. First a guest would open a package, then Bedelia, then another guest. They voted that Charlie play Santa Claus, read the labels, hand out the packages. This made him self-conscious. There was nothing of the actor about Charlie. But as he saw that his friends were more interested in the gifts than in his playing of the rôle, he became comfortable and even jocose.

Bedelia's prodigality astonished them all. These people were not accustomed to lavish giving. Even the richest, those whose safe-deposit boxes were crammed with New York, New Haven and Hartford Railroad Stock, had been taught to be grateful on Christmas morning for an orange, a pair of mittens, a sock filled with hard candy, a copy of the Bible or Emerson's *Essays*. They had all, of course, brought something to the hostess whose Christmas hospitality demanded some return. But nothing to compare with the gifts she had for them. She had packages for the men as well as for their wives. And such luxurious trifles! All from New York stores! Silk tobacco pouches, monogrammed cigar cases, copper ashtrays, inkstands and blotters mounted in hammered brass, and drinking-cups in leather cases.

Mrs. Bennett, who had brought her hostess three gingham potholders bought in August at a church fair and put away for just such an occasion, computed the cost of Bedelia's generosity. 'We've none of us measured up to your wife's extravagance, Charlie. It's not our habit to be so ostentatious as Westerners.'

'Ostentatious' was not the right word for describing Bedelia's pleasure. She found it as blessed to receive as to give. Ordinarily the tidiest of women, she tore off wrappings recklessly and threw papers and ribbons on the floor. Every present seemed splendid to her, every giver prodigal. Charlie saw pathos in her extraordinary pleasure: the orphan made welcome in the warm-hearted family, the little match girl finally admitted to the toy store.

Lucy Johnson's eyes glittered as Charlie handed Bedelia the parcel with gold seals. Under the tissue paper there was a box painted with Japanese characters.

'Vantine's,' whispered Mrs. Bennett loudly.

Several women nodded. They also recognized the box and were wondering why Lucy had gone to New York for the Horsts' Christmas present.

Bedelia held up the gift for everyone to see. On an ebony board sat three monkeys. One held his paws before his eyes, one sealed his ears, the third his lips. The Judge glanced over his spectacles at Wells Johnson.

'Oh, thank you. They're just what I wanted.' Bedelia kissed Lucy Johnson.

Mrs. Bennett whispered to her husband. The Judge glanced over his spectacles at Wells Johnson. The Danbury Express whistled as it rounded the curve. Several men took out their watches to check the time.

Lucy chattered on. She had bought the three ivory monkeys because they reminded her of Charlie.

'Of me?'

'See no evil, hear no evil, speak no evil. Isn't that Charlie all over? His character. I tell Wells that Charlie has the strongest character of any man I know.'

Wells Johnson moved close to Judge Bennett. From behind his cupped hand he whispered, 'Wanted to show my appreciation. Charlie's given me a lot of business this year.'

'Naturally, with the improvements on his property,' said the Judge, who held the mortgage on the Johnsons' house and felt that he deserved an explanation of their extravagance.

'More than that,' Wells hinted.

Curiosity shone through the Judge's gold-mounted spectacles. But Wells cherished his secret like money in the bank. When the Judge had begun to fidget, Wells said, 'Can't talk about it now. Charlie doesn't like it mentioned with his wife around. She's sensitive.'

The Judge sniffed. 'If he didn't carry insurance she'd have reason to be sensitive.'

Bedelia turned her smile upon them and both men grinned self-consciously. She was different from the other women in the room, like an actress or a foreigner. Not that she was common. For all of her vivacity she was more gentle and refined than any of her guests. She talked less, smiled more, sought friendliness, but fled intimacy.

Charlie was restless. When the doorbell rang, he could not wait for Mary, but rushed off to answer it himself.

Two women stood on the porch. One held out her hand and said, 'Merry Christmas, Charlie.' The other shrieked and threw her arms around him.

Charlie had swung his hand toward Ellen Walker, but the greeting was interrupted by the exuberance of Ellen's companion. Ellen's hand fell limply. She followed Charlie and Abbie Hoffman into the hall.

'This is a surprise,' Charlie told Abbie.

'You old hypocrite, you knew I was coming.'

'Of course he knew,' said Ellen. 'I told him weeks ago that you were spending the holidays with me.'

'I remember,' Charlie said.

'You forgot all about me, you fibber,' and Abbie pecked at Charlie's cheek.

He led them to the first-floor bedroom. Ellen Walker took off her hat without bothering to look in the mirror. She had bought herself a new coat that fall and no one liked it. Too mannish, they said. Ellen was a tall girl, but small of bone, delicately proportioned. Thirty years before she would have been called a beauty, but fashions in women change as drastically as in clothes. The Burne-Jones virgin had given way to the Gibson girl, and nowadays Ellen's face was considered too long, her head too narrow, the pale brown coronet of braids absurdly out of style. There was nothing memorable nor distinctive about her looks. A stranger would have remarked that she seemed calm and honest.

Abbie, on the other hand, wore a costume so striking that her face seemed merely an accessory. Charlie thought she looked like a drawing in a fashion magazine, dashing but one dimensional. Her lynx muff was as large as a suitcase and her hat burdened with such a wealth of feathers that just to look at it made his neck ache. On a black net guimpe she wore a brooch so extravagant that it was obviously set with rhinestones.

'Come along when you've made yourself beautiful,' Charlie said and went off in search of his wife.

Bedelia was waiting in the hall. 'We forgot about Abbie,' she whispered.

'It's my fault. I should have reminded you that she was coming.'

'No, dear, you mustn't blame yourself. You've got more important things on your mind. But we can't neglect Abbie. After our wedding present and the way she entertained us in New York.'

Charlie and Abbie Hoffman were first cousins. She had been a Miss Philbrick, his mother's niece. As representative of his people, she had welcomed his bride when Charlie brought Bedelia from Colorado, waiting on the platform for their train and treating them to an expensive lunch at the Waldorf-Astoria.

'You might explain that you ordered a gift and it hasn't been delivered,' Charlie suggested.

'That wouldn't do at all. There ought to be a package under the tree. Abbie mustn't feel neglected.'

The two girls came out of the guest room. Abbie kissed Bedelia and Ellen offered Charlie's wife her hand. As if this were a reception in a New York mansion, Abbie kept on her hat.

'Affected puss,' muttered Charlie, remembering his mother's phrase for Abbie. He stamped off to the kitchen to make some fresh drinks while Bedelia led the newcomers into the living-room. Most of the guests knew Abbie, who had been born a mile down the road and had lived in town until she married. That was the reason why Charlie could not forgive her for carrying her plumes into the living-room.

From the kitchen he heard laughter and shrieks of greeting. Charlie listened and shuddered. As he shook nutmeg into the eggnog, he rejoiced because his wife was without affectation.

The door swung open. 'You'd better fill the bowl, Charlie. Most of the men are ready for more. And two hot grogs,' Ben Chaney said. 'Need any help?'

Mary turned from her dishpan to stare at Ben. He was not tall, but he was muscular and compactly built. Against the gray paint of the kitchen walls his skin seemed almost swarthy, and his abundant hair, curling like a poet's, was shot with red lights. His eyes were pinpoints of curiosity. All at once, irrelevantly it seemed at the moment, Charlie had a solution to the problem of Abbie's Christmas gift.

'Take this in, will you?' He handed Ben the tray. 'And tell my wife I want to see her. I'll be upstairs.'

Mary sighed as Ben left, carrying the tray as if the punch-bowl were the head of a vanquished enemy. Charlie rushed upstairs to wait in the front bedroom for Bedelia.

She did not come at once and he passed the time by looking at himself in the pier glass. It was tilted in a way that distorted his image, making his head seem too large, his torso too long, his legs stunted. This was absurd. Charlie was one of those lank, stork-legged men who could never put enough weight on his bones. His features were neat but thin, and he was too blandly tinted to be handsome. He compared his amiable pallor with Ben Chaney's rugged darkness and ran his hand regretfully through his thinning hair.

Bedelia had come into the room softly. She stood beside Charlie, the top of her head just reaching his nostrils. They had not grown bored with marriage and still enjoyed seeing themselves as a couple. Bedelia's expression changed suddenly, a look of pain crossed her face and she hurried to straighten the pier glass.

'You looked horrid, Charlie. Your lovely long legs, I couldn't bear to see them so short and queer.'

Charlie caught hold of her and held her close, breathing heavily. His eyes clouded. Bedelia slapped his cheek with light fingers. 'We've got guests downstairs, we'll have to get back to them.'

The twilight had thickened. Bedelia went to the window. Her eyes were fixed on some distant point in the dusk. 'Last Christmas,' she murmured. On the flowered drapes her hands tightened. 'Last Christmas,' she repeated in a blurry voice.

'New Orleans?'

'We picked dark-red roses and put them on the table. We had breakfast on the balcony.'

'Are you sorry to be here, Biddy?'

Her mouth, when it was not smiling, was small and perfect, a doll's mouth. There were times when Charlie felt that he knew nothing about her. All that she had told him of her girlhood and first marriage seemed as unreal as a story in a book. When she related conversations she had had with people she used to know, Charlie could see printed lines, correctly paragraphed and punctuated with quotation marks. At such times he would feel that she was remote, like the heroine of a story, a woman he might dream about but never touch.

'I've had an inspiration,' he said. 'A Christmas gift for Abbie.'

'What is it?' Bedelia asked eagerly.

'The pearl ring.'

Bedelia did not say anything.

'Don't you think it's a good idea?'

'We can't, Charlie.'

'Why not?'

'You said it was cheap and vulgar.'

'On you, dear. But Abbie wears artificial stones.'

Bedelia shook her head.

'Why not?' asked Charlie.

'Your sort of people never wear imitation stones.'

Charlie wondered if she was making fun of him. 'Abbie does, my cousin Abbie. Did you notice that brooch?'

Bedelia shrugged and walked away from her post at the window. She seated herself in a low chair which Charlie's mother had used when she sewed. For this chair, Bedelia had chosen a covering of old rose moiré. The drapes and bedspread were of the same fabric, but otherwise the room was just as it had been when Charlie's mother and father slept in it.

'Let's give Abbie the East Indian bangle,' Bedelia proposed.

Charlie was shocked. 'You can't mean that.'

Charlie had bought Bedelia the bangle while they were on their honeymoon. It was of finely wrought silver, as wide as a cuff and hung with small bells. Charlie, who liked to explore odd neighborhoods and queer shops, had wondered how the bangle had come so far west as Colorado, and because it seemed romantic to him had paid twenty dollars for it. This was too much to spend on a Christmas present for Abbie whom he saw not more than twice a year. Bedelia had paid five dollars for the black pearl ring. It was set in imitation platinum and surrounded by false diamonds.

'The bangle's too big for my arm. Too much bracelet.'

'You didn't say that when I bought it. You thought it very handsome when you tried it on.'

The doll's mouth could be petulant. 'You liked it, Charlie, and wanted me to have it.'

'What I don't see is why you're so obstinate about that cheap ring. Since you say you won't wear it yourself.'

Bedelia sighed.

'Of course, dear, if you want to keep it, I shan't insist on your giving it away. But since you said you'd never wear it again . . .' Charlie waited.

She sat like a penitent child with bowed head and folded hands.

'Unless you want to keep it as a souvenir,' he said bitterly. 'To remind yourself that you've married a prig.'

Bedelia smoothed the sheath of her velvet skirt over her legs, looked at the toe of a bronze slipper. 'We can't give Abbie that ring because I don't have it any more.'

'What!'

'I've given it away. You didn't like to see me wear it. You thought it was vulgar.'

'Why didn't you tell me in the first place? Before I'd lost my temper?'

'You didn't give me a chance.'

She looked at him so innocently that Charlie had to laugh.

'What an inconsistent little creature you are, Biddy. To let me argue and make a fool of myself. I've been a bad-tempered boor. I apologize.'

'Charlie, dear, I was horrid to you, wasn't I? Will you forgive me?'

'Forget it,' he said magnanimously.

'Shall we give Abbie the bangle?'

'Just as you wish.'

'You see,' Bedelia said, trying on the bangle and showing him how it slid up and down on her arm. 'It's much too big. You go down to our guests, dear. It'll look queer if we both stay up here too long. I'll wrap Abbie's gift and, when no one is looking, slip it under the tree.'

Charlie could tell by her smile that Bedelia was pleased with her little scheme. He kissed her and left. She packed the bangle carefully and tied it with a red ribbon so that it should look like her other packages.

Then she went to her dressing-table, opened the jewel-box and took out the ring set with the black pearl. She put it into the velvet box in which she had found her new garnet ring, and hid it in the hall cupboard, making sure that it was well back in the shadows.

She returned to the bedroom on tiptoe, fetched Abbie's gift, straightened the red bow, and hurried down the stairs, her high heels clicking on the treads.

The party was over. Of the guests only Abbie, Ellen, and Ben Chaney remained. Abbie had gone back to the guest room to make a ceremony of removing her plumes, and had dragged Ellen with her. Ben was kneeling before the fire. Bedelia stood beside him, holding a basket filled with crumpled tissue paper and ragged ribbons. They watched silently as all the fine wrappings, the silver and gilt, were sucked into the flames.

When all the papers had been burned and the room was neat again, Bedelia excused herself and hurried to the kitchen. Ben took the chair opposite Charlie's and picked up the latest *Literary Digest*. Just as if he belonged here, Charlie thought for a stabbing moment, but dismissed the notion as ungenerous and picked up the new *Atlantic Monthly*.

In the guest room Ellen was washing her hands at the marble stand behind the screen. When she had finished, she started out of the room.

'Stay and talk to me,' Abbie commanded. She had taken off her hat at last and, as she expressed it, her hair was a perfect bat's nest. 'I have a question to ask you. Who's this Chaney?'

'An artist. He's taken Judge Bennett's house for the winter.'

'The summer house? Up there in the woods? Why?'

'How should I know?'

Abbie's head was bent forward and her hair fell over her face like a dark curtain. From behind the curtain floated her curious voice. 'What kind of artist?'

'He paints.'

'Naturally. But what?'

'Pictures.'

Abbie swung back the curtain of her hair and rolled it over her rat. 'You are annoying. What sort of pictures?'

The contrast with Abbie's rich inflection made Ellen's voice a stingy monotone. 'I don't know.'

'You could use a touch of rouge,' Abbie said. 'Everyone does nowadays. Is he single?'

'I've never heard that he was married.'

'Try some of mine, Nellie.' Abbie nodded toward her gold meshbag. 'It's the newest thing, a dry powder, not nearly so vulgar as paint. Is he a gentleman?'

'You sound like a character by Mrs. Humphry Ward,' Ellen said coldly.

'Oh, do stop trying to be a highbrow. You know very well what I mean. Not a teamster or policeman.' Abbie was at last pleased with her hair. After a long scrutiny of her face in the mirror, she said: 'He puzzles me. Not that I mind a bit of mystery in a man. Bedelia seems to like him, doesn't she?'

'Does she?' Ellen tried to sound indifferent.

Abbie gave her a long look. 'You wouldn't be so dull if you'd dress with some dash. There's nothing so abhorrent to the masculine eye as a plaid silk shirtwaist. It simply shrieks old maid.'

Ellen's fair skin flushed. She liked to think of herself as The Tailored Girl and enjoyed wearing suits and shirtwaists.

Abbie took a round pasteboard box out of her meshbag. 'Use this,' she commanded.

'I'd feel horrible.'

Abbie rubbed the puff over a disk of carmine powder and

thrust it toward Ellen. 'With a single man around, I do think you'd try to make yourself more interesting.'

'I'm not one of your predatory females.'

'You'd be better off if you were.' Abbie was merciless. There was no other way of moving Ellen. 'At least you must let me do your hair over. Nobody wears it that way any more.'

'I do. And, moreover,' Ellen challenged, her back rising, 'nothing in the world could induce me to wear a rat. I think they're filthy and disgusting.'

'Then every fashionable woman is filthy and disgusting.

'Bedclia is stunning and she doesn't wear rats.'

'Bedelia has a style of her own. She can afford to be different. Besides, her hair is dyed and quite conspicuous enough.'

'I don't believe that.'

'Touched-up. I'm very sharp about that sort of thing.'

'But Bedelia wouldn't. She's so natural. Why are you so catty about her, Abbie?'

'Why are you defending her, Nellie?'

'Please don't call me Nellie.'

'Why not? We always used to.'

'I don't like nicknames any more.'

Abbie raised her eyebrows. She knew Ellen too well to go on badgering her. Besides, she had other questions to ask. 'Has he money?'

'Who?'

'Don't play innocent. When a single man comes to a town like this, it's every woman's duty to know the facts.'

Ellen relaxed a little. 'I haven't thought much about it, but he's evidently got some kind of income or he couldn't afford to stay in the country all winter and paint. Besides, he has a machine.'

'Let me warn you, my dear, a machine means nothing. Do you remember when my dear Walter bought the electric? We drove around like millionaires and he'd only paid a small deposit on it. You can buy cars on credit, you know.'

Ellen did not approve of Abbie's lightness in speaking of her ex-husband. New York might take divorce for granted, but Connecticut still spoke of it in whispers.

'He gave Bedelia a dozen white roses,' Abbie remarked.

'He gave Charlie a box of cigars. It's only decent of him to repay their hospitality.'

'You needn't snap at me. I merely observed that he buys extravagant gifts. Not a poor man's habit.' Abbie had finished her hair and restored her complexion. She went behind the screen to wash her hands.

Ellen's voice rose above the running water. 'There's something about him. Would you trust him, Abbie?'

Abbie whirled around, holding her dripping hands before her. 'Why must you be so intense? You behave like the third act of a melodrama. What's wrong with him?'

'What do you think of him? Honestly, I mean, not as a bachelor who seems to have money, but as a human being. Would you trust him?'

'Wouldn't you?'

Ellen came close and looked squarely into her friend's face. In spite of her simplicity and Abbie's affectations, they were the same sort—big, bony, honest New England girls. 'It's as if he wanted something of us here. He's made friends too fast. I know that artists are supposed to be unconventional, but that's not it. His manners are good enough on the surface, but there's something about him that I don't understand. He came here in November knowing no one and now he's everybody's chum. And he's always asking women to have tea with him.'

'You are provincial. In New York no one thinks twice when a man asks a woman for tea. Particularly an artist.'

'He asks so many questions,' Ellen complained.

'You sound as if you'd been out to tea with him yourself.'

'I work. I haven't time to go out for tea, but I've had dinner with him at Jaffney's and he's called a couple of times.'

'Then you're not so indifferent, are you? Dinner, evening calls, and he hasn't talked to you about his painting?'

'He doesn't talk about himself.'

'How strange for a *man*.'

'He's always asking about other people's lives, the most personal questions. About their incomes, whether they're well off or not.'

'Sounds like normal curiosity.'

'Evidently New York's made you forget that we were taught never to mention things like that.'

'You're still a child, Ellen. If I didn't know you so well I'd think your naïveté was a pose. Have you asked Bedelia what she thinks of him?'

Ellen seemed not to have heard.

'You'd never catch her dining with a man and not knowing what sort of pictures he paints. And don't tell me he hasn't asked her to have tea with him.'

'He's often here in the afternoon. Sometimes they walk,' Ellen said quietly. 'Of course Charlie and Bedelia are his closest neighbors except for farmers like the Keeleys or those Polish people up the hill.'

The wind had risen. It screeched through the woods, whined around the corners of the house, set shutters to shivering and rattled window-panes.

'Supper's ready. Bedelia wants to know if you are,' Ben Chaney said. He lounged against the frame of the door as nonchalantly as if the house were his own.

'Where did you get your manners?' Abbie asked. 'Weren't you taught to knock when you come into a room?'

'Not when the door's open.'

Abbie looked at Ellen, who looked away.

The house had been more formal in old Mrs. Horst's day. Charlie had been a considerate son who would not distress his dear mother by criticizing her father's and grandfather's tastes in architecture, but before the flowers were withered on her grave he had unlocked the drawer that contained his plans for remodeling the house. In spite of his modern education, Charlie favored the old New England style of building and was one of the foremost architects in the movement to bring back to fashion the best features of the eighteenth and early nineteenth centuries. Before he left for his holiday in Colorado, he had had all the balconies, tower, and scrollwork decorations removed and the house restored to its original lines. The bow window had been left because it was a pleasant place to sit on sunny afternoons.

He and Bedelia had worked together on the interior decoration. All the wallpapers and upholstery fabrics were her taste. They had had only one quarrel and that because she had refused to discard his mother's good Orientals and use rag rugs in their place.

She had a natural talent for housekeeping. With less fuss than his mother had made with her two servants, Bedelia and the young girl, Mary, kept the house like a pin.

Tonight she had left the centerpiece on the table and used her new Madeira doilies under the plates. Red candles shed light upon the meal. She had cooked the main dish herself. It was a casserole of rice cooked with tomatoes, okra, clams, chicken, pimentos and olives, and flavored with saffron. Charlie was not given any. Mary brought him a bowl of plain boiled rice.

'Dyspepsia,' he confessed.

'You!' cried Abbie.

'It must be his nerves,' Bedelia said. 'He works too hard. You'd think his foreman was a complete ignoramus the way poor Charlie has to run to Bridgeport every day.'

Ellen asked if he had seen the doctor.

'I do wish you'd use your influence, Ellen. I beg and beg and he doesn't pay the slightest attention.'

'Let's talk of pleasanter things,' Charlie said.

But Abbie had a theory. 'He probably got it out West. I hear the food is simply . . .' she could not find the right word and wrung her hands.

'You're wrong,' Charlie said. 'There are some excellent restaurants in Denver, and at the hotel at Colorado Springs they had a French chef.'

'I shouldn't like that,' Abbie sniffed. 'If I went to Colorado, I'd expect bear meat or buffalo.'

'Is this a Western dish?' asked Ellen, helping herself to the rice.

'No, it's a recipe I learned in New Orleans. Jambalaya, they call it. They make it differently, with river shrimps and crabs . . .'

'New Orleans,' Abbie interrupted. 'I thought you came from California. Didn't you tell me Bedelia came from California, Charlie?'

'I was born in California, but I've lived in a lot of places. I lived in New Orleans with my first husband.'

'I've always wanted to go there,' Abbie said. 'They say it's quite civilized. Have you ever seen a Mardi Gras?'

'She's as good as Cable when she describes it,' Charlie boasted. 'Tell them about the French Quarter, dear, and the artists.'

'Everything?'

'Why not? Are you ashamed?'

'No, you know I'm not.' Bedelia gave Charlie a warm smile and a small confidential wink. 'But these people are different, dear. They've always been conventional and protected . . .'

'Oh, do tell us,' squealed Abbie.

'It's not that sort of thing,' Bedelia said, laughing. 'You see, we were very poor. Most people would rather confess to sin than poverty, wouldn't they? My husband and I were desperately poor. We lived in a garret.' She was gleeful, as if there was something romantic about it. 'He was an artist, you see, of good family, but his people wanted him to go into business and wouldn't give him an allowance. We didn't mind being poor because we were young and healthy and in love, and most of our friends were poor artists, too. We had lots of fun, and if we could afford a chicken and a bottle of Italian claret, we'd give a party.' Her voice, fading off at the end, hinted at richer memories.

Ellen found the jambalaya too filling. She wished she had not helped herself so greedily.

'If he'd lived, he'd have been an important artist, perhaps a great one. When he died, one of the dealers bought up all his paintings as an investment, knowing they'd be valuable some day.'

'Why, Biddy!'

'What's wrong, honey?'

'You told me his friends had sold them at auction.'

'Oh, oh!' said Bedelia, watching Charlie through her eye-lashes, 'yes, of course, dear, they sold them at auction because the dealer wanted to give me only a hundred dollars. So they made him auction them off instead of just buying them from me, and I got over two hundred. You remember, Charlie, I told you.' Without waiting for Charlie's reply, she went on, 'We're going there some day to see if we can buy back some of the paintings. I'm no critic, but lots of people thought he had great promise.'

Ben had been watching Bedelia. When he caught Ellen staring at him, he picked up his fork and began to eat again.

'You sold them all!' Abbie cried. 'You didn't keep any for yourself?'

'I didn't have a dollar to my name,' Bedelia confessed, quite without shame or embarrassment.

'What did your husband die of?'

'Appendicitis. It was too late when they took him to the hospital.'

She stated the fact simply, and smiled at each of her guests in turn as if to tell them she was not asking for sympathy. Then Abbie asked Ben Chaney if he knew the work of a painter named Cochran.

'The first name was Raoul,' Charlie said.

'Raoul Cochran, that's a queer one.'

'His mother was French,' Bedelia explained. 'Raoul wasn't known in artistic circles in the North. He'd sold a few pictures, but only to people down South.'

Although Ellen disapproved of personal questions, she found herself asking, 'If you were so terribly poor, how did you happen to be spending the summer at Colorado Springs?'

'It does sound extravagant, doesn't it? But I was ill, the shock, you know, it had affected my nervous system, and I lost my baby.' She offered this with appropriate modesty, avoiding their faces. 'The doctor said I must have a change of scene. The mountains had always appealed to me and since the Springs is a health resort, I decided to go there. Of course, I couldn't consider stopping at the hotel. I lived in a cheap boarding-house, but it wasn't uncomfortable and I had a magnificent view.'

'When I met her,' Charlie said, 'she had given herself two more weeks at the Springs. She was hoping to find work in a Denver department store. She had come to the hotel that day to see the fashions.'

'I hadn't had anything new for years and I thought that if I applied for work in a good shop, I'd better show that I knew something about style. So, before I started altering my clothes, I decided to go and see what the Easterners were wearing.'

'She came to look at the millinery, but she found me more interesting.'

'Now, dearest'—Bedelia flirted with her husband enchantingly—'you know that you pursued me relentlessly.'

'From the lounge where you'd been drinking tea to the porch where you'd gone to look at the view. Is that relentless?'

Bedelia included the guests in the next chapter of her story. 'How indifferent he tried to look when he chose the chair next to mine. He put on such a show of not noticing me that I knew precisely why he was interested in the view from that particular angle. It took him almost ten minutes to work up courage to ask if I wasn't awed by the grandeur of the Rockies.'

'We might never have met except for an accident. I'd planned to pack-trip with some fellows at the hotel and one of them sprained his ankle and we postponed it, fortunately for me.'

'And I,' Bedelia added, 'had almost decided not to go to the hotel because the cheapest tea was fifty cents.'

'The gods were good to us.'

Charlie's pious pleasure and Bedelia's nervous assurance annoyed Ellen. The conversation seemed natural, like a scene rehearsed over and over again by zealous actors. Ellen complained, because there was nothing else to fuss about, that the room was too hot. 'It's unbearable in here. Can't you do something about it, Charlie?'

Ellen's shrillness punctured Charlie's mood. He had dwelt for those few seconds among the peaks of the Rockies. He went grumpily to turn off the heat. Then he fetched his mother's white Angora shawl for Bedelia.

'How thoughtful, darling. But you needn't have bothered. I'm not cold.'

'We must be careful now,' Charlie said.

Bedelia shook her head at him.

'What's the matter? Is Bedelia pregnant?' asked Abbie, who had begun to affect frankness.

'Excuse me,' Bedelia said, pushed back her chair and hurried through the swinging door to the kitchen.

'Did I say something wrong?' Abbie was puzzled. 'What's so shocking about babies when people are married?'

'Do hush up,' Ellen said.

'She's sensitive since she lost the last one,' Charlie explained. 'She thinks talking about it might bring bad luck.'

'Superstition,' snapped Ellen, and immediately regretted it.

'We can't all be as rational as you, my dear.'

Bedelia returned with the coffee urn. Mary followed with cups, cream and sugar.

Every time Bedelia served coffee, she enjoyed turning the little faucet on the urn, and Charlie enjoyed the sight of her childlike pleasure. She was composed again, gracious, the charming hostess. 'How do you take your coffee, cream and sugar, one lump or two?'

'How nice you look today, Mary. Is that a new cap?' Ben asked as the young hired girl brought his coffee.

Mary blushed and giggled as she hurried through the swinging door.

'You mustn't tease her, please, Ben,' whispered Bedelia.

'I wasn't teasing. She's a pretty girl.'

'He was driving into town one Thursday when she was off,' Bedelia said, 'so he drove her in and treated her to an ice cream soda. She's got a crush on him.'

'Mary, too,' thought Ellen, and glanced toward Abbie to see if she recognized this as another of his predatory habits.

But Abbie was flirting with Ben. 'That doesn't leave us older girls much chance, does it? With Mary's simple ways and unspoiled charms, she must be very pleasing to a city man.'

'I haven't shown her my paintings.'

'Why should you?' asked Bedelia.

'I've asked you to look at them, haven't I? You're the sort of woman who couldn't possibly have had tea with a man and not know how he paints.'

Ellen tried to look unconcerned, but Abbie accepted the challenge boldly. 'What sort of painting do you do? Don't tell me you're a Cubist.'

'Won't you come and see? A friend of mine is coming

from the West on Friday and Charlie and Bedelia are having dinner at my house. Perhaps you girls would come, too.'

'We'd adore it,' Abbie said before Ellen had time to offer an excuse.

Afterward they sat in the small room, which had been known for generations as 'your father's father's study,' but which Bedelia had renamed 'Charlie's den.' Bedelia brought ashtrays for the men.

'Probably you'd like one, too,' she said, and fetched another for Abbie.

'How did you know my guilty secret?'

'You smoked at the Waldorf-Astoria that day.'

'Were you shocked?' sighed Abbie hopefully.

Bedelia shook her head. 'When you've lived among artists, you're not shocked at anything. But at the Waldorf the people look so respectable that I was afraid you were making yourself conspicuous.'

Charlie had filled his pipe and was about to light it when he remembered Ben's gift. He ought to smoke a cigar, he reflected bitterly, to show appreciation. As he went off to fetch the box, he wondered at Ben's thoughtlessness. They had often smoked together and Ben ought to have noticed that Charlie cared only for his pipes.

He offered the box to Ben, who took a cigar. 'That's funny,' Charlie said to himself, 'he doesn't usually smoke them either.' Both men clipped off the ends and lit their cigars as if it were a regular habit. The room became fragrant with the smoke.

'I do admire your taste, Mr. Chaney,' Abbie said. 'Those are grand cigars.'

'How do you know?' Ellen asked tartly.

'If you'd been with men as much as I have, dear, you'd recognize the smell of a good cigar. Isn't that so, Bedelia?'

'I don't know.'

Bedelia sat stiffly at the edge of the leather chair, her

hands gripping the arms. All the color had been drained out of her face and her eyes had become wary. They were all looking at her and she seemed to be defending herself against their scrutiny. Her voice, giving answer to Abbie's simple question, had been sharp with terror.

Bedelia came into the bedroom. Her hair hung loose. She had on a dressing-gown of royal blue challis printed with roses and bound in rose-colored ribbon. Charlie caught her in his arms and embraced her.

'You smell so sweet. Your skin smells like honey.'

Every night Charlie said this and every night Bedelia told him it was her skin cream. The repetition did not irritate them, for they were still in love. Every trifling incident had either the charm or novelty or the comfort of repetition.

'Well, Christmas is over,' she said.

'A happy Christmas?'

'Yes, honey, of course.'

The blank look had come into her eyes again, and Charlie wondered if she was thinking of Raoul Cochran. There were times when he suffered keen jealousy, when he resented all of her past life, every experience which had not been shared with him, even the poverty and mourning.

'Better than last Christmas?'

Bedelia's eyes met Charlie's and she said reproachfully, 'Oh, darling.'

'Last Christmas you were picking roses.' She was silent and he went on. 'My mother was ill,' as though he were angry with Bedelia for having enjoyed the sunshine and flowers and breakfast on a balcony while his mother suffered in this very room.

His wife untied the rose-colored ribbons and took off her challis robe. Her corset cover and knickers were of fine muslin, lightly starched, embroidered and run through with pink ribbons. Charlie watched with pleasure as she untied the bows and whisked the tiny pearl buttons through minute button-holes.

As she loosened her corset laces, she walked toward the pier glass. 'I am getting stouter.'

'It's becoming.'

'In a few weeks I'll begin to show.'

Charlie went off to the bathroom to wash and brush his teeth. When he came back, Bedelia was in bed, her hair loose on the pillow. His mother had always braided her hair at night, straining it back from a bulging forehead. For Charlie his wife's careless tresses had sluttish charm. Her bedroom slippers were of rose-colored satin with French heels. Her pretty lingerie, ribbons, embroideries, and scents delighted him. Before his marriage he had, like every other respectable man, known a number of wantons. Looking back upon their seductions and comparing them with his wife, he saw the poor girls as drab unfortunates. Bedelia's easy pleasure gave to the marriage bed a fillip of naughtiness without which no man of Puritan conscience could have been satisfied.

He was glad he had married a widow.

'Charlie!' She sat upright and let the covers fall off her shoulders. Her voice was dramatic. 'Your powder! Did you bring the water, dear?'

'I've forgotten. It doesn't matter, though, I feel all right.'

She insisted that he take the powder. For his own good, of course. He had eaten a lot of rich food that day and drunk a number of eggnogs.

'All right,' he agreed, sighing and stamping off to the bath-room. The show of martyrdom was purely a show. Bedelia's concerning herself about his health and keeping powders for him in the drawer of her bed table pleased Charlie. This was another proof of her love for him. The powders, folded into blue packets, were highly effective. She had learned the rem-edy when she worked as a companion to a dyspeptic old lady.

'Drink it fast and you won't notice the taste,' she always

said when she had spilled the powder into the water for him.

As he took off his bathrobe, Bedelia regarded him with shining eyes. 'You're so tall,' she said, and height became the final standard of perfection. 'And your shoulders are so broad. You've got a wonderful physique. That's what your mother always said. "My boy's not handsome, but he has a fine physique." '

Charlie could not enjoy the full flavor of flattery without disturbing the ghosts of Puritan ancestors. To appease certain stones in the churchyard and the bronze figure of Colonel Nathaniel Philbrick, mounted on a bronze horse in the small park downtown, he pretended to reject her admiration. 'Too skinny,' he remarked. Having made this gesture, he laughed and asked, 'Who told you that? Abbie?'

'Ellen.'

'Oh!' Charlie said.

'Poor Ellen.'

'Why do you pity her?' Charlie asked as he got into bed. 'It's no disgrace for a woman to earn her own living.'

'It's not that. I've worked myself. That's not what I mean.'

'I must say I admire Ellen's spunk. She's doing well on the paper. I met Clarence Green the other day and he told me she had real aptitude.'

'I'm sorry for Ellen because she's still head over heels about you.'

Charlie tried to deny it. Bedelia insisted. Ellen's every look betrayed a broken heart. 'But she's a wonderful girl, Charlie. She tries her best to like me.'

Charlie lay on his side, studying the tilt of his wife's nose and the jolly curve of her cheek. He felt unworthy because he was loved by this enchanting woman and by Ellen, who had a strong character. What had he ever done to deserve all this devotion? He was no Casanova. If he had been hard, compact, and wiry, with abundant dark hair and a knowing smile, he might have accepted feminine admiration more complacently. But he was thirty-three, bland, undistinguished, going bald. The virtues he admitted were commonplace, the virtues of an unromantic man, the sort of fellow to whom a nickname like Charlie-Horse could stick for life.

'What about the light?' he asked. 'Shall we try again?'

Without hesitation she replied, 'Yes, dear. We'll really do it tonight.'

He stretched out his hand and the room was dark. Immediately a great variety of noises took possession of the night. The river seemed to rush along faster and to chatter in a wilder voice, the wind wailed, the black walnut tapped its skinny fingers against the windows, the shutters trembled, the panes rattled, and there were scratchings as if an army of rats had invaded the attic.

'Oh, Charlie!'

He took his wife in his arms, held her tightly, whispering. 'There's nothing to be afraid of, Biddy. You've got me here, my sweetheart, my wife, my little love, you're not alone now. I'm here, nothing can hurt you.'

Her tears wet his cheek.

'Just what is it you're afraid of?'

'I don't know,' she wailed.

They clung together. Bedelia made herself small against him so that he should feel larger and more necessary to the frail woman. Since their wedding night he had been trying to help her overcome her fear of the dark. Her efforts had been so sincere that Charlie had never scolded nor laughed at her for the childishness of her terror.

Gradually her fears had infected him. In the daytime he resolved to harden himself against contagion, but when she clung to him in the dark, weeping, his mind filled with strange fancies and his flesh, under the blankets, chilled. By day his wife was earthy, a woman who loved her home and had a genuine talent for housekeeping. In the dark she seemed entirely another sort of creature, female but sinister, a woman whose face Charlie had never seen. It was absurd for a man of his intelligence to let himself be affected by these vague and formless fantasies, and he tried to account for his wife's fear of the dark by remembering that she had lived a hard life. Her girlhood, according to stories she had told them in bits and pieces, a stray anecdote here, a fragment there, had been shadowed by so much misfortune and disillusionment that it would have been abnormal for her to not have been affected.

None of this reasoning did Charlie the slightest bit of good. The phantoms dwelt there as if they had taken a lease on the bedroom. On every other night he had weakened and relit the lamp. Tonight he was determined to prove by disapproval that the darkness was uninhabited and that he had no sympathy for her irrational, childish terror.

A quivering scream rent the blackness. Cold winds swept through the room. Under the blankets Charlie shivered.

'What is it, my dear?'

Bedelia did not scream again. After a silence so deep that she seemed to have stopped breathing, she whispered faintly, 'Did you see it, too?'

'See what?' His voice was crisp with disapproval.

'It moved.'

'Now, Biddy,' he began firmly and coolly.

'I saw it.'

'There's nothing in the room, nothing. It's absurd for you . . .'

She pulled away from him and moved to the edge of the bed. The pillow did not muffle her sobs nor the mattress conceal her tremors. The house was filled, quite suddenly, with small terrible sounds that were closer and more distinct than the rushing fury of the river.

In the ten seconds that passed while he stretched his hand toward the lamp, Charlie recognized the weakness that had taken possession of his spirit. It was a newly acquired quality.

Charlie Philbrick Horst had been trained in the school that rejects idle whims and scorns self-indulgence. Morally sloth-ful, his mother would have called his present state of mind.

'Oh, Charlie-Horse, darling, how good and sweet you are,' his wife murmured. Her tremors ceased. She relaxed, wiped away tears with the back of her hand, offered a dimpled smile.

A small, rose-shaded lamp shed light in a cone on the car-pet. The furniture of the bedroom was real and assuring. Above the mantel hung a portrait of Charlie's mother at sev-enteen, a righteous girl, her lips tight with disapproval. And Charlie would assure himself that it was for his wife's sake that he had turned on the light. In this way he was arming himself against the scorn of weakness which had been planted in him by his mother.

'You're so good, so thoughtful, such an unusual man,' Bedelia whispered. 'I'm sure it's hard for you to sleep with the light on.'

'Oh, I'm getting used to it,' Charlie answered, feeling the chill thaw out of his cramped limbs as he studied his wife's fair flesh, rosy lips, and the curves of her cheeks.

2

'Why do you live way up here in the woods? Are you hiding?'

That was Abbie and typical of her insolence. Ellen, disap-proving, moved to the farthest corner of the cold leather seat. Ben had driven into town to fetch the girls and was driving them back to his house in his automobile. Their coast collars were turned up, their hands tucked in their muffs, their legs wrapped in blankets, but it was still torture to be speeding at twenty miles an hour through the country.

Abbie's question echoed the curiosity of the town. Why had a man who could afford to live comfortably close to his neigh-bors chosen a house in the woods for the winter months?

'A whim,' Ben said. 'I wanted to try painting the country at its bleakest.'

'But why do you have to live in the wilderness? Couldn't you paint just as well if you were comfortable?'

'I couldn't be more comfortable in a New York apartment,' Ben said. And this was true. While his house was remote, it was a modern building equipped with a hot-air furnace and a water-heater. He rented it from Judge Bennett, whose family lived there from the first of June until the Tuesday after Labor Day when they moved back to their stone mansion opposite the Walkers' house in the center of town.

'I'm off the main road,' Ben continued, 'but with a machine it doesn't make much difference. Asa Keeley and his boys cut my wood and do my errands.'

'Besides,' put in Ellen, 'he's got Charlie and Bedelia as his closest neighbors.'

'And Hannah,' Ben said, smiling. 'Hannah gives me more news of the town than I get from your paper, Miss Walker.'

'I believe that,' Ellen said. 'And I hope you've no skeletons in your closet, because Hannah and her sisters and cousins work in half the houses in town, and no secret's safe. She's cousin of the Horsts' Mary, you know?'

'Don't I, though? I'm sure that whenever a button pops off my shirt, Hannah phones Mary about it. Mary tells Bedelia and the next time I see her, I catch her counting buttons.' Ben paused while the girls laughed. 'The latest is the cigar situation,' he confided. 'It seems that Bedelia threw away the cigars I gave Charlie for Christmas. She'd heard somewhere that cigars are bad for the digestion and didn't want him to smoke them. Hannah said he made Bedelia promise not to let me know about it, so that my feelings won't be hurt.'

'I think Bedelia's splendid,' Ellen said. 'She takes such good care of Charlie.'

The Horst house was just off the highway at the junction with the side road that led to the Bennett place. As they turned, they all looked at the Horst house and saw that lights were burning in the front bedroom.

'They'll be over a bit later,' Ben told the girls. 'I told them to come at half-past six. I want to show you my paintings before dinner.'

'Won't they want to see them, too?' Abbie asked.

'No doubt Bedelia's seen them already,' Ellen remarked tartly.

If her legs had not been secured by blankets, Abbie would have kicked Ellen's shin.

'She's seen them often,' Ben remarked, apparently unmoved by Ellen's insinuations. 'She's an excellent critic.'

Ben seemed anxious to show off his work. He hardly gave the girls time to take off their coats and hats before he rushed them into the north bedroom which he used as a studio. Except for an easel, a stool, and a paint-stained table the room was bare. No canvas had been hung, but a number were stacked along the walls. 'I'm sorry you have to see my work by artificial light, but I'm not offering any excuses,' Ben said as he tilted the lampshade so that full light should fall upon the easel. He showed his paintings, one by one, standing by patiently until his guests had enough of each picture.

His work was crude, but not without a certain forcefulness. The paintings revealed characteristics that his amiable manners concealed. He was shrewd and ruthless and saw deeply below the surface.

'You're *fauve*, aren't you?' inquired Abbie.

'Not by intention. It's probably my nature.'

'After seeing your work, I'm rather afraid of you.'

He turned to Ellen. 'Do you think I'm dangerous?'

Ellen lowered her eyes so that she need not look any longer at the painting on the easel. It was of a red barn on the Silvermine River, a favorite subject with the artists who came to Southern Connecticut. Ellen had seen many versions of it. The work of a famous magazine illustrator had been used on the calendar distribution at Christmas by the insurance company for which Wells Johnson worked. Ellen had always thought this a tranquil scene, but in Ben's picture the red barn seemed to be crumbling, the water choked with weeds, and in the flame of autumn foliage there was sense of winter's bitterness.

'It's daring.' Abbie spoke, although she knew it was Ellen's opinion he sought.

'At first it shocks you, but after you're used to it, you find that you rather like it. Like Stravinsky.'

'I'm sure I'd never grow to like it.'

Ellen spoke her mind freely. If she had deliberately set about antagonizing Ben Chaney, she could not have found a more effective method. Abbie tried to signal with her eyebrows.

'At first,' Ellen went on, ignoring Abbie's frantic signals, 'I thought I disliked your work because you deliberately chose ugly things to paint, like slum scenes and garbage cans. But now I see you can also make a beautiful scene hideous.'

'I try to paint what I see. And to see things as they are.'

'Then you find truth ugly when others see beauty in it.'

He shrugged. 'You may be right. I'm not sentimental.'

They heard Charlie's Oakland car puff up the hill. Ben said, 'You've probably seen enough,' and led them out of the studio.

Ellen was glad to return to the glow of the gas logs. She pulled her chair close to the hearth and shivered as if she had just come in out of the cold.

Ben and Charlie drank cider brandy while the ladies sipped sherry. Bedelia was wearing a dress of black crepe de chine, draped at the hips and narrow at the hem. The bodice was cut low, but filled with ruffles of white lace. The dress was both decorous and daring. No woman could criticize, no man fail to notice.

'I'm sorry we're one man short tonight,' Ben explained.

'My friend, whom I'd wanted you to meet, didn't get here after all.'

'So Mary told us,' said Bedelia.

'There are blizzards in the Middle West,' Ben went on. 'No trains moving. I thought he'd arrived in New York this morning, and then I got a wire saying he hadn't left St. Paul.'

Bedelia set down her sherry with an abrupt movement. Some of the wine spilled. She smiled ruefully.

'Is anything wrong?'

Her eyes narrowed and she hung her head.

'Aren't you feeling well?' Ben persisted.

'I got a bit of a chill. Perhaps someone was walking over my grave.' She straightened and gave Ben a reassuring smile to show that the spilled sherry and her sudden alarm meant nothing.

The room was still for a few seconds and then Abbie broke the silence, shrilly. 'Who was this guest?'

'Does it matter, since he's not coming?' asked Ellen.

'We might at least have the pleasure of knowing what we've missed,' Abbie answered with unnecessary venom.

'A friend of mine,' Ben said.

'An artist, too?'

'No, he's in business. Owns a store, two stores, in fact.' Ben's restless glance had circled the room. His eyes were fixed on Bedelia's face again.

'How do you like my new dress?' she cried. The subterfuge was not wholly successful. Everyone could see that she had wanted, desperately, to change the subject.

'Stunning,' said Abbie, 'looks like Paris.'

'I made it myself.'

'No!'

'Yes, she did,' said Charlie, who had been informed of the fact this evening while they dressed.

Abbie shook her head. 'You're a marvel, Bedelia. I'd swear it was an import.'

'Thank you.' Bedelia took another sip of sherry.

'That's how you must sit for your portrait, Bedelia. I want you to wear that dress,' Ben said.

'A portrait of Bedelia!' exclaimed Charlie.

'You don't mind if she sits for me, do you?'

'Of course not.'

'Oh, Ben,' Bedelia shook her head at him. 'Why did you mention it? You've spoiled the surprise.'

'I'm sorry.'

'A surprise for me?' asked Charlie.

'For your birthday, dear.'

'Nothing would please me more.' To the others he said, 'You know I have no picture of her, not even a snapshot.'

'Mr. Chaney oughtn't to paint Bedelia!' Ellen said.

'Why not?' Charlie demanded. 'Why shouldn't he paint Bedelia's picture?'

'Have you *seen* his paintings?'

'Often. Why are you so disapproving?'

Ellen kept them waiting while she thought about it. Finally she said, 'Bedelia's pretty and he seems interested only in making things ugly.'

'That's unjust. I told you I try to paint as I see, honestly.'

'He could never see anything ugly in Bedelia,' Charlie stated flatly.

'Have you seen what he did with the red barn? He's even succeeded in finding evil in that picturesque spot.'

Hannah said dinner was ready.

'You can't find evil where it doesn't exist,' Charlie argued. 'I've no fear of letting him paint Bedelia's portrait.'

'I shall be interested in seeing the finished work,' Ellen said.

'You'll be the first to have a chance to criticize it,' Ben said, as he rose and led the way to the dining-room.

The meal began, as Mary had informed Bedelia, with clams. Bedelia had already warned Charlie against the first course. He nibbled a dry cracker.

Ellen, who was sitting next to him, asked why he wasn't eating. 'Not dyspepsia again, Charlie?'

'I'm not hungry.' Hoping to avoid any more discussion of the loathed subject, he said, 'You're looking unusually well tonight. What have you done to yourself, Nellie?'

Ellen's fair skin turned scarlet. Long ago, when Charlie had taught her tennis and sat next to her on hayrack rides, his name for her had been Nellie. *Seeing Nellie Home,* he used to sing out of tune but cheerfully. She felt the heat of the blush and feared that her burning cheeks must reveal her shame. But the flush was becoming. Abbie had lent her a dress of gray wool bound in cerise silk.

'What's the secret, Nellie? Is it love that's causing you to bloom?'

Hannah thrust a plate of hot biscuits between them. Ellen buttered hers with an air of severity. Chilled by her extraordinary tension, Charlie gave ear to the conversation between Ben and Abbie.

Bedelia was listening but taking no part in it.

'At first,' Ben told Abbie, 'I'd thought of painting her as she looked to Charlie that day on the hotel veranda. All in black, the widow. As background the stony peaks of the Rockies to show the cruelty and indifference of Nature, and the harshness of the world against which a frail woman must battle.'

'It sounds stunning. Why have you changed your mind?'

'The obvious lack of mountain scenery.'

'Couldn't you do it from photographs?'

'That's not the way I work. Moreover, my model would no longer be the slender and ardent widow pursued by our friend Charlie from the hotel salon to the veranda. I found the story romantic when I first heard it and was tempted to work from imagination rather than reality.'

'But the story is true.'

'The subject had changed. Instead of that pensive widow

we see a buxom wife. The lines are no longer angular but . . .' he carried out the idea with his hands. 'This is to be the portrait of a woman who's satisfied with her life because she's succeeded at a woman's most fundamental job, which is to make a man comfortable.'

'Very flattering,' said Charlie.

'You smug thing!' cried Abbie, playing with the East Indian bangle which she wore over her tight black satin sleeve.

Ben saw that his guests were through with the clams, and he rang the bell for Hannah. Then he turned to Bedelia and said, 'When you sit for your portrait, you must wear the black pearl.'

'Black pearl!' exclaimed Abbie, looking at Bedelia with new respect. 'Don't tell me you own a black pearl.'

Bedelia glanced at Charlie. It was fortunate, her eyes seemed to be saying, that she had had her own way about Abbie's gift. Ben might have embarrassed them by remarking that he had seen Bedelia wear the ring. 'Oh, it's not real,' she explained. 'I picked it up in a novelty shop in New York. It cost five dollars. Charlie thought it looked cheap, but I'm so ignorant that it looked like a real one to me.'

'A remarkable imitation,' Ben said. 'I'm no judge of jewelry, but when I first saw it I thought the platinum and diamonds genuine, and that the pearl might be worth a thousand dollars.'

Abbie played with the bangle. 'It sounds stunning. Why don't you wear it, Bedelia?'

'My husband doesn't approve of artificial stones.' Bedelia spoke without resentment, simply stating fact.

'I'm sorry I noticed the ring that night,' Ben said. 'If I hadn't admired it quite so much, Charlie would probably never have noticed it.'

'Not notice a black pearl!' cried Abbie as if she were speaking of mortal sin.

Charlie wished they would quit talking about it.

'I'm sure he noticed,' Bedelia said. 'It was much too conspicuous for him not to. But he didn't want to hurt my feelings by criticizing my taste, so he controlled his own, although he detested the ring.'

Charlie sighed.

'My sensitive ear perceives the overtones of a domestic quarrel,' Abbie said brightly.

'Charlie and I never quarrel, do we, dear?'

Again Ellen felt, as she always felt when people were oversweet or used too many pet names, that underneath the sugar frosting the cake was sour.

Hannah passed roast beef, Yorkshire pudding and all the trimmings. Charlie barely touched the food and only wet his tongue with Burgundy. His head had begun to pound. 'Nerves,' he told himself disapprovingly, 'nothing but nerves.' Instead of the round table set with Mrs. Bennett's second-best dishes, he saw a square corner table at Jaffney's Tavern, and Ben as host again. The picture in Charlie's mind was like one of those Impressionist things, all angles and disharmony; a gleaming tablecloth, a long-necked bottle of Rhine wine, Bedelia's hand stretched across the table over a platter of lobster and wedges of lemon, resting in Ben's swarthy hand, and Ben bending over to examine the black pearl. Charlie, usually observant, could have sworn he had never noticed the ring until that night, but Bedelia had assured him that she had been wearing it all that week. Charlie had reflected upon the scene, analyzed his emotions and blamed his bad temper upon the flash of jealousy which burned when he saw his wife's hand in Ben's.

'What a prig you are,' Abbie said, not knowing she salted a wound. 'And how like my dear Aunt Harriet. I can just hear your mother, Charlie. ' "I do not like to see a member of my family decked out in artificial jewelry." ' The mockery was precise. Abbie had caught the quality which had made the late Mrs. Horst such an annoying woman.

'All right, I'm a prig. I acknowledge it and I'm sorry.'

'You were right,' Ellen said. 'I detest artificiality in any-thing.'

'Of course he was right,' Bedelia added. 'Everyone has a right to his own taste, and Charlie's is so much better than mine that I could never be comfortable wearing anything he dislikes.'

'Bravo!' Abbie shouted. 'A truly feminine speech, and how much more successful'—she addressed this to Ellen—'than any of your feminist attitudes.'

'My wife is an unusual woman,' Charlie boasted. 'Instead of reproaching me, as most wives would, she gave the ring away.'

'Gave it away! Not really!' shrilled Abbie.

Ben's face tightened.

'Gave it away because I didn't like it,' Charlie said.

Bedelia lowered her eyes modestly.

Abbie said: 'I'd never have given it away. But that's the difference, I suppose, between a successful wife and a failure like me. If I ever marry again, I'll come to you for advice, Bedelia.'

'Thank you, Abbie.' Bedelia straightened her ruffles. On her right hand gleamed Charlie's Christmas gift, the gold ring set with garnets.

For dessert they had mince pie. Charlie was not given any, Hannah brought him a custard. That, of course, was Bedelia's doing. She had heard the menu from Mary and told her to let Hannah know that Mr. Horst must have a simple dessert.

He ate only a small portion of the custard and felt worse than before. The pain in his head had become a dull beat. When Hannah brought around the cheese, he put a little on his plate. Bedelia shook her head at him.

'Not Gorgonzola, Charlie.'

It was a half-whisper, but everyone heard and laughed. Later, after Charlie was stricken, they remembered Bedelia's solicitude.

The party broke up early. It had not been a very successful evening. The dinner had been too heavy and the guests were dull. Charlie and Bedelia left at half-past ten. It was fortunate that they did not stay longer. Otherwise Charlie would have suffered his attack at Ben's house and there would have been no end to the confusion.

He had not been home for more than ten minutes when it happened. Bedelia had gone upstairs ahead of him because Charlie never went to bed without trying all the locks and taking a final look at the furnace. When he came into the bedroom, she was standing before the pier glass in her black silk corset. Charlie thought this the most seductive garment he had ever seen and, whenever Bedelia wore it, he wanted to make love to her.

She saw his face in the mirror. Whirling around she cried, 'Oh, Charlie, darling, you're not going to be ill, are you?' she said.

'I'm all right,' he said.

'You felt sick at Ben's house, I know you did. That's why I suggested coming home early. You look awful.'

The creature who stared back at Charlie from the pier glass had sunken eyes, colorless lips, and a pistachio green complexion. But Charlie was determined not to be ill and he squared his shoulders and began briskly to undress.

Bedelia mixed him a sedative. Her hand trembled as she poured the powder from one of the blue packets into the tepid water. 'Drink it fast, you won't notice the taste,' she said. As he drank the foaming stuff, she watched him anxiously. 'Feel better now, honey?'

At that moment he did feel better. He watched Bedelia loosen the laces of her corset. 'If you weren't my wife, I'd say that corset looked fast.'

She was hurt. 'If that's the way you feel about it, I'll never wear it again.'

'Don't be so sensitive, Biddy. I meant it as a compliment. A woman who has had two husbands should know that a touch of suggestiveness is appealing to the masculine eye. As Herrick put it, "A sweet disorder in the dress kindles in . . ." '

That was as far as he ever got with Herrick. Bedelia, who had gone to the closet for her nightgown, heard him gasp the last word. She turned quickly and saw that he had begun to vomit. He was bent over, steadying himself against the footboard of the bed. She saw him stagger backwards, let go of the footboard, and fall.

For a moment she did not stir. She stood at the closet door, her hand tight on the china knob. Charlie lay on the rose-colored carpet, as white as death and as silent. Painfully his wife opened her fingers, released the doorknob, and crossed the room. Her knees were shaking so that she walked like a drunken woman, and when she knelt beside him and lifted his wrist, she could not take his pulse because her own hand was so unsteady.

Mary rose early the next morning. She could hardly wait until it was late enough to call Hannah without disturbing the Horsts or Mr. Chaney.

'Guess what?' she said when finally she had gathered enough courage to use the telephone.

'Hen Blackman's popped the question,' Hannah guessed. Hen Blackman was Mary's steady fellow.

Mary was so eager to spill out her news that she did not bother to tease Hannah. 'Mr. Horst's awful sick. Almost kicked the bucket last night. The doctor was here when I got in from the dance.'

'Mr. Horst! Why, he was here for supper. Must have been awful sudden. What's wrong with him?'

'Poisoned.'

'You don't say. Poisoned? By what?'

'Something he ate,' said Mary.

Hannah served Ben Chaney the news with his breakfast. 'Couldn't be nothing he ate in this house. No one else got sick, did they? Mary acted like it was my cooking done it, but I'm telling you . . .'

Before she had a chance to tell him anything, Ben Chaney was at the telephone. He slammed the studio door in a way that showed Hannah he did not want her to hear what he was saying. He tried to get hold of Doctor Meyers, who was out on a call and could not be reached. Then Ben asked the long-distance operator to put in two calls, one to New York and one to St. Paul. Afterward he changed from his painting smock to his tweed jacket, pulled on his overcoat, grabbed his hat, and was out of the house before Hannah could ask whether he'd be back for lunch.

He did not ring the Horst doorbell, but went around the back way and tapped at Mary's kitchen window. She hurried to open the door, smoothing her hair and wiping her hands on her apron.

'I didn't want to ring in case Mr. Horst was sleeping. How is he?'

'He's still asleep.'

'And Mrs. Horst?'

'I brought her her coffee up to bed. The doctor says she should stay in bed this morning. She was all wore out, he says.'

Ben took off his overcoat and seated himself in one of the kitchen chairs. 'Mind if I smoke?'

Mary gave her permission with a flourish. 'Like something to eat, Mr. Chaney? Or a cup of coffee? I just made a big pot in case somebody'd want it in a hurry. In an emergency it's always good to have hot coffee.'

'If it's not too much bother, Mary.'

She fetched a Limoges cup from the pantry. When Ben

suggested that she sit down and have coffee with him, the girl giggled happily. She poured her coffee into one of the heavy kitchen cups, but tried to be elegant and serve him cream and sugar like Mrs. Horst at the dining-room table.

He asked her a great many questions, but Mary did not think this odd. Small-town people do not hide their natural interest in the affairs of their neighbors. Mary told him precisely what she had told Hannah, which was all she knew.

'Are they getting a trained nurse? Has the doctor suggested it?'

Mary nodded. Doctor Meyers had told her last night that Mrs. Horst wanted to take care of Mr. Horst herself, and the doctor said that Mary was to be responsible for the house. 'Mrs. Horst, she'd rather take care of him herself with me looking after the house for her than have a stranger in to nurse him. With me responsible for the house, she can nurse Mr. Horst all right. She'd rather do it herself.'

Ben looked out of the window. Mist was rising from moist ground. Mary cried, 'Oh!' and clasped both hands over her heart. Ben turned and saw Bedelia at the kitchen door. He was no less startled than Mary had been. Bedelia had appeared silently, and she stood so quiet that she seemed an apparition that had materialized out of the dark air of the corridor.

He rose and went to her. Taking her hand, Ben said, 'Bedelia! Good morning. How are you?'

She did not greet him and stood there, looking past him or through him as if she were not aware of his presence. She was highly agitated, her mouth working and her eyes narrowed to dark slits.

'Mrs. Horst, what's the matter? Can I do something for you?' asked Mary.

Bedelia raised her shoulders and shuddered delicately as if she were shaking off an evil mood. Smiling, she bade Mary good morning. Then she looked down at her hand which lay in Ben's. She continued to smile but in a different way. Her upper lid curled back over her teeth and her eyes were guarded.

'Good morning, Ben.'

'How's Charlie? If there's anything I can do for you, Bedelia, you must tell me. Anything at all.'

'It's good to have friends. At a time like this, it's all you have to . . .' she paused, seeking the right words, '. . . to give you courage. Oh, Ben, if anything should happen to Charlie!'

'He'll be all right,' Ben said.

She let Ben lead her to the den, pull a chair close to the hearth, and light the coal fire. She was still agitated. Her pointed pink fingernails clawed the leather of the armchair.

'You're sure you're all right, Bedelia?'

'That's what Charlie asked me as soon as he became conscious last night. Was I all right? You'd think I was the sick one.' Bedelia had become herself again, composed, gentle, all curves and sweetness.

Ben chose a chair opposite Bedelia's. They sat there without talking. The rain had started. Wind sighed through bare branches. The river charged angrily over the rocks. Ben looked from the dripping window back toward the blue flames of the coal fire, and then at Bedelia again.

Her hands lay limp in her lap. She seemed sunk in complete lethargy as if the preceding mood of nervousness and agitation had exhausted her.

Mary stamped into the room. Bedelia looked straight at the girl without seeing her. Shuddering, Mary said, 'Mrs. Horst.' Her voice was unsteady.

Bedelia slid forward in the chair. Her eyes widened and her hands tensed again.

'It's not Mr. Horst? There's nothing wrong upstairs, is there?'

Mary shook her head. She had interrupted only to tell Mrs. Horst that Miss Ellen Walker had called to say she had heard about Mr. Horst and to ask if she could do anything. 'Thank you,' Bedelia whispered, dismissing the girl. She hugged her knees and looked into the fire as if she were alone in the room.

A few minutes later Doctor Meyers rang the doorbell. Ben hurried to open the door.

'Well, how's the patient?' the doctor asked as he pulled off his rubbers. Then he noticed Ben and said, 'My wife tells me you called this morning, want to see me about something?'

'After you've seen Charlie.'

Bedelia went upstairs with the doctor. Ben picked up the *National Geographic* and looked at maps of the Caucasus. Mary came into the room with a dustcloth and asked if her work would disturb him. He did not answer, and Mary scurried away to dust the living-room gently as if the furniture were ill, too. After a while Bedelia came downstairs. Her eyes were moist and bright. She sniffed at her handkerchief, which was scented with a flowery perfume.

'The doctor's a long time,' Ben said.

'Yes. He wanted to know everything Charlie's eaten for a month. And you know Charlie. He never remembers from one day to the next what he's had for dinner.'

She had changed into a house gown of maroon wool banded in black velvet and bound her hair with a maroon ribbon. The doll's mouth was as red as a cherry.

'You'll be ill yourself if you worry,' Ben said. 'If it's food poisoning, as the doctor suggests, Charlie'll be all right in a few days.'

She retreated again to the leather armchair. Apparently the flames could not warm her, for she rubbed her hands and shivered. 'I've been unlucky all my life.'

The wind echoed her sigh.

When the doctor came downstairs, she fairly leaped from her chair. 'How is he?'

'Much better. His pulse is slow but not dangerously so. You'll have to keep him in bed a few days and feed him carefully. It's been a shock to his system.'

Bedelia nodded.

Charlie tells me you gave him a powder last night. Why didn't you tell me?'

'It was only a bromide,' she said. 'It couldn't possibly have hurt him.'

Ben was frozen. Nothing seemed alive in him except his eyes. They searched the doctor's face and then fastened on Bedelia's and remained there, steadily.

'What kind of bromide?' Doctor Meyers asked.

'It was a prescription a famous specialist in San Francisco gave an old lady I used to work for.'

'And you gave it to Charlie?'

She nodded.

'Don't you know it's dangerous to give people medicine that's been prescribed for others?'

'There was nothing dangerous in this. I've often taken it myself. For gas. It was very soothing.'

'I'd like to see it,' the doctor said.

She left the room. Both men watched until she was out of sight.

Ben said, 'Food poisoning, are you sure that's the cause of Mr. Horst's illness, Doctor?'

Doctor Meyers, affronted by this tone of authority from a man who was no member of the household and hardly more than a stranger in town, bent over to fasten his shoelace. 'I hear he had dinner at your house last night, Mr. Chaney.'

'Several people dined at my house. They all ate the same food. None of the others were stricken.'

'Mrs. Horst says that he had a special dessert served him, a custard. The rest of you ate pie. What was in the custard?'

Ben shrugged. 'Hannah Frost, my hired girl, can tell you. But I hardly think a simple dish like that could have caused it. And the rest of the custard is probably still in the pantry if you'd like to have it analyzed.

The doctor took his coat off the hook. With his back to

Ben he asked: 'Is that what you wanted to see me about, Mr. Chaney? Because one of your guests was poisoned by something he ate? When I discover what caused it, I'll let you know.' He wrapped a knitted muffler, irrelevantly gay, about his neck.

'Don't you think he ought to have a trained nurse?'

The doctor wheeled around. Since he had suggested a nurse and then allowed Bedelia to change his mind for him, the question made him angry. 'Why are you so interested, Mr. Chaney?'

'As a friend I want to see everything done that can possibly be done for Charlie. Besides'—Ben moved closer to the old man—'we have to think of Mrs. Horst's health. Do you think she's strong enough to nurse him . . . in her condition?'

Bedelia leaped out of the shadows of the stairs, hurried to the doctor, clung to his arm. 'I'm going to have a baby.'

'Oh! I wondered about you. You're putting on weight. Better let me look you over one of these days.'

'I feel fine. I've never felt better in my life,' Bedelia said. Then she handed him the box that was filled with packets of the sedative powder. 'Here it is, Doctor. I had it made up at Loveman's Drug Store. Mr. Loveman knows all about it.'

The doctor put the box in his overcoat pocket. 'Charlie looks pretty good to me, Mrs. Horst. Just let him rest and eat lightly. I'll stop in tomorrow.' He opened the door and a blast of cold air blew in upon them. 'Good-bye, Mr. Chaney,' the doctor said and slammed the door.

Bedelia stood with her hand on the post of the staircase, looking after him. Rain beat a sad rhythm on the roof. Currents of warm air moved through the house from the steam radiators, but they could not defeat the chill of the hall. Bedelia shivered. When she saw how steadily Ben was watching her, she raised her shoulders in a delicate shrug and turned and walked into the den.

CHARLES HORST STRICKEN
Local Architect Felled By Sudden Attack

Ellen typed the story on an Oliver machine with a broken D. Her hand was unsteady and she made more than her usual typographical errors. She had been assured by Doctor Meyer's wife that Charlie was not in danger, and Mary had said that he was resting comfortably. 'Mr. Horst was married last August to Mrs. Bedelia Cochran, widow of the late Raoul Cochran, a distinguished artist of New Orleans, La.' Ellen's desk stood in a row of broken-down, dusty, splinter-rough desks in a noisy loft with a cement floor, plaster walls, and a deafening echo. 'They met in Colorado Springs, Colo., where Mr. Horst had gone for a holiday after the death of his mother, Mrs. Harriet Philbrook Horst, one of our most beloved citizens.'

At five minutes after twelve she covered the typewriter and left the office. There was a rumor going through the town that Madame Schumann-Heink was arriving from New York to visit a musical family who had recently bought a house in the neighborhood. Although the newspaper office was but three blocks from the railroad station, the rain was so heavy that Ellen had to take the streetcar. The wind blew furiously. An umbrella gave no protection. Women's skirts were blown high above their shoe-tops, but the tough boys who usually hung around the street corners, hoping to catch a glimpse of ribbed black stockings, had sought shelter in saloons and poolrooms.

The railroad station smelled of rubber, moist wool, and steam. Ellen waited behind a dripping window, watching the passengers alight from the New York train. There was no one who could be mistaken for Schumann-Heink. She saw Ben Chaney hurry along the rainswept platform and wondered whether she dare ask him to drive her home. But when she saw that he was meeting a woman, her courage failed, and she pressed into the shadows so that he should not see her as he and his companion left the station.

Ellen hurried through the rain to the streetcar. The ten-minute ride seemed interminable. Lunch was even worse. Ellen's parents were the high-thinking sort, retired school-teachers, and gossip was not permitted at the table. As soon as she could politely do it, she urged Abbie to come upstairs with her. She closed the bedroom door and plunged into a description of the scene at the railroad station.

Abbie was not impressed. 'If you'd spoken to him, you'd probably have been introduced to his dear godmother or maiden aunt.'

'She didn't look auntish. They seemed terribly absorbed in whatever they were talking about, as if they shared some passionate interest.'

'But you said she was homely and oldish.'

'I didn't mean it was romantic. They seemed to be excited about something.'

Abbie puffed on her cigarette and reflected upon the ugliness of Ellen's bedroom. When they had been chums at grammar school and Abbie had brought her secrets to Ellen's room, the white iron bed had stood in the same corner, the Morris style dresser and desk had been adorned with the same scarves and pictures. On the wall hung faded photographs of the Parthenon frieze, the Forum, and of Michelangelo's *David*.

'Do you think he knew Bedelia before he came here?' Ellen asked.

'What a suspicious nature you've got,' Abbie said. 'I've never in my life heard anything so vicious. Whatever makes you think that?'

'He's not really interested in anyone else. It's a sort of pre-occupation with him. Haven't you noticed the way he always watches her?'

Abbie crushed the stub of her cigarette into a saucer which had been sneaked upstairs for that purpose. To cleanse the air of the tobacco smoke, she opened the window. 'What about his dates with other women? Those tea parties with Lucy Johnson? And you and Mary among the others?'

'To disguise his real interests.'

'What a wild imagination. You ought to write penny-dreadfuls.'

'I'm not suspicious by nature,' Ellen said. 'At first I thought I was getting these ideas because I was jealous of Bedelia.' It cost Ellen some effort to say this, but she had made up her mind to speak frankly, and she gritted her teeth and went on. 'You know that I tried to like Bedelia and trust her, and I'd have succeeded if it weren't for this Chaney affair.'

Abbie was warming herself over the register. Her skirt filled with hot air and spread out as if hoops supported it. 'You've chosen a strong word. Do you believe that of Bedelia?'

'I'm not so low.' Ellen's eyes were upon a snapshot of Charlie framed in raffia. He wore tennis flannels and carried a racket, and his hair was abundant.

'My guess is that Chaney's in love with her. But you can't blame Bedelia for that. She's the sort that men die for.' Abbie stepped off the register. Her skirt fell limp about her legs.

'Die for? That's pretty romantic, isn't it?'

'A slight exaggeration. What I mean is that Bedelia's a man's woman. Men fall in love with her because she's crazy about men, and they sense it. She exists only for her man, her whole life is wrapped around him. Without a man she couldn't live.'

'And we can, I suppose?'

'Unfortunately,' sighed Abbie. 'You and I, pet, have got too far from the harem. You earn your living and enjoy it. I have an income and live quite adequately alone. Men aren't our lords and masters. And they resent us.'

'Let them. The harem doesn't hold any charms for me,' Ellen said angrily. She took one of Abbie's cigarettes, placed it between her lips and drew in her breath as she touched a match to it.

Abbie watched with a gleam in her eye. The stairs creaked, but Ellen did not put down the cigarette.

'Bravo,' whispered Abbie.

'I'd like them better without the perfume.'

'We must be feminine.'

'That's a compromise. Either you smoke or you don't.'

Abbie laughed. Ellen's mother creaked past the door. If she had come in, Ellen would have continued to stand there with the cigarette in her hand as if smoking were her daily habit. The cigarette was not so much a symbol of defiance as proof that she had rejected the harem.

As she dressed to return to the office, she decided to quit thinking about Charlie, and to get rid of the souvenirs which cluttered her room. There was not only the picture of Charlie in tennis flannels, there were old cotillion favors and faded dance programs, and all of the presents he had ever given her, starting with the copy of *Elsie Dinsmore* he had brought to the party celebrating her ninth birthday.

Now that he was comfortable and free of pain, Charlie was less concerned with his own condition than with its effect upon Bedelia. The trick which Fate had played upon her was in bad taste, Charlie thought. How ironic, after the sudden death of her first husband, for her to see her second in the throes of an almost fatal attack.

'You're sure you feel all right, dear?' he asked for the twentieth time. 'You're a bit pale. What a brute I was to give you such a shock.'

'Don't be silly, Charlie. It wasn't your fault.'

'Whose fault was it? Do you by any chance blame yourself?'

Bedelia's eyes wore the blank look. She stood at the foot of the bed, her hands tight on the rail.

'I've been careless,' Charlie went on. 'I've worked too hard, enjoyed the holidays too much, not rested enough, and have been careless about eating. I was most inconsiderate. For your sake, sweetheart, I should have been more careful.'

Bedelia's eyes filled. She rubbed them with her knuckles. Charlie saw in her movements the pathos and helplessness of childhood. He was deeply moved.

'Come here, Biddy.'

She waited, then took an irresolute step toward him.

'My goodness, are you afraid of me?' teased Charlie.

She went to him and he took her hand. He felt closer than he had ever been to her guarded and delicate spirit; as if he saw through walls of tissue and bone and concealment; as if there had never been any Cochran nor any past he could not share, nor any blank, remote looks to protect her from curiosity. She pressed his hand and looked into his eyes, searching, too, Charlie thought, for the part of him that she knew not.

The sound of the doorbell caused her to start and shrink, and when she heard Doctor Meyers's voice, her nostrils quivered and her cheeks seemed to become hollow. Terror possessed her. She seated herself on the edge of the bed, clutched the post as if for support.

'Mary, I'm making you responsible for Mrs. Horst's health,' they heard the doctor say. 'She's not feeling too well, and I don't want her to do any work in the kitchen. You must do all the cooking without any help from her.'

'Yes, sir.' Mary's voice rang with pride.

'Has he had lunch?'

'Yes, sir. Mrs. Horst fixed him the gruel like you told her.'

The doctor bounded up the stairs. 'How are you, Charlie?' he called from the hall.

'Feeling fine.'

As he entered the bedroom, the doctor looked at the tray

and the empty bowl. 'How'd the lunch agree with you? Any pains? Nausea?'

'Why did you come back?' Bedelia asked, her voice unsteady. 'You said you wouldn't come until tomorrow. Have you found out something . . . about Charlie?'

The doctor answered her with his eyes on Charlie. He seemed withdrawn, as if he were determined to have no contact with her. 'I stopped to say I'd changed my mind about a trained nurse. I've called the registry and they're sending a woman this afternoon.'

Bedelia stood up. Her skirt caught in the bed and she jerked it free with a graceless movement which made her for the moment a stranger to Charlie.

'But you said I could take care of him. Why have you changed your mind?' She waited impatiently for the doctor's answer. His silence increased her alarm. Charlie saw that her chest was rising and falling and that she had frequently to moisten her lips.

'Please tell me the truth,' she said curtly.

'I'm more worried about you than about Charlie, Mrs. Horst. When I said that you wouldn't need a nurse, I didn't know of your condition. You've had a shock and I don't want any after effects.'

'It's worse than you told me, and you don't think I'm capable of nursing him.'

'I fear you'd nurse him too well for your own good.'

'So you know our secret,' Charlie said to the doctor. 'When did my wife tell you?'

'This morning,' Bedelia answered quickly.

The doctor insisted that she go downstairs and eat a good lunch. 'I don't hold with these female habits of picking food here and there at irregular hours. You need nourishment, Mrs. Horst. Eating for two, aren't you? Run along and I'll keep Charlie company until you return.'

The doctor seated himself in the rocker and folded one leg

over the other. Bedelia lingered in the room. It was clear that she did not want him to tell Charlie anything that she was not to hear. After Charlie joined forces with the doctor and urged her to eat a sensible lunch, she left. The smell of her perfume remained in the air.

'Mind?' asked Doctor Meyers, and pulled out a thin cigar. A gold cutter, the gift of some grateful patient, hung with his Masonic medal on a gold chain. As he exhaled a cloud of smoke, the scent of Bedelia's perfume was lost.

The doctor studied his cigar, the hand that held it, the weave of the carpet, the tips of his pointed shoes. His tranquility alarmed Charlie. When Doctor Meyers had good news he danced about and talked in such a rush that all the words ran together. Why, then, this long scrutiny of cigar and carpet? Immediately Charlie suspected the worst, a fatal disease, long months of suffering, a losing fight against pain. Cancer, was it? Or heart disease?

Doctor Meyers spoke at last. His voice was dry and he brought out the words with effort. 'The nurse will be here this afternoon. I don't want you to eat or drink anything, not even a sip of water, unless she gives it to you.'

'Why not?'

The doctor waited until the full meaning of his warning had touched Charlie.

'Why not!'

The doctor cleared his throat. 'Just an idea of mine.'

'Are you crazy?'

'Perhaps.' The doctor tugged at his Van Dyke. 'I'm a cantankerous old fool. Maybe I ought to turn my practice over to a younger man. But give me a couple of days, Charlie, to have an analysis made. Unfortunately, the excrement had all been removed before I came last night, but after I'd pumped out your stomach, what remained . . .'

'What are you inferring?' Charlie shouted.

'Nothing, Charlie. Keep calm. We'll have to wait a couple

of days. I'm having the work done in New York. I don't like the laboratory here, there's too much gossip, everybody who works in the hospital is intimate with somebody in town, and you can't keep anything quiet. Do what I say, Charlie, promise you'll eat nothing except what the nurse gives you.'

Charlie was livid. He almost leaped out of bed.

'Get back under the covers and keep calm. It's probably nothing but a fool idea of mine, but I don't want you to take any chances. That's why I mentioned it. Now don't go getting any ideas in your head.'

'How can I help it when you make these absurd insinuations? I'll eat anything I damn please. And if you don't take back what you just said, I'll sue you for malpractice. Or libel. God damn it, I will!'

'Sure, but don't eat anything except what the nurse gives you. Is that clear?'

'You're a senile fool.'

The ash had grown long on Doctor Meyers's cigar. It spilled on his vest. He whisked it off carefully, and holding his hand like a cup, sought the wastebasket. 'Why don't you keep an ashtray up here?'

'You have just made a filthy rotten insinuation against my wife,' Charlie said solemnly. He had grown calm all of a sudden, his high color had faded and he was as pale as a tallow candle. 'I can't allow you to say things like that. I won't stand for it.'

'Don't,' said the doctor. 'I wouldn't stand for it either. But I'd keep my head and follow the doctor's instructions.'

'God damn you!'

The doctor did not mind being sworn at. He quite approved Charlie's resentment. It showed that Charlie was well on the road to recovery. But he begged him, for the sake of his blood pressure, to remain calm.

'Listen,' Charlie pleaded, trying to be cool about it and hoping that his own good sense would bring the old man around to a saner point of view. 'I've had a lot of indigestion lately. I told you that this morning.'

'You didn't tell me how long you'd been having it. When did you first notice it, Charlie?'

'After we finished doing the house over. I've been working too hard; first, the house, and then the supervision on the Maple Avenue stores and the Bridgeport job.'

'October, did you say?' The doctor pulled at his beard.

'What of it?'

'Don't lose your temper again, Charlie. Keep calm. It's probably nothing but acute indigestion. As soon as you're on your feet, I'll give you a thorough going-over. And just humor me in this one thing, don't take anything from anyone but the nurse.'

'I'll see you in hell first.'

'Very well. It's on your own head.'

The silence that followed was an armistice, not a declaration of peace. Charlie was sorry he had lost his temper. Had he, in that first explosion, acted as if he had taken the doctor's theory seriously?

There was the flowery fragrance again. He looked up and saw Bedelia beside the bed, blithe and fresh. The hot lunch had restored her color. And she was smiling, showing her dimples, changing the very atmosphere with her perfume and the rustle of her petticoats.

'I was upset when you sent me downstairs,' she confessed in light, rapid tones. 'I thought you were sending me away because you had something to tell Charlie that you didn't want me to hear on account of my condition. But when you began shouting, I knew it was all right. Charlie would never have raised his voice if you'd brought him bad news. What were you arguing about? Politics again?'

'Yes,' Charlie said quickly. And to the doctor, 'Where my wife comes from it's no sin to be a Democrat. She's used to your party brothers, Doctor.'

Bedelia laughed. 'You know I don't understand anything about it, dear. As long as you're well enough for an argument, I don't care who you vote for.'

'Come here, my love.' Charlie wanted her close beside him, he needed the assurance of her physical sweetness, and he hoped to make a show of defiance before that old fool of a doctor.

The shrewd eyes looked on and the pointed face became more wrinkled and simian. What Doctor Meyers saw before him was a demonstration of faith. No spoken declaration could have made the point more clearly. Charlie was investing his faith in Bedelia. A charming picture it made, husband and wife holding hands, looking fondly into each other's eyes, flaunting their love.

The doctor walked to the wastebasket and flicked the ash off his cigar. Then he returned to his chair and sat, rocking and smoking, until the doorbell rang and Mary came upstairs to say the trained nurse had arrived.

3

During the night the storm ceased. Charlie lay alone in the wide bed and wished that he had his wife beside him. Bedelia had moved into Charlie's old bedroom. The nurse had ordered the change.

Since she had arrived that afternoon, held a conference with Doctor Meyers in the den, marched up the stairs and changed her drab dress for a blue-and-white striped uniform, this woman had ruled the household. Charlie and Bedelia had hated her on sight. Nevertheless, they let her intimidate them. She used her ugliness as other women use beauty to give her authority. If a country fair had offered prizes for the most unattractive female on exhibit, Miss Gordon would have captured first honors. Below dusty hair, tightly netted, bulged a forehead like a parenthesis. Between this bulge and the crag of her chin, her face curved inward like a soup plate. Her nose was broad but so flat that it gave slight relief to the concavity. Her body was squat, her wrists red, and her disposition sour.

By her order Charlie slept alone. The night was still. He heard only the chatter of the river, a sound so familiar that he could shut it out altogether, and give attention to whatever moanings and creakings there were within the house. By habit and profession he was able to locate every sound. He recognized a steely whine as the complaint of bedsprings in the room where Bedelia was spending the night.

The floor creaked lightly under cautious footsteps. Charlie turned hopefully toward the door. The footsteps came closer. His heart began to pound in anticipation. The darkness was so solid that he could not see the door open when he heard its hinges creak. But he smelled the flowery perfume.

Then a fresh sound smote his ears, and a hoarse voice croaked, 'Is that you, Mrs. Horst?'

'I was just going to get a drink of water,' he heard Bedelia say. 'I thought I'd see if Mr. Horst wanted anything.'

'I'm here to take care of that, Mrs. Horst.'

'Yes, but I was worried. On account of last night, you know.'

'He's asleep. I wouldn't disturb him if I were you. Go back to bed, Mrs. Horst. I'll bring you a drink of water.'

The hinges creaked, the door closed, the voices ceased. The down quilt and wool blankets could not warm Charlie's cold flesh. Why had he allowed the nurse to send his wife away? Had he, in spite of all his logical excuses, been swayed by the doctor's warning? 'No! No!' he snarled at the blackness that surrounded him. It was a long time before he could fall asleep.

In the morning as the nurse gave him a sponge bath, he said, 'It's kind of you to take such good care of my wife, Miss Gordon. I heard you last night.'

'She oughtn't to wander around at night, not in her condition. She might catch cold or stumble over something in the dark.'

As she bathed her patient, exertion and the heat of water caused her coarse skin to redden. Revolted, Charlie decided that he would get rid of this witch as soon as he was strong enough to argue with the doctor.

He did not wish to be discourteous and tried to make conversation.

'You're not a native here, are you?'

She shook her head.

'I knew that at once. You see, I've lived here all my life and know nearly everyone in town.' This information had failed to interest her, but Charlie went on bravely. 'Where do you come from?'

'N'Yawk.' The accent made it authentic.

'Have you been here long?'

'Couple of months.'

'What made you come here?'

'It's no worse than any other place.'

He heard Bedelia moving about in the other room and shouted to her impatiently. She hurried in to him, holding her challis robe about her shoulders like a shawl. Her eyes were heavy with sleep and her mouth round and pouting like a child's.

Miss Gordon looked on coldly while they kissed. 'You'd better put your robe on, Mrs. Horst. You'll catch your death.'

'Thank you,' Bedelia said humbly and obeyed.

Miss Gordon's vigilance made husband and wife feel like secret lovers. Caresses and confidences had to be stolen while the nurse was absent from the bedroom, attending to her most personal needs (in which she showed unusual self-control) or when she was downstairs in the kitchen preparing her patient's meals. She would accept help from no member of the household. Mary was insulted three times a day, and if

Bedelia tried to perform the slightest service for Charlie, she was officiously brushed aside.

'You must be careful, Mrs. Horst, in your condition.'

'Millions of pregnant women scrub floors and do the family washing,' Bedelia protested. 'I'm perfectly healthy and there's no reason why I can't fill the Thermos.'

Miss Gordon took the vacuum bottle in her capable hands, washed it thoroughly and filled it herself. There was no way of escaping her devotion. Bedelia was slightly awed and greatly puzzled by it. Miss Gordon considered herself on twenty-four-hour duty.

To Charlie it was clear that the nurse was following Doctor Meyers's explicit instructions. She was the only one who ever gave the patient a drop of medicine or a drink of water. Charlie did not demur. He did not believe there was the slightest reason to exercise such caution, but he was afraid that any protest would result in Bedelia's discovering the doctor's suspicions. Loving his wife so dearly, Charlie could not bear to hurt her by letting her know that she was the victim of the old fool's hysteria.

Charlie had not been able to forget the doctor's warning, but he found what he considered a satisfactory explanation. Doctor Meyers was incompetent. Because he could find no scientific name for Charlie's attack, he had invented an excuse. The old man's judgment was weak, his imagination fertile. When he was up and about, Charlie decided, he would go to a younger man for a check-up.

On the second afternoon of Charlie's illness, Ben Chaney drove over and suggested that he take Bedelia for a drive. The weather had repented its bad behavior and was now mild and dry. Bedelia, of course, refused to leave her husband's bedside. The argument took place in the hall on the first floor. Miss Gordon, who heard everything that went on in the house, looked up from the drab sock she was knitting and told Charlie that he ought to insist that his wife accept the invitation. For the sake of her health, the nurse said, Mrs. Horst ought to have at least an hour's fresh air every day.

And each afternoon thereafter, Bedelia went out for a drive in Ben Chaney's car.

On New Year's Eve Charlie was allowed to get out of bed. He was much improved and so rested that he looked better than before he was stricken. He dressed in dark trousers and his purple silk smoking-jacket, and chose one of the fine silk ties which Bedelia had given him for Christmas.

Miss Gordon would not let him leave the bedroom. 'Not without the doctor's permission.'

'Then call up and get the doctor's permission. And ask Meyers why the devil he hasn't come to see me.'

'I do not like profanity, Mr. Horst.'

'I beg your pardon, Miss Gordon. But tell the doctor I want to see him today.'

'You know, Mr. Horst, that Doctor Meyers has been confined to the house with a cold. I've reported to him twice a day, and since there's no change for the worse in your health, there's no reason why he should risk pneumonia or bring infection into this house.'

'But I want to see him.'

'I'll tell him,' she said.

Doctor Meyers said that Charlie had better stay in his room for another day, and promised that if he felt well enough tomorrow he might go downstairs.

'Is he coming over?'

'He'll try to get here tomorrow.'

'The old faker,' murmured Charlie.

'Did you say something, Mr. Horst?'

'When Miss Walker and Mrs. Hoffman arrive, have them come upstairs.'

'I'll tell Mary. I'm going to lie down and take a little nap.'

Charlie's jaw dropped. Miss Gordon did not usually practice such self-indulgence. She might have taken her nap,

Charlie reflected, while Bedelia was at home. But it was like the nurse to overlook everything but her patient's physical needs.

Soon afterward Abbie and Ellen arrived, Abbie with a jar of calf's-foot jelly, Ellen with Albert Bigelow Paine's *Life of Mark Twain*. The room was filled with laughter and gossip, and Abbie, who was to leave town the next day, shrieked her opinions of her old friends. Presently Bedelia returned and with her Ben Chaney. Although he had called at the house every day, this was the first time he had been allowed upstairs.

'It's good to see you,' Charlie said. 'After all this female society, it's pleasant to see a pair of pants.'

'Now, darling,' Bedelia pouted.

'Doctor Meyers has been to see you, hasn't he?'

'He's worse than an old woman.'

Ben had brought Charlie a bottle of sherry and Bedelia suggested that they open it. She went downstairs to fetch it and some sweet biscuits. As Charlie was supposed to be an invalid, Ben did the honors. He uncorked the bottle, poured a bit of wine into his own glass, then filled the others. Bedelia carried a glass of wine and a biscuit to Charlie.

'Mrs. Horst!'

Miss Gordon stood at the door. She walked silently on low-heeled shoes and no one heard her enter. Everyone looked at her. Ellen drew in her breath.

'What are you giving Mr. Horst?'

'It's quite all right, Miss Gordon. The doctor said he should drink a glass of wine every day. Mr. Chaney's brought him some sherry. Will you have some?'

'I never take spirits.' Miss Gordon stood rigid, inspecting Charlie's guests scornfully.

'Has Miss Gordon met these people?' Charlie asked. 'Miss Gordon, Mrs. Hoffman, Miss Walker, Mr. Chaney.'

'How do you do,' Ben said.

'Pleased to meet you,' said Miss Gordon.

Ellen gasped. For the rest of the visit she perched at the edge of her chair and plucked at her skirt with nervous fingers.

'What got into you this afternoon?' Abbie asked when they were home again and safe behind the locked door of Ellen's bedroom. 'You were fidgeting like an idiot. Why are you so nervous?'

'I could have told you at the beginning that there was something sneaky about him.'

'Ben? But he's a very well-bred fellow. I can't understand your aversion to him, unless you're prejudiced against eligible men.'

'Listen!' Ellen whispered. 'I've discovered something. That nurse is the woman he met at the station. I told you about it, Abbie. His godmother, my neck! And they acted as if they'd never seen each other before when Charlie introduced them.'

'Are you sure?'

'Could you make a mistake about that face? I'd swear it in court, I'd risk my life on it. But why should they want to hide it?'

Abbie gave up. Here was a problem that her worldliness could not solve. Ellen unbuttoned her mannish coat. From an inside pocket she pulled out a yellow paper packet of cheap cigarettes and, as calmly as if she'd been doing it all her life, lit one.

The next morning Charlie made a resolution which, unlike most New Year's vows, was carried out at once. Nothing could start the year more unauspiciously, he decided, than a breakfast served by Miss Gordon. Without permission he got up, took a warm shower, dressed, and went downstairs. Miss Gordon, coming through the swinging door with his breakfast tray in her hands, found him at the table.

'Why, Mr. Horst!'

'I'm having breakfast with my wife this morning.'

'But . . .'

'Will you join us, Miss Gordon? And incidentally, Happy New Year.'

'Happy New Year,' she said ungraciously.

This victory was tonic to Charlie. Bedelia's pleasure strengthened his resolution. When breakfast was over, he said, 'Miss Gordon, I wish to thank you for your services during my illness.'

'I've only done what I was paid to do.'

'I want you to enjoy the holiday. You gave up your New Year's Eve festivities for my sake, but I don't want you to sacrifice today's ceremonies, too.'

'I haven't planned anything particular.'

He waved away the excuse. 'I know you'd rather be with your friends. And since I don't need a nurse any longer, allow me to show my gratitude by paying you for the next couple of days, and take a holiday.'

Bedelia did not laugh, but the dimples were dancing on her creamy cheeks.

'We'll call McGuiness to take you to town.'

Miss Gordon sat firm. 'Aren't my services satisfactory, Mr. Horst?'

'Quite, Miss Gordon. But I'm fully recovered and shan't need a nurse any longer.'

'We shall have to ask Doctor Meyers about that. He is the only one from whom I am allowed to take orders.'

'I won't ask him, I'll tell him.'

The coffee-cup hid the lower part of Bedelia's face, but over it her dark eyes encouraged Charlie's rebellion. Feeling himself a man of authority, he hurried to the telephone.

To his great surprise, Doctor Meyers readily agreed that Charlie no longer needed a nurse. While Miss Gordon packed her bag, Charlie and Bedelia embraced. Forty minutes later she was driven off in McGuiness's hack, and the Horsts were alone at last. Mary had the day off, too. Her young man, Hen Blackman, had driven over from Redding in his father's buggy, and Mary, wearing Bedelia's kid gloves and one of Bedelia's hats, departed ecstatically.

'I hope she gets back in time,' Charlie said as he watched the buggy turn out of their drive to the main road.

'In time for what, dear?'

'Looks like a heavy snow.'

Bedelia nodded vaguely. She had gone to the what-not to restore order to the chaos created by Mary in dusting the shelves. Whenever the hired girl's back was turned, Bedelia went through a ritual of moving bric-á-brac. Charlie watched indulgently. He could have prophesied her every movement. Bedelia had such a love for little ornaments that she suffered if she saw the snuffboxes, miniature furniture, carved ivory animals and statuettes out of place.

Ben Chaney and Doctor Meyers arrived from different directions at almost the same moment. There was much shaking of hands and offering of good wishes for the New Year.

'I've come to call for my passenger,' Ben said.

'I can't come with you today, Ben. Miss Gordon's gone. I don't want to leave Charlie.'

'Miss Gordon's gone, has she?' Ben said.

The doctor slanted a curious look at Ben, then turned to Bedelia. 'You'd better get a little air today, Mrs. Horst. Looks like we're in for a bad storm and this might be your last chance for several days.'

There was some argument before Bedelia could be persuaded to leave her husband, and the doctor had almost to order her to take the drive.

As soon as she had gone off with Ben, Charlie folded his arms across his chest, looked down at the doctor and said, 'I want to know the meaning of what you said the other day.'

'Forget it, Charlie.'

'What do you mean? "Forget it, Charlie." What were you trying to do, pull my leg?'

'There's nothing to it. I've had reports form the laboratory. I'd rather have had the original excrement, but she'd cleaned it all up before I got here. But I'm certain that if there had been a toxic agent present, it would have shown in the specimens I sent to the laboratory.'

'I still don't understand you. What were you looking for? Poison?'

The word hung in the air. But having said it, Charlie felt better.

'Have a cigar, Charlie?' The doctor offered a pair of cylinders wrapped in tin foil. 'Christmas present from a patient. With a family like mine you don't often get a chance to smoke Corona Coronas.' The doctor did not speak again until he had cut off the tip, lighted the cigar, and enjoyed the first puff. 'I admit that your symptoms puzzled me, Charlie. I could find no cause for that sudden attack. After I went home that morning and talked it over with my oldest boy—there's no one who diagnoses so daringly as a medical student—I decided to take no chances.'

'But I'd been having dyspepsia all along.'

The doctor sighed.

'It's not like you to alarm your patients. Frankly, I don't understand your actions.'

The doctor did not immediately answer. After a while he said, 'I sometimes think my wife is in her dotage. She fancies those animated photographs which are becoming so popular with the children, and often drags me into town to see them.' He shivered slightly. 'No doubt my mind has been affected by the lurid quality of these entertainments.'

Charlie got up. 'Why are you lying, Doctor?'

'Don't shout. My hearing is perfect.'

'I beg your pardon. But I insist that you tell me the truth.'

'Aren't you glad to know that it was nothing more than an old man's overzealous imagination?'

'If it was nothing but imagination, why did you tell me about it? I should think you'd have tried to save me the anxiety.'

'I felt it my duty to warn you in case my premonitions meant anything. If there had been danger and I had failed to warn you, I should have been responsible.'

'Perhaps you fail to realize the gravity of the charges you made again an innocent person.'

'I made no charges.'

'You insinuated that I had been give'—Charlie cleared his throat— 'given poison by . . .' He could not continue.

'Your attitude surprises me. One would think I'd brought you bad news today. I confess that I'm relieved to find that it was nothing more than an attack of acute indigestion, and I beg your pardon for having caused you any anxiety.'

Charlie sank into a chair. His eyes were wet. The doctor turned away tactfully and walked to the bow window. Snow was falling, but so lazily that the ragged flakes seemed suspended in the air. The landscape bored Doctor Meyers and he moved from the window. He saw that Charlie had not recovered composure and fixed his attention on the opposite corner of the room. There stood the what-not with its absurd collection of silver, ivory, porcelain and enameled toys. For the life of him, Doctor Meyers could not understand why grown women treasured such trifles. One group attracted him by the very virtue of its inanity. A Dresden china marquis in a coat of ripe-plum red held his pale hands over the eyes of a lady whose lace-trimmed skirts billowed over a chair decorated with gilt arabesques and painted rosebuds. As he examined the piece, the doctor heard Ben's automobile drive up and stop at the door. He replaced the ornament upon the shelf guiltily, for he knew how his wife scolded if the symmetry of her shelves were destroyed.

Charlie blew his nose and returned his handkerchief to his pocket. He looked guilty, too.

Bedelia opened the door with her key. Ben lingered in the hall to take off his hat and coat, but Bedelia hurried into the living-room with the snowflakes shining on her velvet hat and on the sealskin collar of her coat. Her eyes were bright, her cheeks rosy. She touched cold lips to Charlie's cheeks.

'It's snowing quite hard. Ben thought we ought to turn back before the roads were all snowy. It was such a lovely drive, Charlie, with the snow beginning to fall and the sky that peculiar shade of gray-blue like lead. How I love your Connecticut.'

'His Connecticut,' sniffed the doctor.

At the sight of Bedelia's pretty face and the memory of his ridiculous fears, relief welled up again in Charlie and he was compelled to blow his nose loudly. Bedelia noticed the waxen color of his skin and the contrast with his reddened nostrils and eyes.

'Oh, my dear, what has the doctor been telling you?'

'I'm afraid he's caught my cold,' Doctor Meyers remarked. To give his excuse authority, he pulled out his handkerchief and sniffed at it with dry nostrils. 'I'd better be going before the snow piles up.'

'I insist on knowing what you told Charlie.'

The doctor smiled over Bedelia's shoulder at Charlie. 'He'll tell you the good news.'

'Good news?' said Ben, coming into the room. 'What good news?'

'Let Charlie tell you,' the doctor said with a contemptuous glance at Chaney. Then he wished them all a Happy New Year and left.

'What was it?' Bedelia demanded.

'Now that it's over,' Charlie said, 'I can tell you that he had certain apprehensions . . .'

'What sort of apprehensions?'

'Very stupid and exaggerated. Now he's come to his senses and discovered that there was nothing to his suspicions.'

'What were they?'

Charlie shrugged. 'I can't give you the technical name, it's merely that he warned me to prepare for a shock. And now he's confessed that his fears were unfounded.'

Ben stood with his legs apart, his hands clasped behind his back, his eager eyes on Charlie's face. He had not moved, but his expression had become more alert and his lips had tightened.

'I'm so happy, dear.'

'We've nothing to worry about. I'm fully recovered and ready to resume my routine. The day after tomorrow I'm going back to work.'

As Charlie said this, the pattern of his life became normal. He looked around and saw the room as it had been when he and Bedelia had finished redecorating the house. There were not even the Christmas wreaths and ribbons left to remind him of holiday disruptions. The love-seat had been moved back to its place in the bow window.

The snowfall was heavier, the wind rising. A light blanket of snow concealed the darkness of the earth. Twilight entered through the uncurtained windows. Bedelia lighted the lamps. Then she saw how Doctor Meyers had disarranged her shelves and hurried to restore order.

'I had a wire from my friend in St. Paul,' Ben said. 'The blizzards are apparently over in the Middle West and he's coming here, after all. You'll meet Keene Barrett in a few days.'

The ornament slipped form Bedelia's hands. The Dresden lovers lay shattered on the floor. The marquis's white-wigged head rolled into the corner, the porcelain lace of his mistress's skirt powdered the rug.

Bedelia's face had been drained of color. Her empty hands were circled before her as if she were still holding the ornament.

'Biddy, my sweet!' Charlie took her in his arms. 'Don't be upset. The thing has no value and, just between you and me, I'll confess that I always thought it hideous.'

She lowered her unsteady hands. Her rings sparkled in the lamplight. Her eyes had become blank, all expression was erased from her countenance, and it was clear that she had not heard what Charlie said. He led her to the couch, sat with his arm around her swelling waist. Soon he and Ben were talking casually again, about motors, comparing the merits of their machines and discussing the improvements which were being made by manufacturers. Bedelia sat beside her husband quietly, sunk in reverie, hardly aware of the men's voices. Presently Ben rose and said that he must leave. Charlie asked him to stay for supper. Bedelia did not repeat the invitation.

Long after Ben had gone, his voice echoed in Charlie's ears, rising louder than the shrieks and wails of the storm. Ben had used the commonest phrase of the day, Happy New Year, but Charlie could not purge his mind of the cheerless tone of the greeting.

While Bedelia prepared their light supper, Charlie sat in the kitchen. He enjoyed watching her work. She went about it with zest and competence. The kitchen, more than any room in the house, was her own. The room positively glistened. The floor was laid in black-and-white linoleum, shelves and cabinets were painted a clean gray, and all the pulls and handles were of white china imported from Holland. Mary had starched the ruffled curtains like Sunday petticoats.

Bedelia had tied over her blue dress an apron as crisp and clean as the curtains. She looked less like a housewife than a character in a drawing-room comedy, the maid who flirts with the butler as she whisks her feather duster over the furniture. The kitchen, with its neat shelves, starched curtains, and copper pots, made Charlie think of a stage-setting. And when Bedelia brought out her red-handled egg-beater and started whipping up a froth in a yellow bowl, he was enchanted. He had to hug her.

She did not use her work as a protest against his love-making. She set the bowl upon the table and lay back in his arms. It was then that he saw that she was trembling. This surprised him. She had gone about her tasks with composure.

'Dearest, what's wrong?'

She did not answer. Charlie tilted her chin backward and looked into her face. He caught there the shadow of the terror he had noticed when she dropped the Dresden lovers. Her lips were parted but she did not cry out. Immediately her mood was communicated to Charlie. He felt a tension within him, a pulling and straining of his nerves.

Presently Bedelia disengaged herself and went back to work. She folded the beaten whites into the seasoned yolks of the eggs and poured the mixture into one of her copper pots. She had a child's ability to shut out everything except the task at hand. If Charlie had not been so much in love and so sentimental in his attitude toward the delicacy of women, her indifference might have offended him. But his mother had made him sensitive to women's sufferings. No man, thought Charlie, would ever comprehend the tortures suffered by the more exquisitely wrought female.

Her mood persisted. At supper Charlie was almost ashamed of his good appetite. Behind her untouched plate Bedelia sat with idle hands and impassive face.

'You're not eating,' he said.

For all she heard, he might have been talking to the coffee-pot.

'Bedelia!'

She roused herself, sought his eyes, apologized wordlessly for inattention. Then she made a great effort and her lips curved into a smile.

How gallant she was! thought Charlie. How courageously

she tried to overcome her sensitivity! And for his sake. He said tenderly: 'What's worrying you, Biddy? Not that ugly little ornament you broke today. Why, I'm glad it's gone. I've always disliked it. Those gingerbread things are in bad taste, I think, and besides, it was given Ma by her old friend, Adelaide Hawkins, whom I loathed.'

'Charlie, let's go away.'

'Are you crazy?'

'I want to go away from here. Now, at once, please.'

'My dear girl—'

'I want to go away.'

'Why?'

'I don't like this place.'

'You said this afternoon that you loved it.'

The wind had become stronger. It tore across the fields and over the small hills, whipped around the house, churned up the river, sent drafts whistling down the chimney. Walls, doors, and storm windows could not shut out its fury.

'Don't let the storm worry you, dear. It's always like this. The house seems to shake on its foundations, but it's firmly built, it's stood for a hundred and nine years, and will probably be standing when our grandchildren come of age.' This failed to move Bedelia, and Charlie added, 'If you're afraid of the river, I guarantee you it won't flood us. This isn't the season, and since we put in the stone terrace . . .'

'We could leave tomorrow morning.'

'Whatever has got into you?'

'I want us to go,' she said, leaning across the table and turning her eyes upon him with full awareness of their appeal. All of her will was concentrated in the need to dislodge his objections and get her own way.

'My dear,' he said, in the patient monotone of a parent pleading with a stubborn child, 'I can't just pack up and leave because you get a sudden idea that you want to go away. I haven't the slightest understanding of this whim, for I told you the winter here would be severe and you said you'd enjoy the new experience. We may be snowbound for a few days, but otherwise we'll suffer no discomfort. The house is warm and secure and there's nothing to be afraid of.'

'Don't you love me?'

'What a question! This has nothing to do with love. I've got my business, it's important for me to get the Bridgeport job done well. My future depends on it.'

'We could go to Europe.'

'You sound insane.'

She nodded.

'This is the maddest thing I've ever heard. In the middle of winter.'

'The *Viktoria Luise* sails next Thursday. We could stay in New York until then.'

Charlie was too intent upon his own arguments to wonder why or how she possessed this information. He talked about his home, his work, and his bank account. He had spent a lot of money that year, traveled, married, bought the automobile, Bedelia's wardrobe, and done over the house. Of his mother's legacy little remained. Their income depended mainly upon his work. He had explained this to Bedelia before they were married so that she should not think she was getting a rich husband, and she had laughed, telling him how poor she had been, and how rich he seemed to her, and how little it mattered.

'Please, Charlie.'

'Have you gone mad?' Although he tried not to show it, Charlie had become angry. His voice betrayed him.

Bedelia was crying. The tears overflowed her eyes and sobs shook her shoulders. Charlie's anger melted. He ran around the table to her, embraced her, touched his lips to her wet cheeks. To this physical assurance of his love she yielded at once, resting in his arms and enjoying his strength. But her sobs did not cease. She was torn by her sorrow, inconsolate, like a child who knows no cause for its racking grief. Charlie led her to the stairs, half-carried her to the bedroom, seated her in the pink chair while he uncovered the bed. She remained in the chair while he ran about collecting her night things and rubbing her forehead with cologne.

While he tended her, Charlie asked and found a satisfying answer to the question of her conduct. Other women woke at midnight and asked for dill pickles; some craved strawberries in January. Charlie thought about the week just ended, the excitement of the holidays, the work of preparing the Christmas party, the shock of his attack, the doctor's uncertainty and the tragic memories which all of this must have awakened in her. The day, too, had been filled with small annoyances. Most terrifying of all to a person accustomed to milder climates must be the thundering of the winter storm, the wildness of wind and river.

He cursed the storm and begged God for its cessation.

Bedelia lay in bed and watched as Charlie hung up her dress, set her shoes on the shelf, rolled her corset in its string and put it into the proper drawer. The room smelled of sachet, cologne, and the dry heat of the steam radiator.

'Don't ever believe a word Ben tells you,' Bedelia whispered.

Charlie whirled around. 'Ben? What's he got to do with it?'

'He's against us.'

Charlie sat on the edge of the bed, took Bedelia's cold hand, and scowled down into her face. 'Don't be ridiculous. Ben's a fine chap. You've always liked him.'

'He's against you, Charlie.'

'I don't know what you mean.'

'He'll hurt us. That's all he cares about, to hurt us and ruin our lives.'

Charlie looked at the window, tried to measure the storm's intensity, wondering whether it would be possible for the doctor to reach the house that night. The curtains had not been drawn and the darkness outside made the window a mirror so that Charlie saw reflected the lamplight, the pink chair, and himself at the edge of the bed, holding his wife's hand. It was a reassuring picture. Solid walls shut out the blizzard.

'Please, Charlie, let's go away. I don't want to stay here any longer,' she said pathetically. She made it sound as simple as if it were an afternoon's excursion that she had suggested.

'What's the matter? Has Ben done anything to you? Has he insulted you?' The blood ran hot in Charlie's veins, his fists clenched, his head throbbed. He recalled Ben Chaney's way of watching Bedelia, remembered the night at Jaffney's Tavern when she had worn the black pearl and her white hand had rested in Ben's swarthy hand above the platter of lobster and lemon wedges. 'By God, I'll strangle him.'

She had buried her face in the pillow and was shaking and sobbing again. The wind split the world, shattering rocks, dividing the rivers. The sky was about to fall, the earth to explode, the waters to rise up and devour them.

Against his wife's hysteria Charlie was impotent. And impotence aggravated his fury. He was wildly angry, his eyes bulged out of his head, his face was stained a purplish red, and when he spoke his voice shook with anger. 'Tell me,' he implored. 'Tell me!' he commanded, but all in vain. She burrowed deeper in the pillows, hid her face, stiffened if his hand brushed against her.

The storm's fury died. The wind retreated, the waters were lulled. The earth became solid again. And Bedelia fell asleep, her head on her bare arm. Emotion had exhausted. She slept like a child, breathing aloud. Charlie covered her, lit her night lamp, and went downstairs.

He vowed that he would think calmly, he swore that he would banish all suspicion from his mind, he struggled to find reasons for his wife's sudden hysteria. And this was as vain as his commands and his pleadings to Bedelia. Why had she begged him to run off with her? Why was she afraid of Ben Chaney? *He'll hurt us.* Why, for God's sake? *That's all he cares about, to hurt us and ruin our lives.* If this were true, if Ben were, as Bedelia had argued, against them, why had he shown no signs of enmity until today? Had he tried to be . . . or, God deny such treachery, been . . . Bedelia's lover? Was he urging her to desert her husband and run off with him? Had he, when Bedelia refused his entreaties, threatened to expose her infidelity?

Charlie could not believe it. The idea of such betrayal was the fruit of a sick imagination, rotten fruit fertilized by suspicion, fear and lack of self-esteem. In Charlie's house there was no room for such treachery. Infidelity had never dwelt in the old Philbrick house, could never dwell there. The ceilings would rot, the walls cave in, the floors lose their solidity.

Charlie was ill with anguish. The day's emotions had been too violent for a man just risen from a sickbed. He was almost too weak to climb the stairs, clung to the rail and pulled himself up like a cripple. So that he should not disturb Bedelia, he undressed in the bathroom, and when he got into bed, lowered himself cautiously onto the mattress. She did not twitch a muscle. In a few minutes Charlie was sleeping soundly, too.

The room had been lighted by Bedelia's night lamp. Charlie awoke in unbroken darkness. At first the strangeness of this did not occur to him, for he had been sleeping alone in a dark room all the time he was ill. As he became aware of the storm crashing about the house, the river's rage, the passion of the wind, he was struck suddenly by the sense of darkness and was convinced immediately that he had gone blind. He groped for the night lamp, turned the switch. The room was still black.

For a nightmare moment he could neither speak nor move.

He tried to call, but he had no voice. When he stretched out his trembling hand, he could not find his wife in bed.

On icy, uncertain legs he traveled through infinite darkness to the electric switch on the wall. He felt it, heard the click and waited for the light. Darkness remained. He was sick, faint, bilious, recalled in minutest detail the sensations he had suffered before his attack and thought he was about to fall unconscious again. All the while he groped for the china matchbox on the mantel. He struck a match. Out of the darkness jagged a small yellow flame. Relief surged through him. His skin grew damp with grateful sweat. Unsteady hands found the candle, touched flame to wick. In the first rays of flickering light he saw the old gilt-framed portrait of his mother above the mantel. At once intelligence returned, he became his rational self, knew the storm had disconnected electric wires, and assured himself that other of his sick fancies could be as sensibly explained, cursed himself for allowing his mind to become infected by the virus of fear, and knew that he would find Bedelia sleeping gently on her side of the bed.

She was not there. Nor had she gone off to sleep alone in the room she had used during Charlie's illness. She was nowhere on the second floor, and when he, candle in hand, went down the stairs, calling her name, there was no answer. Through the house he went, searching every room, but all that remained of Bedelia were the clothes that hung in her closet, the copper pots and contrivances she had bought for her kitchen, the smell of her perfumes and unguents, the fabrics she had chosen for pillows and furniture, her hyacinths growing in the blue pot.

'Bedelia! Biddy! Where are you?'

Only the wind answered.

4

Of the world outside there was nothing but white motion. Snowflakes tumbled out of clouds like feathers from a torn pillow. Snow rose, too, and whirled off in gigantic spirals like ghosts leaving the churchyard. No sane person could have gone out in this storm, Charlie told himself, as he took the oil lamp from its hook in the shed. He had put on trousers, a flannel shirt, his mackinaw and a cap.

The lamp hung from his wrist as he cupped his hands before his mouth calling, 'Bedelia! Bedelia!' He squinted through the snowfall, but could see nothing but the white restless circles rising from the ground and the white flakes falling from the burdened sky.

He pushed his way through the drifts and worked up the slight slope that led to the gate. The snow was high and although it was dry and light, the ground below was uneven and he could not be sure of his footing.

On the road he stumbled over something, saw a dark patch in the snow. As he leaned over, the wind seized his cap and whirled it away. He clapped his hands over his ears, which had begun to sting as if a swarm of bees had been at them. A wraith of snow rose, filling his eyes with its bitter powder. Tears prevented his seeing properly and it was through a cloud that he recognized the dark patch as the traveling bag of ox-blood morocco which he had bought as a birthday present for Bedelia.

A few feet farther on, half in the ditch and almost covered by the snow, lay his wife. 'Thank God!' cried Charlie. The wind seized his voice and whirled it away along with the cold and the snowflakes.

He picked her up and struggled with her to the house. It took all of his strength to get her across the yard to the door of the shed. There he almost collapsed, and he leaned against the wall to rest and recover his breath. When he had finally got her into the house and laid her on the linoleum of the kitchen floor, he knelt beside her and listened for her heartbeat. In his excitement he missed it. He lifted the still figure, clasped it to his breast, forgetting suspicion and anger, forgetting that she had tried to run away, remembering only that he loved her and had been happy with this woman.

She did not open her eyes until he had carried her to the couch in his den and covered her with a fur rug. A shadow crossed her face as she looked around the room, recognizing the house from which she had not been able to escape. She closed her eyes again, shutting out the sight of her failure. Her suffering was acute.

Charlie hurried to the basement, heaped coal on the fire, rushed back to the den, turned on the radiator. When the room was warm, he uncovered her and removed her wet clothes. She opened her eyes and looked at him squarely. A wan smile curved her lips. Charlie rubbed her with rough towels until her flesh was red, but she did not cease shivering. The pathos of her dark eyes, the tremors and muteness, reminded him of a spaniel he had owned when he was a boy, and he felt sorry for her as he used to feel sorry for the dog because it depended on him for food and affection. He wrapped her in blankets and carried her up the stairs to bed. Not once while he was working over her did he show resentment nor ask the reason for her strange conduct.

'Now, my dear,' he said tenderly, 'you're to have brandy and hot milk, and then you're going straight to sleep.' He covered her with wool blankets, the down quilt and the comfort his mother had stitched in the Snake and Apple design.

She drank the milk and brandy like a good child, her dimpled hands clasped around the old silver mug. And with the same docility she obeyed Charlie's command to sleep.

He left the room on tiptoe. There was nothing more that he could do for her, but he decided that he had better consult the doctor anyway. While he was on way to the telephone, he wondered what to say if the doctor should ask how his wife had got such a severe chill. Then he discovered that the line was dead. The storm had disconnected the telephone wires. Charlie was glad of that. A sense of duty had prompted him to call Doctor Meyers, but he was relieved when he found that he would not have to answer any questions.

All this effort, the strength he had expended and the anxiety, should have wearied him. But he was wide-awake and restless. In vain he tried to quiet his curiosity. When Bedelia had recovered from the chill, he would ask her a few important questions. He would approach the subject calmly, show neither anger nor distrust, but prove by his love and firmness that she might fearlessly confide in him. As he planned it, Charlie saw himself and Bedelia beside the fire, heard his voice gently urging her to full confession. The vision did not quiet him. He could not help recalling his talks with Doctor Meyers and wondering whether she had overheard the doctor's warning. But if this were so, why had she waited four days before wounded pride forced her to flee? And what had it to do with her sudden rage against Ben Chaney?

His thoughts traveled in dark circles and left him bewildered. At the end of a tortured hour he was no wiser than he had been at the beginning. Then he remembered the traveling bag and went outside for it. Ordinarily Charlie would not have opened his wife's bag nor examined its contents. This would have been cheap and unworthy, the action of a man who would consider it right to read his wife's mail. He had an excuse, however. The bag was wet and its contents would become mouldy unless they were taken out and dried.

Bedelia had packed stockings, a change of underwear, a nightgown, slippers, a black silk crepe kimono with a turquoise-blue lining, and an extra shirtwaist. There were also her toilet things, the padded leather box in which she kept her knickknacks, and a sheaf of travel folders showing schedules of Cunard, White Star, and Hamburg-Amerika sailings. The discovery of these pamphlets unnerved Charlie. They were evidence that Bedelia's idea of running off to Europe had not occurred spontaneously at the table last night.

Idly he opened the leather box. It contained trifles, the sort of souvenirs that young girls cherish. In a heart-shaped locket he saw Bedelia's dark eyes under a mass of fair curls and he wondered why his wife had never showed him this picture of her mother. A pressed rose, dry and breaking apart, and a spray from a cerise plume were in a faded lavender envelope. There was a miniature Japanese fan, a penknife with a mother-of-pearl handle and broken blade, and a round pillbox with a blank label. In it was a white powder like the powder his wife used for polishing her fingernails. Last of all he pulled out the swollen velvet box which had held his garnet ring.

He snapped it open. There was the black pearl in its setting of platinum and diamonds.

We can't give Abbie that ring, Charlie, I don't have it any more. I've given it away.

Hastily Charlie replaced the ring and put the velvet box back in the padded leather container. He put away the travel folders, too, and the rest of his wife's tawdry souvenirs.

'Are you angry with me, Charlie?'

He pulled down the shade. The light disturbed him. He did not wish to look at Bedelia's face nor show his to her. 'We'll talk about it later. How are you feeling?'

'I've caught a bad cold.'

'Yes. You'll have to stay in bed.'

Dark hair outlined the pale oval of her face. She moaned lightly.

'Are you in pain?'

'My chest hurts. It's my own fault, though. I've been naughty, I deserve punishment.'

She waited for Charlie to comment upon her naughtiness. The word she had chosen was far too frivolous to describe her thoroughly abnormal conduct. Charlie could not speak at all. Pretending to be busy with the knob of the radiator, he kept his face toward the wall.

'Charlie!'

'Yes?'

Huskily she whispered, 'Have you heard from Ben?'

Charlie turned, still squatting beside the radiator, glared across the room at his wife. His voice was thickened by new, coarse notes. 'No, and we're not likely to for a few days. The road's blocked, the electricity's off, and the telephone wires are down.'

'Oh!' Bedelia said, and after she had thought about it, laughed lightly. 'Snowbound, Charlie! Are we snowbound?'

'Yes.'

'When I was in school we studied a poem about a family who were snowbound. Do you know it, Charlie?'

He could not answer. Bedelia was making an effort to restore the old relationship; she was pretending that there had been no attempt to run off, no lies, no unanswered questions.

'You must know it,' she persisted and her voice was actually blithe. 'You know so much poetry, Charlie. I think it's by Lowell.'

'No, Whittier.'

'Yes, of course, Whittier. I wish I had your memory, dear.'

He looked at her obliquely and saw that she was smiling and trying to win him. It was as if nothing extraordinary had happened, as if they had gone to bed comfortably last night and awakened side by side that morning.

'After we've had breakfast, I want to ask you some questions, Bedelia.'

She pushed up in bed. 'Yes, of course, dear. But we must have breakfast first, I'm hungry. Will you pull up the shades, please?' There were the dimples again, dancing in her cheeks, the shining eyes, the creamy luster of her skin. She was rosier, too, flushed with fever but prettier for it.

'What about Mary? Didn't she get back?'

'Not in this storm,' Charlie said. 'She's probably snowed in at Blackman's farm.'

'With her young man,' Bedelia laughed. 'I hope she makes the most of her good luck.' Then the smile disappeared and she frowned and sucked in her cheeks, worrying about the housekeeping. If Mary was away and she was ill in bed, how was Charlie to be fed and the house kept clean?

'Leave everything to me, I'll take care of it.'

'But you can't do housework, Charlie.'

'Why not? I can't get to the office.'

'I don't like to see a man do housework.'

There was no other way of handling it. Charlie fled gladly to the lonely kitchen where he need not face deceit, nor suffer remorse because he had not the courage to ask his wife a few questions. This was weak of him and he despised himself for it, but he knew that once he had put them into words his fears would have substance and reality, and he would be forced to take action.

Bedelia had no excuses to offer. So long as Charlie avoided the questions, she was content to let the answers wait. One would think she had caught cold shaking her rugs out of the window. As the day passed, both she and Charlie seemed to have forgotten that she had tried to desert him. Whatever urge had sent her off in the midst of the blizzard was lost in the lethargy of fever and comfort.

If Bedelia had sought a way, deliberately, to recapture Charlie's love, she could have found none more effective than fever, confinement in bed, helplessness. The more she depended on him, the richer grew his affection and the firmer his belief that strength such as his was capable of forgiveness. His enjoyment of her weakness was no sign of cruelty in him. It carried out the pattern of his training. He had been taught that man is strong, woman frail; that devotion and self-sacrifice are love's glowing crown. He cooked, washed dishes, carried trays, cleaned lamps, ran gladly whenever she had an errand. She had given in completely to her illness, enjoying the weakness that made him her slave. She leaned upon his arm while he arranged her pillows and depended upon his moral strength in trusting him to abandon his grievance.

In the afternoon she felt better, wanted to sit up in bed, and asked him to bring one of her robes from the closet. Charlie chose the black crepe kimono with the turquoise lining.

As he held it for her, he said, 'I unpacked your bag, you know.'

'Thank you,' she said.

She knotted the sash, straightened the seams and pulled at the wide sleeves. 'This is pretty, don't you think?'

'Uh-huh.'

'Would you get me my silver mirror, please? And my brush and comb. I'd like my powder and chamois, too. And yes, Charlie, that naughty little box.'

Charlie frowned.

Bedelia laughed. 'So you've discovered my little secret? I hope you don't despise me for it.'

'Bedelia,' he said, determined to have it out with her now, 'I have become more and more mystified by your behavior. There is nothing funny about this to me, and I shall be grateful if you'll explain the situation.'

The wayward creature laughed even more frivolously. 'Oh, Charlie, don't be so pompous. I'm talking about the little box that contains the secret of my pretty red lips and cheeks.'

'I'm sorry, I don't understand you.'

'Rouge,' she said merrily. 'Paint, if that's what you call it. Abbie paints, too, but she uses that horrid dry powder. She thinks it doesn't show, but even a blind man would notice.'

Silently Charlie watched while she brushed and combed her hair, braided it and wound the braids in snails over her ears. She smiled and winked as she dipped her little finger into the rouge pot, reddened her lips and rubbed color into her pale cheeks.

'I do look better now, don't I?'

'Are you quite done?'

She put her hairbrush and cosmetics in the drawer where she had left his digestive powders. 'I'll keep these handy so you won't have to do so many errands.'

'Bedelia!'

'Yes, dear.'

'There are some things we ought to discuss. I believe you're well enough now.'

'Why are you so cross, darling? Have I done something again?'

Her teasing made Charlie feel that he had been pompous. He had been standing before the mantel with his arms crossed on his chest. He relaxed, slouched forward, and put his hands in his pockets so that he should not appear so formidable. But his voice was cold. 'My dear, I should like some explanations of your conduct.'

She examined her fingernails.

'Why did you run off? Is there anything here that you're afraid of?'

'I was afraid that you didn't love me anymore.'

The simplicity of her statement astonished Charlie. He could think of nothing to say.

'You were unkind the other night. I thought you were tired of me and wanted me to go.'

'Bedelia, look at me.'

Her eyes met his.

'You tried to run off in the midst of a blizzard, you risked your life to get away from this house. Surely it couldn't have been because I refused to listen to your irresponsible talk of running off to Europe. There must have been more to it than that.'

'I love you so much, Charlie, and I'm always afraid I'm not good enough for you.'

'Biddy, my dear, please be sensible.'

'You're so much more intelligent that I am. Whenever I see you with Ellen, I realize how much better an intellectual woman would have suited you.'

'If Ellen had suited me better, I'd have married her. You ought to understand that. Now tell me honestly, why did you run off?'

'You were horrid to me. You hurt my feelings.'

'I?'

'You made me feel like a silly goose.' Tears gathered and she groped among the pillows for her handkerchief. Finally she had to ask Charlie to get one out of the top drawer.

He felt sorry for her. This was not reasonable, but he could not help himself. 'I don't remember being cruel, and if I happened to say something out of the way, I'm sincerely sorry. But was that your only reason? Did you actually rush off like that because you thought I'd quit caring for you?'

She bowed her head.

Charlie prepared gloomily to speak his mind. Bedelia wiped her eyes and reached for the hand mirror. When she caught Charlie staring, she smiled ruefully.

He began clearing his throat. Then, 'I also have something to confess. When I unpacked your bag, I discovered something.'

'You mustn't blame yourself for that, dear. Anyone would have done the same thing. I think it was sweet of you to unpack for me.'

'I discovered something!' He came closer to the bed and squinted down at her, expecting guilt or fear to be written on her face. She was not discomposed. He went on, 'I discovered, first of all, that your flight was not unpremeditated.

There were a number of travel booklets in your bag. You
knew when certain ships were sailing. It's clear you've been
thinking of this for some time.'

'Yes, I have,' she said amiably.

'You don't say!'

'Listen to me, Charlie. It's not easy to say what I'm going
to say now. When I married you, I was very fond of you. I
thought you were the sort of man who could make a woman
happy, and I needed a man like that. I pretended to be more
in love than I really was.' A penitent sigh escaped. 'I can tell
you this now because I am in love with you now, Charlie,
desperately. It took me a while to understand how wonderful
you are. And when I discovered that I was passionately in
love with you, I began to be afraid. I felt that I wasn't half
good enough nor clever enough to be your wife, and I voiced
that if you should ever get tired of me, if I ever discovered
that you were unhappy or sorry you had married me, I'd run
off.' She spoke readily, the words tumbled out, and she was
soon out of breath.

'Why, Biddy,' Charlie said, shaken by her intensity.

'I'd die before I hurt you, Charlie.'

Charlie sat down at the foot of the bed. He was moved by
his wife's outburst, but also bewildered. If love had sent her
rushing out into the snowstorm to desert him because she had
felt herself unworthy, why had she asked him, several hours
earlier, to flee with her? He was tempted to ask that question,
but unwilling to hurt her by showing that he lacked faith in
her excuse.

'I know what you're thinking,' Bedelia said. 'You're wondering where I'd get the money for a trip like that. I've got
something to confess, dear.'

Now that he was close to the truth, Charlie was not sure
whether he wanted to hear it. His forefinger traced the curves
of a green calico snake quilted into the white muslin of the
comfort. Better to live happily, he told himself, than to suffer

painful knowledge. The trunks of the quilted apple tees were russet-colored, the foliage green with small white dots. In every fourth patch was stitched a round apple of scarlet cotton.

'I got a little money in November, money of my own.'

'How?'

'A legacy. Raoul's grandmother died. She left it to him and it became mine legally. His people didn't want me to have it, they were always against me, but they were afraid I'd make a scandal and show how mean and greedy they were, so they had to give it to me.'

'Why didn't you tell me?'

She sighed. 'Darling, darling Charlie, I hate to reproach you, but'—she uttered a slight, deprecating chuckle—'you are a bit jealous, you know, even of poor dead Raoul. So I decided to keep this fund secret and have a little money of my own to buy Christmas presents with. So I could be as extravagant as I liked, and not feel that I was wasting your money.'

'Then you lied about saving the money out of your household allowance?'

'Yes, dear.'

'I'd rather you told me the truth.'

'Forgive me, Charlie, please say you'll forgive me.' She extended her hands. Charlie did not take them and they lay cuplike on the quilt. 'I'll die if you don't forgive me.'

'That's extravagant talk.'

'Don't be so horrid to me, Charlie. I love you. I live only for you.'

Her fervor embarrassed him. He rose and walked away from the bed, and looked at his mother's portrait above the mantel. Harriet Philbrick had never colored her lips and cheeks with rouge. Only righteousness had adorned her countenance. She sat upright in the carved Victorian chair and faced the world with full assurance of her superiority. Emboldened by the look in his mother's eyes, Charlie whirled around and said in the voice she had used when she wished to show displeasure, 'Why did you lie to me about the ring?'

'What ring, dear?'

'Please don't lie, Bedelia. I know you didn't give away the black pearl. I saw it in your bag.'

'Oh, that. Yes, of course, you found it in my bag. Since I thought I was leaving you, it didn't matter whether I wore it or not. You see, dear, you haven't improved my taste at all. I'm still fond of that imitation pearl.'

'But you said you'd given it away.'

'No, I didn't. I never gave that ring away.'

'You told me you had.'

'What a funny idea!'

'Look here'— Charlie almost shouted it—'you told me that on Christmas. I wanted to give Abbie the ring and you said you'd given it away.'

She shook her head.

'I distinctly remember,' Charlie said. 'On two occasions you said it. The night we dined at Ben's.'

'No!' she interrupted. 'No, I didn't say it at all. You said it, I remember now that you told Ben and Abbie I'd given the ring away. I didn't say anything then because I didn't want to contradict you in public, particularly after Abbie made that flattering remark about me and what an unusual wife I was. I wondered where you'd got the idea, and I meant to ask you about it when were alone, but you had your attack that night, and I was so frightened I completely forgot.'

'Do you mean to stand there and say you didn't tell me on Christmas that you'd given the ring away?'

'I'm not standing here,' Bedelia said, 'I'm lying here in bed, sick as a dog, and it's very cruel of you to stand there and say I told you anything like that.'

'I could have sworn it,' Charlie said.

'You probably imagined it. You've got an awfully vivid imagination, Charlie.'

He could think of nothing to say. She might be right. He had been certain that Bedelia told him she had given the ring away. Was it only imagination? Was his memory unreliable, his truth illusion, his reality mere fantasy?

One question honestly answered might have cleared away all the confusion. But Charlie was loath to ask his wife about her relations with Ben Chaney. How much happier he would be if he attributed all suspicion to the workings of an over-wrought mind. The truth was that Charlie did not want to know the truth, and willingly allowed himself to be confused by Bedelia's air of innocence and melted by her charms.

That night Charlie was awakened by the touch of icy fingers on his face. He had gone to bed in his old room, the one he had used when he was a boy and his parents were alive. While Charlie was ill, Bedelia had occupied this room. She had left her handkerchief on a table beside the bed, and as he drifted off to sleep, Charlie had been aware of the fragrance.

He smelled it again, but the odor was stronger and closer to him. Believing this and the icy finger to be part of a dream, he kept his eyes closed and turned toward the wall. The fragrance lightened, but the fingers seemed to be pulling at his flesh and through the walls of his drowsiness he heard his name spoken.

Bedelia bent over the bed. In one hand she held the candle which Charlie had left burning at her bedside. It had been a tall candle when he left it there at eight o'clock, but now it was burned to a half-inch stub. The white Angora shawl was slipping from Bedelia's shoulders, and her hair hung in dark tangles over it. Her eyes burned with an uneasy fire that seemed to be constantly heightening and dying. Her cheeks were scarlet.

Curiously there darted into Charlie's mind the echo of Doctor Meyers's voice and the old man's warning. He shook off this terror, remembering the doctor's apology, and so awakened himself that he sat up straight, and said in a firm voice, 'What's the matter? Are you in pain? What is it?'

Bedelia could not speak. She looked less feverish than frantic; wild, like a frightened animal. Her throat had swelled and in it a pulse beat. She managed finally to whisper, 'There's someone downstairs.'

'That's impossible,' Charlie said.

'I heard him, someone moving.'

Charlie leaned over and pulled the shawl up on her shoulders. 'You oughtn't to be wandering around in the cold, dear. Go back to bed. We're completely cut off from everything. No one could possibly reach us.'

Unheeding, deaf to his words, she whimpered, 'I'm frightened. Someone is here.' She leaned toward the door, listening.

Charlie heard the river spilling over the rocks, the usual creaks and groans of the old house. He put on the new green robe that his wife had given him, tied the belt tight around his waist, took the candle from her hands and lit his own candle. Bedelia crouched beside the bed, watching him.

As he started out, she cried, 'Wait! Don't go!'

'Don't be foolish. I'm sure there's no one there. I'm just going down to make sure so that you won't worry. Go back to bed and put on plenty of covers. I'll heat some water for the bag.'

'I love you so much, Charlie, I'll die if anything happens to you.'

He led her back to the front room, tucked the covers around her. She watched anxiously as he left, the candlestick in his hand.

Why, if there was no possibility of an intruder's entering the house, if they were so completely isolated that no one could reach them, why did his heart pound as if he, too, had heard Bedelia's enemy and feared meeting him in the dark? He walked cautiously, on tiptoe, holding the candle in his left hand so that he had his right free and ready. In the dancing shadows cast by the candle, he saw movement in the shadows, and every corner was occupied by a waiting foe. As he opened doors and entered dark rooms his flesh crept.

He searched the house through, looked into closets, behind sofas and chests. No one was there. Their isolation was as complete as it had ever been, the night as quiet, the snow unscarred. Outside nothing moved except the river, winding like a black snake between snow-covered rocks. But the terror would not leave him. As he moved about the kitchen defiantly, heating a kettle of water, he found himself straining for unfamiliar noises.

Bedelia said, 'I'm sorry that I disturbed you. Will you forgive me, dear?'

He filled the rubber bag, covered it with a towel and laid it under her cold feet. 'Why are you so nervous? Perhaps you'd better talk to the doctor about those nightmares. They can't be normal.'

She kissed him and said that she was too tired to talk about it now. Would he please forgive her and let her sleep?

In the morning she was feeling much better. The nervousness had died with the fever and she was in a most winsome mood. 'You've forgiven me for disturbing you last night, haven't you?' she pleaded.

Charlie stood at the window, his back toward the bed. Frost had crusted the snow so that it shone like frosting on a wedding cake. No human, no animal, no vehicle had scarred the surface.

'I can't understand how you happened to think that someone was in the house last night. You knew we were completely cut off.'

She did not immediately answer. Three seconds later Charlie felt her warm moist lips against his cheek. She smiled up at him, telling her husband with the kiss and the smile that she wished to forget her horrid nightmares. Her arm linked in his, her soft weight against him, she begged, 'Please don't be angry. I'll die if you turn against me.'

'Why do you always say that, Bedelia? No one's turned against you.'

'People talk behind my back. You don't know. They're trying to turn you against me.'

'That's absurd. What people? Besides, nothing could turn me against you. You're my wife and I love you dearly. But I can't help being hurt and upset when you tell me lies.'

She changed the subject. 'Look at the river, how black it looks against the snow. Doesn't it ever freeze?'

'Not here. It's moving all the time. Down near the mill the ice must be solid now. When you're over your cold, I'll teach you to skate.'

'How soon will the snow melt?'

'Not for weeks unless we get an early thaw.'

'Shall we be snowbound all that time?'

'No, indeed. They ought to be clearing the road by this time. There must be a lot of snow in town.'

'Perhaps they'll never clear it.'

'If they don't, I'll quit paying my taxes. This road is always cleared. It's a through highway.'

'What about the side roads? Will they be cleared?'

'Not till Nature does the job.'

'Then Ben will be snowed in a long time?'

Charlie nodded. Bedelia made no attempt to hide her pleasure.

She wanted to stay up, but Charlie insisted that she spend another day in bed. He worked as industriously all morning as a cleaning woman at twenty-five cents an hour. Bedelia called to him several times, begging him to spare himself, but he enjoyed the labor. The physical effort kept him from thinking, and by twelve o'clock he felt as rugged and witless as an athlete.

'From now on,' he said as he carried Bedelia's lunch tray

into the bedroom, 'I'll have no more compassion when women complain about the work of housekeeping. How much pleasanter it is than using your brain.'

Bedelia laughed. She looked very pretty sitting up against the pillows in a pink wool bed sacque. She ate all of her lunch and thanked Charlie extravagantly for being so very good to her. He had carried wood upstairs and made a fire in the bedroom.

'You're so good, darling. You're much too fine for any woman. I didn't think a man could be so good.'

'You sound as if you hadn't much faith in men.'

'Men are rotten!'

'My dear child, that sounds very bitter.'

'You don't know, Charlie. There aren't many men like you in the world. Men are awful. When they made you, they destroyed the mold.'

'You've been unfortunate. You've met a few bad men and you judge the whole sex by them. Most men are pretty decent.'

'No! No! You don't know. They're rotten! Beasts!'

Charlie was shocked by her bitterness. He remembered certain stories she had told him, and he felt sorry for her because she had suffered when she was very young and had lost faith in human nature. This accounted for her prejudice and a lack of balance in her emotions. Because she was plump and radiant, he had thought of her at first as a healthy woman, but he looked upon her now as an invalid whose health could be restored only by constant love and tenderness. She must learn to trust her husband implicitly, tell him the truth, and purge herself of hatred and bitterness.

Feeling more like a father than a husband, he leaned over the bed and kissed her forehead. Her arms twisted about his neck, she pulled him toward her convulsively and pressed her lips against his mouth, his chin, his cheeks.

Charlie stayed with her until she fell asleep, her hot hand

clasped around his hand. He unlocked her fingers gently, pulled up the covers and left her.

Her lip rouge had left a crescent-shaped scar on his cheek.

He washed the lunch dishes and put them back on the shelves. Then he went into his den and filled his pipe. As he pulled the Morris chair to the window, he decided that he would quit worrying about Bedelia. In time, if he was patient and sympathetic, she would confide in him. It would be better to learn of her sins . . . or her folly . . . through such voluntary confession than by forcing the facts out of her. By seeking evil he was sure to find it a good deal blacker than if he relaxed and learned the truth in a gentler way. The footbar of the Morris chair slid out and Charlie stretched himself in it comfortably, puffing at his pipe with great contentment.

A shadow passed the window.

Charlie sprang up.

The shadow moved past the window and went around the corner of the house to the front door. It was Ben Chaney who had come down the hill on snowshoes.

The doorbell rang.

'How are you?' Ben asked. He bent over, leaning against the wall to unfasten the snowshoes. He was wearing a city overcoat with velvet lapels, a derby hat, a red woolen scarf and earmuffs.

'How are you?' said Charlie.

'I've managed to survive. It's hard to believe, isn't it, that we're only sixty miles from Herald Square? I feel like an Eskimo.' He looked up, examining Charlie's face. It showed no expression. 'Believe me,' Ben went on, 'if I were an Eskimo, the last person I should want in my igloo is Hannah. I've learned the history of every uninteresting inhabitant of this community. Aren't you going to ask me in?'

'Come in.'

Ben's eyes scanned the hall and staircase, and before he

followed Charlie into the den, he peered into the living-room. 'I tried to phone you, but my wire was disconnected.'

'Ours, too.'

'A damned nuisance. I haven't been able to get word from my friend who's on his way to visit me. The man from St. Paul, you know. I suppose the railroads are all blocked.'

'Probably.'

'To New York certainly, but I'm wondering if he was able to get that far. No doubt he's marooned somewhere, Ithaca or Rochester.' Ben stood over the radiator, rubbing his hands.

'Are you cold?' Charlie said. 'Would you like something to drink?'

'Not a bad thought. A slug of c.b. would hit the spot.' He followed Charlie to the dining-room, still rubbing his hands. 'What do you think about me as the snowshoe kid?'

Charlie brought out the decanter of cider brandy, set it with a single glass upon the tray and led his guest back to the den. 'I had no idea you knew how to use them.'

'Neither did I. I'd given up hope of being rescued and was resigning myself to slow death by boredom when Asa Keeley's boys arrived on snowshoes and brought me these.'

'You've learned quickly.'

'I stumbled about at first, but the kids gave me a few pointers and here I am, no bones broken.' He laughed heartily. The release from his house and Hannah's company had raised his spirits. 'To your health, Horst. Aren't you drinking?'

'I don't feel like it,' muttered Charlie, who was in no mood to touch glasses with Ben Chaney.

'Well, your health!' Ben gulped down the cider brandy. 'How are you?'

'All right,' Charlie said grudgingly.

'And Bedelia?'

'She's not well.'

'I'm sorry. What's wrong with her?'

'A bad cold and a fever. I think it's la grippe.'

'Too bad. Have you had the doctor?'

'How could he get here?'

Ben laughed. 'I'm still the city man, you see. Well, this has been an experience. It's good to see you, Charlie.'

While he had been talking in this inconsequential way, Ben had been looking around. Not an inch of the room had escaped his scrutiny. At one time Charlie had believed this habit of observation to be the sign of an artist's sensitivity to shapes and surfaces, but now he decided that it denoted an undue interest in Bedelia and her surroundings. In spite of his growing aversion to the man, Charlie recognized in Ben's vitality, in his taut darkness, in the distinctive modeling of his face with the thin nose and high cheekbones, qualities which would attract a woman.

Charlie grew angry. He looked at Ben, who had taken the Morris chair for himself and who was stretched out at ease, playing with Charlie's grandfather's ivory paperknife.

'What have you done to my wife? What has made her so miserable?' Charlie demanded.

The question startled Ben. The very shape of his face seemed to change. He caught Charlie's glance and immediately altered his expression. With eyes whose glassiness disguised all feeling, he said, 'I've done nothing to your wife.'

'Don't lie to me. I've got to know what this is all about. You've done something or said something that's brought her to the verge of nervous prostration. What was it? If you've insulted her . . .' Charlie's voice dwindled. In spite of the wish to guard himself, he showed tremendous passion. His face had become beet-red, a vein throbbed on his forehead, and he kept clenching and unclenching his fists.

Ben sat back in his chair. He tried to give the appearance of composure, but he was watching Charlie closely and guarding himself at the same time. 'Did Bedelia tell you I'd insulted her?'

'I'd take my wife's word, Chaney, before I'd believe you. I know Bedelia's honest with me, so there's no use in your beating around the bush. What happened between you and her the other day?'

Ben did not immediately answer. Charlie felt derision in his silence and thought Ben must be taking time to manufacture some lie with which to soothe the deluded husband. The longer Charlie had to wait, the stronger grew his determination to get a straightforward answer.

'What has your wife told you about me?'

The insolence of the question stunned Charlie. What right had Ben Chaney to demand explanations of him? He the injured one, the aggrieved husband? But his position was insecure, his righteousness unstable because he had not had the strength to force the truth out of Bedelia. His ignorance left him defenseless. He covered it with bluster. 'Damn it, man, you've got no right to question me. Tell me the truth or . . . or I'll beat it out of you.'

Ben raised his eyebrows. 'I can't defend myself until I've heard the accusation. Tell me what this is about and I'll answer you truthfully.'

Charlie would rather have fought it out than compromise, but there was nothing to fight. Bedelia had never confessed infidelity and Charlie had discovered nothing compromising in her relations with Ben. On the contrary, she had expressed her fear of him.

'Why is my wife afraid of you? Tell me that honestly,' Charlie challenged.

'Is she afraid of me? I didn't know that. The last time I saw her she was very cordial.' Ben's voice was serene, but his eyes burned brilliantly. He was not as composed as he tried to look.

'What happened the other day that made her try to run off at the height of the storm?'

Ben leaped up. 'Tried to run off! When?'

Their positions were reversed. Ben had become the curious, impatient one, Charlie armed with knowledge and the power to tantalize.

'Come, tell me.' Ben made no attempt to hide his eagerness. 'She ran off at the height of the storm, you say? After Doctor Meyers and I were here the other afternoon?'

'She says you're against her. What does that mean?'

Ben returned to the Morris chair. For a time he seemed lost in thought. He had picked up the paperknife again and had poised its point against the back of his hand. Finally, avoiding Charlie's face, he said, 'To hell with it! I'll have to tell you.'

'Then you have something to confess?'

'Sit down.'

Charlie did not want to sit down, but he could not afford to waste time in argument. He sat at the very edge of the couch and drummed his fingers against the wooden frame.

Ben quit stabbing his hand and used the padded arm of the chair as his target. 'It's a long story. I'll begin by telling you about Barrett?'

'Who the devil is Barrett?'

'Keene Barrett, the man from St. Paul. You may remember that I mentioned his name the other day.' Ben studied Charlie's face to see whether his words had any effect.

'Did you? I probably wasn't listening. What's he got to do with you or my wife?'

'Keene Barrett was to have arrived the night you came to my house for dinner, but there was a storm in the Middle West and his train was delayed. He'll be here as soon as the roads are open.'

A silence followed. It was not the comfortable silence that punctuates good talk between friends, but the dismal silence of apprehension.

'What has this Barrett to do with me?' Charlie asked querulously.

Ben had decided upon a way of telling his story and he would not let Charlie's impatience divert him. Leaning back in his chair, dropping the paperknife, he began:

'Keene Barrett had a brother, Will. They owned . . . Keene Barrett still does . . . a couple of drugstores, one in Minneapolis, the other in St. Paul. Their business was good because they were smart business men as well as good pharmacists. They put in soda fountains and dressed up their windows and had the best trade in the Twin Cities. Keene was the merchant, Will the druggist. To the day he died he liked making up prescriptions.'

'Look here, I'm not interested,' Charlie grumbled. 'I asked you a question and . . .'

'You'll find out soon enough,' Ben interrupted and went on with his story. 'Keene had a nice fat wife and had three children. He was always urging his brother to try matrimony. Mrs. Keene liked to arrange little parties, invite nice girls and get brother Will to take them home. Finally she thought she'd found him a prize package, a girl whose father had a seat on the Minneapolis Stock Exchange.'

Charlie sighed loudly, hoping to distract Ben and make him quit the story. Ben made a motion with his hand for silence.

'Two years ago Will had pneumonia and went off to recuperate at Hot Springs. One day his brother got a telegram saying that he'd met a lady he liked enough to marry. And a week later they got another wire saying that Will was bringing home his new wife. Mrs. Keene was disappointed, but Keene said that his brother's life was his own business, told his wife to forget the Stock Exchange and welcome her new sister-in-law. The whole family went down to the train to meet her.'

Ben had begun to toy with the paperknife again. 'I'm making it a hell of a long story. But you ought to know the details.'

'In the name of God, why?'

'You'll see soon enough. The new wife turned out to be a peach. In a week Mrs. Keene confessed that she was just as glad they'd lost out on the daughter of the Stock Exchange. Everyone loved Maurine . . . that was her name . . . Maurine Cunningham. At the whist club she was a howling success and all the ladies gave luncheons for her. Will Barrett had never been so happy in his life and he'd tell his brother every day what a wonderful woman his wife was. She was a wonderful wife, jolly, affectionate, even a good cook. They took one of those furnished hotel apartments, but Maurine wasn't satisfied with the equipment, she was always buying new pots and dishes. Sometimes Will would work in the Minneapolis store at night, and Maurine used to come and sit on a stool in the prescription room to keep him company. On the way they'd stop in some garden or rathskeller for a glass of beer. Will was fond of his beer.'

'I fail to see why you're telling me all this,' Charlie interrupted. He was pounding his fists against the frame of the couch, preparing to strike a more satisfying blow. 'Let me tell you this, Chaney, if you're trying to avoid my questions . . .'

'Keep your shirt on,' Ben ordered. 'I told you there was a reason for my telling you this story. You'll understand soon enough, maybe too soon for your own peace of mind.'

'All right, but hurry. I don't care for the trimmings. The domestic life of the Barrett family sounds pretty dull. What happened anyway?'

'It was in March that he married her. Early in June there was a druggists' convention in Chicago. The Barretts decided to make a holiday of it and take their wives along. They took a train to Duluth and there boarded a lake steamer. While they were sitting on a deck, a man came up to them. "How are you, Mrs. Jacobs?" he said. They thought he was crazy, but he looked straight at Maurine and went on, "I always knew we'd find you. I've got some good news."

'She seemed utterly bewildered. "I'm sorry, but I don't know you," she said. The man asked if he wasn't addressing Mrs. Arthur Jacobs of Detroit.

'Will said, "You must have made a mistake, this lady is my wife." The man apologized and said he hoped he hadn't offended anyone. There happened to be a remarkable resemblance between Mrs. Barrett and Mrs. Jacobs. This wasn't extraordinary, it happens to everyone, and they thought little about it. Late that night, when the others had gone to bed, Keene Barrett was taking a walk on deck and this man took a turn with him, and told him why he was so disappointed at not finding Mrs. Jacobs.

'He was an insurance agent and Arthur Jacobs, a jeweler, had been his client. Jacobs died and his wife collected around fifty thousand dollars. There were a few fees and assessments and costs deducted. Later on it was discovered that someone in the bookkeeping department had made an error and the company still owed Mrs. Jacobs two hundred and fifty dollars. They tried to communicate with her, but she had moved without leaving a forwarding address. The insurance company, knowing how much criticism is directed at the corporations these days, wanted to pay every cent it owed to any beneficiary, and asked this agent, who had originally sold Jacobs the policy, to find her. No one knew where she was, neither Jacobs's people in Detroit, his lawyer, nor any of his friends.

'As he remembered Mrs. Jacobs, the agent said, she seemed lighter in coloring than Mrs. Barrett, but since Mrs. Barrett had been wearing a hat, he might have been mistaken. Keene thought the whole thing a fake, for the man insisted upon giving him his business card, and it looked like an insurance agent's trick to strike up an acquaintance. On his way back to his stateroom, Keene tore up the card and scattered the pieces over the rail.'

Ben paused and poured himself another drink. Charlie winced. He was sick with impatience.

'After they returned from the convention,' Ben continued, 'Will rented a summer cottage on the shore of Lake Minnetonka. The Barretts were outdoor men, fond of boating and fishing, and winter sports, too, skiing and snowshoeing. Maurine wasn't so fond of sports, but Will enjoyed teaching her to swim and sail. She enjoyed the country, though, insisted on doing her own housework, and when Will was in the city at his work, she'd bake cakes and sew and read novels.

'One Saturday the Keene Barretts came out to have dinner with Will and Maurine. Will drank a few bottles of beer and got sort of jolly. He wanted them to go out for a sail in his canoe. Mrs. Keene was horrified. She told Will that he must not, in any circumstance, take Maurine canoeing late at night in her condition.'

For the first time Charlie showed an interest in the story. 'She was pregnant, too?'

Ben nodded. 'Will got angry at his sister-in-law for scolding and said the sail had been Maurine's idea. They often went canoeing at night. Anyway, as the evening progressed, Will got drowsy from the beer and nothing more was said about going out on the lake. At eleven the Keene Barretts left. Maurine was tired and said she'd be asleep in five minutes.

'The next thing Keene Barrett heard, his brother was dead. In the morning Maurine had run a quarter of a mile to the nearest neighbor's, pounded on their door and asked for help. Her husband had disappeared, she said. His bed hadn't been slept in all night. The neighbors and his sons came back with her. One of the boys saw the canoe floating on its side. They found Will's body under the pier. It looked as if he'd tipped over while getting into the canoe, had fallen into the water and had been caught between the posts. That could have happened to a man used to boating if he'd been drowsy and fuddled after too much beer.'

Ben waited then for Charlie to say something.

Charlie cleared his throat. 'What about the wife?'

'She collapsed. Keene was cut up about it himself, but he and his wife felt it their first duty to look out for their brother's widow. Financially Maurine was provided for. Will had taken out a thirty-five-thousand-dollar life insurance policy. The amount staggered Keene. It was a big load for Will to have carried. The drugstores were prosperous, but they cost a lot to run and the brothers' incomes were mostly from the salaries they drew. Still, Keene was glad that Maurine and her unborn child would be taken care of and there'd be no burden on him.

'About six weeks after Will's death, Maurine decided that a change of scene would take her mind off the tragedy and went to visit an aunt in Kansas City. She'd given up the cottage and had been staying in St. Paul with the in-laws, and she left a lot of stuff in their attic, pans and fancy dishes, winter underwear and her fur coat. The whole family took her to the train. She kissed them fondly and there were tears in her eyes when she thanked them for their kindness.

'That was the last they saw of Maurine.'

'What! You mean they never saw her again?'

'Never.'

'How did that happen?'

'They had a couple of letters, one written on the stationery of the Mühlbach Hotel, and one written on the engraved paper Charlie had bought her from one of the salesmen who sold gift stationery to the drugstore.'

'You said Charlie.'

'I meant Will Barrett.'

'The room's getting chilly,' Charlie said, and turned on the radiator. 'I've been keeping the fire high on account of my wife's cold, but it got too hot down here and I turned off the heat.' Steam hissed through the pipes.

'One day,' Ben went on, 'Mrs. Keene said she was worried about Maurine. The poor girl had borne the shock bravely, but her nervous system might have been affected more than they thought. Mrs. Keene called the family doctor and asked when Maurine's baby was due. The doctor said he hadn't known she was pregnant. Not that it wasn't possible. He'd taken care of her for a nervous collapse, but there'd been no trouble on the other score so he hadn't made an examination.

'Keene got to worrying about it then. He wired Maurine at the Mühlbach. His telegram was returned with the information that Mrs. Barrett was not at the hotel. Keene sent another wire, asking if she had left a forwarding address and was informed that she had never been registered there. They were holding mail for her, however. This turned out to be mail from Hazel and Keene Barrett.

'Time passed. Keene tried to keep his wife from worrying by saying that Maurine was careless and lazy, and some day she'd surprise them by wiring them to meet her at the railroad station. She'd want her winter things and the fur coat she'd left behind.

'One day, when Keene was cleaning out his desk, he came across an envelope containing the stubs of the stateroom reservations from the Chicago trip. He showed them to his wife, who cried and remembered how happy they had all been and wondered if poor Maurine had been killed in a streetcar or railroad accident and been buried without identification in some potters' field. To Keene the ticket stubs brought back another memory; the insurance agent, the story of Mrs. Jacobs, and the curious similarity of the two cases.

'He wrote the insurance company and asked if they had the address of the widow to whom they had recently paid thirty-five thousand dollars. A few days later he was visited by two men, one the vice-president and general manager of the insurance company and the other a private investigator.'

'Go on,' Charlie said.

'Keene had not mentioned the Jacobs incident in his letter, but the insurance people connected it at once with Maurine's disappearance, and told him of another case in Memphis.

These stories had certain points in common with the story of Will Barrett's courtship, marriage, and sudden death. McKelvey, the Memphis man, died of ptomaine poisoning after a fish dinner. His wife had eaten a warmed-over chop, as she had always disliked fish. Several of McKelvey's friends and relations remembered that, when they went to the Peabody Hotel for those famous frogs' legs or red snapper, she ordered chicken or pot roast. There was no autopsy. Too many people have died from eating bad fish.

'Jacobs, the Detroit husband, fell asleep in the bathtub and was drowned.'

'Indeed,' said Charlie.

'McKelvey, the first husband on our list, was a newspaper editor who had gone to Asbury Park for a summer holiday and there met a charming widow named Annabel Godfrey. Jacobs met Chloe Dinsmore on a train bound for the Kentucky Derby, took a cinder out of her eye, and told her how to place her bets. His people were pleased with the marriage, although they were Jewish and the bride a Gentile, because she was a sweet, steady girl and they thought she'd keep him from gambling away so much of his money.

'In every case the woman was pretty, winning in her ways, and quite able to charm the man's family. In every case she was a widow who met her husband at a resort, or, in Jacob's case, on the way to the races. Mrs. McKelvey and Mrs. Barrett said they were pregnant when their husbands took out these big insurance policies. We don't know about Mrs. Jacobs. Although she had dinner with her mother-in-law every Friday night, she whispered no secrets. But men like Jacobs are good providers anyway, and since he gambled away a large part of his income, it wasn't remarkable that he'd insure his life for fifty thousand dollars.'

In an even voice Charlie asked, 'Why are you telling me this story?'

Ben looked up. On Charlie's lip curved the stain left by

Bedelia's lip salve. 'Arthur Jacobs was a jeweler. He collected black pearls.'

'An interesting story. Have another drink?' Charlie tipped the bottle over Ben's empty glass. His voice and hand were steady, his expression calm.

It was Ben who showed nervousness. He scorched his throat with the drink, shook his head and grimaced. 'I don't like telling you this, Horst, you're a hell of a nice fellow, and since I've been living here, I've . . .' he broke off and brought his fist down upon the arm of the chair. 'The hell with it, you'd have to know sooner or later.'

Charlie looked at the floor.

'I paint,' Ben said grimly, 'only as a kind of hobby. It helped me in this case. She said her first husband was an artist. Let me give you my card.' He took out his wallet and gave a card to Charlie. On it was printed 'Benjamin Wallace Chaney & Sons, Private Investigators,' and an address on Broad Street, New York, and in the lower left-hand corner, 'Mr. B.W. Chaney, Jr.'

Charlie threw the card into the wastebasket.

'At present we're doing a job for the Federal Insurance Company, the South & Western, The Household, and the New Colonial & Family Life.' The last named was the company in which Charlie's life was insured for sixty thousand dollars.

'Since last winter these companies have combined in an effort to trace the woman or women involved in these cases. It's been mostly a routine job because we've been looking into the lives of women whose husbands have taken out policies or increased their coverage to a figure which is out of proportion to their earnings. Mostly the wives of overinsured men are nervous, spoiled, and afraid of being left alone. You can check up on these women in a few days. They have families, friends, school records. But when a woman tells you about a past that can't be checked, when you can't locate a single old friend, nor a house in which she's lived, nor a store where she's traded . . .'

Charlie had controlled himself admirably through the earlier revelations, but all of a sudden, he began to shout. 'Get out of here! Get out!'

Ben noted the red stain on Charlie's lip, the scar left by Bedelia's affection, and he smiled a little. That smile was too much for Charlie. He leaped and struck. Ben was unprepared. The breath was knocked out of him. Charlie stood above the Morris chair, his clenched fists raised and ready to strike again. This was not decent fighting. But Charlie had no regard now for the rules of the game. His anger was hard and hot and every instinct urged him to punish his enemy.

He lunged forward, fist aimed at Ben's chin. Ben was on his guard and, although still seated, he struck hard. Charlie lurched backward. Ben leaped up. Charlie recovered and moved forward again. Ben was a smaller man, but he had training and experience in fighting. Charlie had not used his fists since he was a freshman and had only anger to guide him. He fought ruggedly but ineffectually. Ben caught him around the waist and with a twist of his right arm threw Charlie to the floor.

Charlie started up, but Ben was upon him. His every movement was easy, economical of effort, swift and certain. Charlie would not give in until his rage was satisfied. He fought wildly. They rolled the length of the room. Finally Ben pinned him down and kneeled upon him in a way that left him completely helpless. Charlie was red-faced and weary while Ben seemed hardly to have exerted himself. He got up, straightened his coat, pulled at his tie and smoothed his hair. Until Charlie was on his feet, Ben kept his back turned so that Charlie should not feel his humiliation too keenly.

Charlie stood in the center of the room, his hands hanging

loose and his arms suspended weakly from his defeated shoulders. He had lost the fight and had been allowed to dust himself off. He saw that the struggle had been senseless. Even if he had trounced Ben, he could not have changed any of the detective's facts.

When Charlie spoke again, he chose his words with care and enunciated clearly. 'I think I know why you told me that story and what you want me to believe. But you're wrong. You've followed a false lead. I don't want to hear any more about it.'

'I don't blame you,' Ben said smoothly. 'I'd have done the same thing to anyone who made that kind of remark about my wife. But the fact remains . . .'

'I don't want any more of your facts!'

'Maybe they'll seem more interesting after you've had a dose of poison in your boiled rice.'

'You can go to hell!' Charlie shouted.

'There had probably been a sedative in Will Barrett's last stein of beer. She could have got hold of all the opiates and poisons she needed while she sat in the prescription room with her husband. If he went to the toilet or out to wait on a customer, she could have sneaked a little out of this jar or that. Probably cached away plenty of it for future business.'

'That's just a conjecture. Proves nothing.'

'A fellow in Topeka, Kansas, Alfred Hall, a meat jobber, died after sprinkling insect powder on his French toast instead of powdered sugar. He was off on a fishing trip and cooked his own meals. His wife had planned to go with him, but she was having heart palpitations and the doctor warned her against all exercise. So the poor husband had to go alone. The night before he left, he packed his kit, a very handsome and expensive kit it was, all fitted out with tin plates and containers for food. His wife had given it to him for his birthday. Some neighbors had stopped in that evening and Hall showed them the new kit before he went into the kitchen to pack it. A few days later, some Boy Scouts found his body beside his dead campfire. And there was insect powder in one of his tin shakers. Hall was nearsighted and must have mistaken it for powdered sugar when he packed.'

'Accidents happen,' said Charlie.

'Indeed they do. And nobody blamed the poor wife. This isn't one of our cases, so we're not investigating the widow. Hall had neglected to insure himself properly and all she got out of it was about forty thousand in cold cash. I'm only telling you about Hall to show you how careful a man's got to be with French toast.'

Charlie tried to show indifference.

'You're not nearsighted, but you have indigestion. Now don't get sore again,' Ben hastened to say. 'It's only that a lot of men have been trapped by their weaknesses, one nearsighted, one with a taste for fish, one who couldn't take his beer without getting drowsy. And always such careful planning. Palpitations of the heart, doctors' warnings, convenient birthday presents, an aversion to fish, a passion for moonlight sails.'

'So that's where Meyers got the idea? From you?'

'I wanted to get my operative in here, not only to keep an eye on things, but to see that nothing was slipped into your food or medicine. If you had died after all those authentic symptoms, it would have been the most natural thing in the world for the doctor to write Acute Indigestion on the death certificate and let it go at that.'

'But it was acute indigestion. You know very well I'd been having dyspepsia for some time.'

'That it can be brought on artificially, too?'

'Nonsense.'

'There are a number of drugs that could have done it. Digitalis, for instance. And she had been giving you that sedative . . .'

'A simple bromide that Loveman mixed for us.' Charlie

had become peevish. 'I don't want to hear any more of your filthy suspicions. The doctor got his analysis, didn't he? Didn't it show? You know as well as I that I had an attack of acute indigestion, nothing more.'

'I was here when you told your wife about it,' Ben reminded him. 'You may remember that it was right after that that I mentioned Keene Barrett's name for the first time. I did it with a purpose. I wanted her to know she wasn't as safe as she supposed.'

'Damn you!' cried Charlie, the cords rising in his neck and his voice tightening. 'What right have you to speak of her in that fashion?'

'It would have been greatly to her advantage to have had the analysis made and proved negative. Another attack would seem quite normal. And if it had been fatal, she'd have blamed poor old Meyers for faulty diagnosis and improper care.'

'You've got no proof of anything.'

'Did you notice,' Ben asked slyly, 'how she acted when she first smelled the smoke of your Christmas cigars?'

'What was there to notice?'

'Odors are potent in stimulating the memory. McKelvey smoked that brand. They were specially made in Cuba for members of his club. She wouldn't have reacted so violently to the smell of ordinary cigar smoke.'

'Thanks for your thoughtful Christmas gift,' Charlie said.

'You know there was never a Raoul Cochran in New Orleans?' Ben waited for Charlie to answer the question. Charlie looked as if he had not heard. 'None of the artists had ever heard the name, nor any of the landlords in the French Quarter, and none of the stores that sell artists' supplies.'

'They lived quietly in a cheap flat. Probably they paid their rent in cash. They didn't know many people.'

'What about those parties they gave whenever they could afford a chicken and a bottle of claret? And what of the friends who insisted that his paintings be sold at auction so the dealer couldn't cheat the poor widow? And where's the dealer?'

Charlie had no answer.

'I know artists,' Ben said. 'I've lived in colonies in summer, and have spent as much time as I could afford with painters. They're alike in one thing . . . they'll talk about their work to anyone who'll listen, and most of them ask for credits from the fellows who sell brushes and canvas. How is it, then, that nobody there remembers a painter named Raoul Cochran and his pretty wife? For God's sake, Charlie, wipe that red stuff off your face, it makes you look like a damn fool.'

'Red stuff?'

'Evidently you've been kissed.'

Abashed, Charlie pulled out his handkerchief.

'On the left side, just above your mouth.' Ben spoke testily. 'There were no paintings with the signature of Cochran, no dealer, no friends, no credit at the stores, no trace anywhere of Raoul or Bedelia.'

Charlie looked at the red stain on his handkerchief.

'Neither the City Hall nor any hospital has a record of Cochran's death.'

Charlie managed to produce a frigid, disdainful voice. 'I met a number of people who knew her.'

'In Colorado Springs? They'd met her there, hadn't they? Just as you did.'

'Just the same, I don't think there's any connection.'

'You may be right. I have no evidence that Annabel McKelvey, Chloe Jacobs, and Maurine Barrett are the same woman. But they had one trait in common. They photographed so badly that all of them, pretty woman, too, were more afraid of cameras than of pistols . . . or poison. Have you ever taken a picture of your wife?'

Charlie could not answer. He had lost his expensive German Kodak when he was off on a jaunt in the mountains with Mrs. Bedelia Cochran. She had let him take several snap-shots of her, and then his Kodak had, quite by accident, fallen off a cliff.

'When I suggested that she sit for her portrait,' Ben said, 'she hesitated at first and told me she was a bad model. Cochran had tried several times to paint her, but had to give up, she said. I begged her to let me try and finally she con-sented. In fact, we had quite a conspiracy about it, for she decided to give you her portrait for a birthday present, and insisted that she would pay me for it. I knew, of course, the portrait would never be finished.'

The Kodak had been a gift from his mother and Charlie had always been careful with it. He could almost remember placing it with his coat and knapsack beside a rock at a safe distance from the edge before he went off to gather wood for their fire. Afterward Bedelia said that he had been absent-minded. She had noticed that he left the camera near the edge and had meant to speak of it, but disliked reproaching him.

'These wives,' Ben continued, 'had another trait in com-mon. Annabel, Chloe, and Maurine were always sweet-tempered, docile, and patient. McKelvey, Jacobs, and Barrett were unusually happy husbands. I guess a woman who regards her marriage as temporary can afford to be easy-going with a man. She doesn't have to worry about giving him a finger and having him take the whole hand. No wonder Mrs. Barrett thought her sister-in-law spoiled her husband.'

Charlie went into the hall and looked up the stairs. He had heard something on the second floor. Or perhaps he had only imagined he heard his wife coughing. But when he climbed the stairs, he discovered that the bedroom door was closed tight. For this he was grateful. What if Bedelia had heard Ben's story? Charlie was ashamed because he had listened to all of it and he despised himself for having lost the fight.

He opened the door softly, crossed the bedroom on tiptoe. As his eyes became accustomed to the dim light, he saw his wife's features clearly, the proud little nose, the doll's mouth, the curling lashes and the rounded chin. She slept as peacefully as a child.

Downstairs again, facing Ben, he said, 'Please don't talk so loud. I don't want anyone to hear what we're saying.' He would not use his wife's name nor even refer to her by a pronoun. Charlie was calmer now, and better able to handle his end of the argument. The visit to the bedroom and the sight of his wife's innocent slumber had restored his faith. He had been tempted to abuse Ben, to scorch the man's pride with fiery insult, but this, he saw now, would be no more effective than the use of his fists.

'I can't think of a single reason why I should believe you,' Charlie began. 'You came to my house under false pretenses, you've been dishonest with me since the day we met, you've accepted our hospitality and pretended to be our friend while you were spying on us. Why should I believe you?'

'Quite a shock, wasn't it, when she heard me use Barrett's name?'

'Was it?' Charlie asked coldly.

'Why did she break that ornament? It slipped out of her hands when she heard me say that Barrett was coming here.'

'Might have been an accident.' Charlie managed a condescending smile.

'Did she say anything about it afterward?'

'Nothing. You're the only one who's ever mentioned Barrett's name around here.' That was literal truth. Bedelia had not mentioned Barrett as her enemy; that was Ben Chaney's role. *He'll hurt us. That's all he cares about, to hurt us and ruin our lives.* Her voice echoed in Charlie's ears and he could see her shadowed eyes and furrowed brow as she leaned over the plate of untasted food.

'When Barrett gets here, he'll identify her if she is Maurine,' Ben said. He went into the hall and took his overcoat off the tree. 'I didn't like telling you this, but you asked for it. I'd planned to wait until we were sure.' He put on his mittens and wrapped the scarf around his neck.

Charlie had nothing more to say and Ben left without a farewell. Some impulse sent Charlie to watch his visitor depart. He stood in the living-room window waiting while Ben fastened his snowshoes. It seemed to take him a long time to tie them on. Finally Charlie saw him push off, moving clumsily at first, and then finding his balance and gaining speed. Ben crossed the bridge and climbed the hill on the opposite side of the river. It was not yet four o'clock, but dusk had fallen. There was no wind and the world was utterly still except for Ben's dark shape against the snow. The shape dwindled and disappeared over the top of the hill.

Charlie turned from the window. In the dim room he saw the shapes of things, chairs, tables, the sofa and love-seat, and the spaces between these things, and he remembered how he and Bedelia had moved the furniture again and again until they were satisfied with the arrangement. Bedelia's living in it had changed the old house. Her stamp was on everything, the wallpaper and upholstery fabrics, the mirrors and sconces; her workbasket had been left on the lowboy, and on the dining-room table bloomed the white narcissus she had grown in a pottery bowl.

The silence was torn by a scream. Charlie thought the wind had risen to trumpet the coming of a new storm. In the second shriek he recognized his wife's voice. Had Maurine Barrett cried out when they came to tell her that her husband's body had been caught between the posts of the pier?

He rushed up the stairs. His wife's voice floated toward him through the darkness of the hall. 'I had a nightmare, Charlie. I dreamed that you were dead.'

5

'Why are you staring at me like that?'

Bedelia sat high against the pillows. She had asked Charlie to bring her the pink bed sacque, and when she had tied the pink bow under her chin, combed her hair and touched up her lips, she was as rosy and pert as a schoolgirl. The room was dry and warm, and the scent of her cosmetics gave it the oversweet atmosphere of a hothouse.

'You're looking at me so strangely, Charlie. Are you angry, dear?'

Charlie walked toward the bed. Bedelia held out her hand. He took it and she drew his hand to her face and rested her cheek against it. Ben's facts receded into the distance. Charlie saw innocence in a pink jacket, heard rosy lips asking for his love, smelled her seductive perfume, touched a warm hand. His senses knew reality. The session with Ben became a dream. This woman was his wife, he knew her intimately, was not blind to her faults and weaknesses. He had been madly in love with her, dazzled by her charms, but he had not lost his head so completely that he had mistaken a vulgar adventuress for a sincere woman. And the woman Ben described had been far worse than an adventuress, she had been a hideous monster, a siren, a blood-sucker, Lucrezia Borgia and Lady Macbeth, all at once. Charlie was no fool. He might have been oversanguine, more trustful of strangers than a lot of people, but he had his standards of character and expected his friends to live up to these standards. Barrett's wife had been mercenary. Mrs. Jacobs was a cold woman. Annabel McKelvey could not offer affection with such pretty impulsiveness.

'I'm hungry,' Bedelia said.

'I'll fix you some supper. Won't take ten minutes,' Charlie promised.

He was glad to leave the bedroom. In her presence it was not possible to think clearly. He stamped down the stairs, telling himself in sound sentences that Ben Chaney had made a hideous mistake, that the black pearl was what Bedelia claimed, a five-dollar imitation. Last week Ben had made melodrama out of a case of common indigestion; now he was magnifying a molehill of coincidence into a mountain of evidence. A detective! Had Charlie known this at the start, he would never have become intimate with Ben Chaney. Perhaps he was a snob; the Philbricks had always been snobs, but they had successfully protected themselves against the humiliation suffered as a result of intimacy with inferiors. Would his mother have asked a detective to dinner? He could hear her answer, 'One might as well dine with a burglar.' Let Barrett come! At the first glance the man from St. Paul would destroy Ben's fine theories.

While Charlie was slaying dragons on the staircase, a miracle took place. Light! Light after darkness! Could there have been a clearer symbol of hope? Of course, if he were to quarrel with Providence and seek scientific explanation of the miracle, it could be attributed to the workings of the Connecticut Light and Power Company whose linesmen had restrung the wires which the blizzard had disconnected. The sudden burst of light in the dark hall was due to Charlie's own negligence in forgetting to turn back the switches which he had thoughtlessly turned on while the power was off.

In his present mood Charlie preferred the miracle. Faith is nourished not by intelligence but by emotion, and emotion is the product of desire. By wishing hard enough you can make yourself believe almost anything. The Kodak had fallen off the cliff by accident. Charlie had a most reassuring vision, could see himself leaving it carelessly at the edge.

He set about making tea. The kitchen reflected his wife's soundest qualities. In every copper pot its bright miniature was repeated. Charlie sang as he made toast in Bedelia's new electric machine, cooked a rarebit in her chafing dish. He felt superior to Ben's nonsense, aloof as a god. His voice seemed to him only slightly inferior to Caruso's. All at one time he had to keep his mind on the toast in the electric machine, the melting cheese in the chafing dish, the water in the kettle.

The kitchen floor was spread with newspapers. Charlie had laid them there when he finished scrubbing the linoleum. That was Charlie all over, an architect, successful in his field, making good money, but not too proud to scrub the kitchen and spread newspapers on the floor. As he crossed from stove to table, the kettle in his hand, an item attracted him. He bent down to read it, forgot everything else, and there was havoc in the kitchen. The kettle tipped, the cover slid off, hot water spilled, the toast burned, and the rarebit thickened in the chafing dish.

The newspaper item told of the conviction of a bachelor, forty-seven years old, elder in a New Hampshire church, for the murder of his spinster sister. Witnesses said the sister had tried to separate him from the piano teacher with whom he had been having an illicit affair for seventeen years. Charlie seldom read such stories. The sort of people who committed murder, or allowed themselves to become victims of murder, were to him as incomprehensible as savage Igorotes, and such crime as remote from his understandings as hara-kiri or child marriage. A medicine man who painted his skin and danced to exorcise devils seemed no farther off than a New Hampshire elder who could suffocate his sister with a green silk sofa pillow.

Boiling water spread and darkened the newspaper. From the toaster came a charred smell. The cheese sauce bubbled angrily. There were switches to be turned off, plugs to be pulled, the floor to be mopped, fresh bread to be cut, new water boiled, cheese to be grated. Charlie worked defiantly. He sang loudly, rattled dishes, banged away with the pots. The medicine men dance to exorcise civil spirits. Charlie

Horst tried to imitate Caruso. In fear of excess he spared the tea, shut off the current before the toast was brown, made a watery rarebit. Yet he continued to sing loudly as though the courage of his voice could thicken sauce, brown toast, strengthen tea, disperse the shadows on the stairs, and revive the faith that had seemed so firm when he started work in the bright kitchen.

Maurine Barrett had been a good housekeeper, she had equipped her kitchen with all the latest conveniences, her egg-beaters and can-openers had been the most recent inventions, and when she went away, she had stored them carefully in her brother-in-law's attic.

'Charlie, dear, it's delicious,' Bedelia said of the rarebit. 'You're a much better cook than I am.'

'It's a bad supper and you're a gallant liar.'

'No, you mustn't say it's bad. It's delicious.' Bedelia smiled, dimpled, her dark eyes worshiped her husband, and the room was sweet with the scent of her perfume.

That evening a bell rang. Charlie and Bedelia were startled. They had forgotten about the telephone. 'We must be connected,' Charlie said.

Bedelia nodded. She had a crochet hook in her mouth and could not speak.

The operator was calling to see if their line worked. The trunk wire had been disconnected, she said, and the telephone company was glad to inform its subscribers that service had been restored.

Charlie was not as happy about the restoration of the telephone wire as he had been about the electric light. This was not a miracle but an omen. His house was again part of the world from which it had been separated by the storm. Next the snow shovels would come, and then there would never be peace in his home again.

'So the phone's connected,' Bedelia said.

'Yes.' His voice was brusque. More than four hours had passed since Ben had left the house, and nothing had been said of his visit.

Charlie pulled a chair close to the bedroom fire. Bedelia went on with her crocheting. From time to time she measured the unfinished slipper against the finished one.

'When will the snow be cleared away?'

He scraped his throat, tried to soften the hard tones. 'I don't know. Why are you worrying about it so much?'

'It's such fun to be alone with you, dear. I don't want us ever to be rescued.'

'We'd starve to death.'

'We'll live on biscuit. There's plenty of flour. I'd rather live on biscuit with you, Charlie, than roast goose and oysters with anyone else.'

He stared into the fire. A sudden wave of anger had risen in him, resentment at her airs and graces, the guilelessness and girlish prattle. His anger was futile, of course. When he turned and saw her, rosy in the lamplight, the pink bow tied under her chin, his resentment turned upon himself for allowing his faith to be shaken.

'Don't you believe me, Charlie?'

'Believe what?'

'That I love you better than anything in the world?'

'Don't be foolish.'

'I don't know what you mean by that. I don't know whether you mean that I ought to know that you believe I love you and am foolish to be asking about it, or whether you don't believe I love you more than anything else in the world.'

How was it possible for a small woman to have drowned a man who had been boating and swimming all his life? If Will Barrett had drunk too much beer, he might not have known it was she who pushed him off the pier, but he should have been restored to his senses by the shock of the cold water.

Thinking of it, Charlie experienced all the sensations. He lost his balance, fell, shuddered as the water closed over him, floundered about, held his breath, struggled and tried to reach the surface. His arms flailed about in the effort to swim blindly toward the posts that held up the pier. Drunk or sober, he would not have allowed himself to drown, he thought. But if he had been drugged, if he were not wholly conscious, the water might not have revived him.

'Great God, I'm getting morbid.'

'Did you say something, dear?'

'No.'

'Why are you so cross with me?'

'Am I cross? I'm sorry.'

'Perhaps you're bored being stuck in the house without any company but me. I know I'm not very intellectual, but I try not to be a bore.'

'My dear, you're not the slightest bit of a bore.'

The telephone rang. Charlie was glad that he had an excuse to run down the stairs.

Ellen was calling. 'Hello, Charlie, are you all right?'

'Hello, how are you? Dug out yet?'

'Good gracious, yes. We were only snowed in a day down here, worse luck. I've had to go to work as usual. It's pretty bad out there, isn't it?'

'We're comfortable,' Charlie said.

'It's been terribly exciting in town, everybody dug and shoveled, not only the poor who were getting paid for it, but the Mayor and City Council and all the storekeepers and bankers. The poor were angry because other people were doing the work that's rightfully theirs, taking away their chance to make a little money, but there was so much snow that there'll be work for them for days to come. They're coming out your way tomorrow.'

'That's good.'

'You don't sound enthusiastic. What's the matter? Don't

you want to be dug out?' Charlie did not answer, and after a little pause Ellen added with unconvincing gaiety, 'I suppose when you've been married just a little while, you don't mind being cut off from the world. How's Bedelia taking it?'

'She's in bed with a cold.'

'Oh, what a nuisance. Do give her my love,' Ellen said dutifully. Her voice revived as she exclaimed, 'Charlie, I've got the most astonishing news for you! A letter from Abbie. What do you think?'

'Bustles in style again.'

'Now, Charlie, don't tease. This is important. About someone quite close to you.'

His heart missed a beat.

'Your neighbor, Mr. Chaney.'

'Oh!'

'It's quite shocking. Shall I read you what she says?' A paper rustled. 'Before I read it, let me tell you one thing, Charlie. I never did trust him. You can ask Abbie. I thought he was sneaky right from the start.'

'Go on, read it.'

'I won't read the whole letter, you know how Abbie goes on, just the part that's apropos. Quote, "The most ironic joke has been played on us by Fate and your dear Charlie"'—a giggle traveled over the wire—'"is the victim. Last night I went to a New Year's reception at the Hattons', who were good friends of ours when I was married to Walter. I joined a group of people I knew. They were listening to an elderly gentleman tell some fascinating stories about crime and graft in Kansas City, etc., and I thought he must be an editor or journalist like Norman Hapgood or Lincoln Steffens. Believe me, he was quite distinguished. I had not caught his name and later I went up the punchbowl and asked my hostess to identify him. Imagine my surprise when she told me he was a *detective!!*"

'Oh?'

'Abbie has it underlined and two exclamation points.'

'What else does she say?'

'"My hostess explained that he was not like a policeman, but is a private investigator with a very interesting history. He had taken a house next to their summer place in Mamaroneck and she had been shocked when she heard he was a detective, but found that he was quite decent and respectable, and his daughter, Beatrice Chaney, had gone to Mount Holyoke. After that I managed to have a heart-to-heart with the old gentleman. When I said that I had met a young man of that name, he interrupted and asked if I'd seen his son's paintings. Evidently he doesn't care any more for Benjy's art than you do, pet. I told him I thought his son's work clever, but somewhat *fauve*, and he remarked that most young ladies felt just as I do about the lad.

'"They are evidently well-bred people, and if he can afford to give his son a machine and let him spend his life painting, they must have money. There is no reason why you should be such . . ."' Ellen stopped reading.

After a silence, marked by the humming of the wires, Charlie said, 'Go on. What else does she say?'

'It's nothing. Abbie said something silly.'

'That you were a snob, or a prig?'

Ellen laughed self-consciously.

There was another silence, and then Ellen said, dryly, 'She thinks any single man ought to fascinate an old maid.'

Charlie laughed mechanically. 'Why, you're still a spring chicken, my dear. And Ben's an attractive fellow. Abbie may not be so silly after all.'

'I'm not interested.'

Charlie was pleased. It was selfish of him, after he'd gone off and married another woman, to cherish Ellen's affection, but he was human, and his admiration of Ben had been grudging. 'I don't think he's your type, Nellie. He's not good enough for you.'

'Oh, Charlie!' Ellen's laugher was freer and lighter.

The banter had lightened Charlie's spirits. As he hung the receiver back upon the hook and started up the stairs, it seemed that his life had been restored to its normal pattern. He saw himself as Ellen saw him, a man who had married impulsively but with good sense.

'Ellen certainly talked a long time,' Bedelia said as he returned to the bedroom.

Charlie was paralyzed. Had the door been open all the time? How much had his wife heard of Ellen's talk about detectives?

'She'll never fall in love with him,' his wife continued.

Charlie found that he could move gain, and speak. He studied Bedelia's face and observed nothing more than curiosity written upon it. It had been Ellen, he recalled, who had mentioned detectives; he had said nothing about Ben's work.

'It's Abbie,' Bedelia said shrewdly. 'She's probably trying to push Ellen off on the first man who comes along so she won't be an old maid.'

This phrase, used humbly by Ellen and by Bedelia derisively, irritated Charlie. 'Ellen's not an old maid. She's still young and a handsome girl.'

'You needn't worry about Ben. She'll never fall for him. She's still too much in love with you.'

'That's nonsense,' snapped Charlie, blushing.

'She'll never get you, though. I won't let her. You're mine.'

Charlie shrugged as if he considered the conversation too trivial to be continued, and walked away from the bed.

Bedelia's voice pursued him. 'Ellen wishes I'd die so she could marry you.' This was stated so calmly that it seemed no absurdity, but honest fact.

Charlie wheeled around. 'It's not worth talking about. I wish you wouldn't make such crazy statements.'

'Do you wish it, too? Do you want me to die so you can marry Ellen?'

'That's the most ridiculous thing I've ever heard. Ellen's a fine, good-hearted girl. Such a thought would never enter her mind.'

'She's against me, Charlie. She and Ben are working together.'

He turned away again and found himself face to face with his image in the pier glass. He felt that he had changed and expected to find evidence of it in his appearance. The change was there, but not sufficiently developed to show in his manner, his speech, nor the expression of his face. It was rather in his searching of Bedelia's manner, speech, and facial expression that the change manifested itself.

She went on quietly. 'You aren't very clever about people, dear. You trust them too easily. The ones you admire the most turn out to be the rottenest.'

He turned around and stared at her, wondering if Bedelia had chosen this oblique way to tell him about herself. 'I don't quite understand you.'

'You can't tell what most people are thinking,' she went on, almost blithely. 'Nor what their plans are nor how they feel about you. Those who look the most innocent are often the most deceitful.'

Jacob's family had been fond of Arthur's new wife, Chloe. She had been a sweet, steady girl and the old-fashioned Jewish family had not minded her being a Gentile.

'You're so good, Charlie, that you don't see the evil in others. Just because you're so decent yourself, you think everyone else is decent, too. You have no idea how rotten people are.'

Charlie returned to the fireplace. His body had become heavy and his mind rusty with fatigue. He knew that there was something grave beyond Bedelia's words and he was afraid she would tell him more than he could bear to hear. He called himself a coward, but wished just the same that they could return to the smug safety of Christmas Day.

Bedelia's calm had fled. She watched Charlie, aware that he had not been moved by what she had said. She hurried to tell him again that, if he knew the world as she knew it, he would realize how vile people are, and how rare were his own virtues. 'You're unusual, Charlie, you're sort of pure, you don't know that people are always plotting things against each other. That's why I love you so much because you haven't a suspicious bone in your body. You trust everyone, you think we're all as good as you are.'

'My dear,' he said, exercising such control that he managed to speak smoothly, 'you're letting yourself become hysterical.'

'When you were so ill that night, I was almost out of my mind. I was afraid you'd die. If you had, I'd have killed myself. I was afraid you'd die and I'd be alone again. Do you believe me? I wanted to kill myself that night.'

'Please, Biddy . . .' he said gently, 'you mustn't get so excited. We'll stop talking about it. You'll be feverish again.'

'What would I have to live for without you?'

'That's a perfectly natural way to feel when you're in love. You think your life has no reason except for that. But you do survive and after a while you probably find that there's a lot of pleasure in living.'

'I wouldn't. Not without you.'

Charlie drew a deep breath. 'How about Cochran? You said you loved him, but afterward you managed to live quite well without him.'

'Charlie, I have something to confess.'

Charlie edged closer to the fire. A shiver ran through him. He rubbed his hands.

'Women are sometimes deceitful. They're afraid men don't love them enough and they tell little lies to make a man jealous. When I first knew you, Charlie, and told you about myself, I tried to make you jealous by saying I loved Raoul and had been happy with him. That was a lie. I wasn't happy. I've had a hard life and I was never happy till I married you. Before that, dear, believe me, I didn't know what love was.' She whispered the last phrase as if the words were too sacred to be spoken aloud.

Raoul Cochran had seemed real, almost alive, when Bedelia told Charlie her stories of life in the New Orleans studio. Charlie's jealousy of the dead husband had been a lively emotion. Now the jealousy was dead. Ben's facts had killed, and Charlie mourned his dead jealousy and wished he could feel its flush again.

'The baby, our baby, I needn't have had it, it's only because I love you so much,' Bedelia murmured in a husky voice.

It had not been his wife who suggested that he increase his life insurance. That was his own, not Bedelia's doing. When she had told him that she was pregnant, he had seen fear in her eyes and known that she was remembering insecurity. 'I'm going to increase my life insurance,' he had said, and her eyes had filled with grateful tears.

Bedelia took up her crocheting. Her fingers jerked the wool as she talked. 'One night, Charlie, in the bathroom . . . your old gray and red robe was hanging on the door . . . so plain and ugly . . . but it made me think of you, how plain and good you are, how little you care for yourself . . . and suddenly it came to me, why shouldn't I have a baby? With you, Charlie . . .' Her hands were so unsteady that she had to put down her crocheting again, and she laughed out of key. 'I had always been afraid and I knew that night . . . when I looked at the ugly bathrobe . . . that I didn't have to be afraid any more. Do you understand?'

Charlie was not certain of his voice, and he nodded swiftly.

'Are you glad?'

The nod was briefer this time.

'I never thought I'd tell you. But you're not like those others, Charlie, you're a good man, a woman could tell you anything and you'd understand.'

Her voice trembled and her eyes shone with sincerity. Barrett had rejoiced when his wife told him that she was pregnant, and McKelvey had probably passed around those excellent Cuban cigars. It was not known whether Chloe Jacobs had whispered any such secret, but Jacobs hadn't needed the inspiration toward bigger life insurance.

This time Charlie closed the door before he went downstairs. He telephoned Doctor Meyers.

'Hello, Charlie. I've been thinking about you. Tried to call you yesterday, but you were disconnected. How are you?'

'Fine.'

'How's the digestion?'

'Pretty good.'

'No more dizzy spells? Nausea?'

'I've called you about my wife, Doctor.'

'What's wrong with her?'

'I want to ask you a question.' Before he spoke again, Charlie arranged and rearranged the words in his mind. 'Look here, she's got a bad cold, la grippe, I think. I want to know . . . is it dangerous in her condition?'

'Keep her in bed.'

'Yes, I have. But I want to know about . . . well, you know she's pregnant, of course.'

'Naturally. I examined her the other day.'

'You did!' Charlie's heart began to race. 'Then she really is . . . I mean, Doctor, is she all right?'

'Didn't she tell you? What's the matter, Charlie? Why are you so nervous?'

'I just wanted to be sure she was all right,' Charlie said.

'I've heard of women getting crazy notions,' the doctor laughed, 'but this is the first time I've found symptoms in the father. Don't you worry about it, Charlie. Your wife's a healthy woman and don't let anyone tell you it's dangerous after thirty. You ought to have two or three more . . .'

Then Bedelia was pregnant. The lie she had told her other husbands was no longer a lie. And no wonder she was so sensitive about it. Ghosts of old falsehoods had come back to haunt her. She had lied so often that she was afraid of the truth. The fact that this was a real pregnancy, along with the analysis that proved that Charlie had not been given a dose of poison, showed that Bedelia was not planning her husband's death. She was carrying their child, planning their future. What had seemed hysteria was the lifeline to which she clung with frail, desperate persistence. She loved him.

'Good God!' Charlie exclaimed as he saw the irony of her situation.

'Darling, why are you staying down there such a long time?' called his wife.

'I'll be right up,' he promised.

He did not return immediately to the bedroom. He had to examine his thoughts and review the situation. For a moment he had admitted the possibility of his wife's guilt. Suppose she were proven innocent; could he, like the old doctor, drop the belief as neatly as the knife is dropped after the operation is over? *Your wife's a healthy woman . . . you ought to have two or three more.* Could you, during Christmas week, suspect a woman of giving her husband poison, and in the first week of the new year offer your blessing to the virtuous wife and mother? Should Ben Chaney's story be proven untrue next week, could Charlie shed suspicion with the same ease?

Suppose Ben had made a mistake, followed the wrong clue, suspected an innocent woman? Suppose poor Bedelia was the victim of a monstrous practical joke? Ben might not be a detective at all; he might be a clever lunatic.

For thirty seconds these happy hopes dwelt in Charlie's heart. He breathed freely and started up the stairs to the room where his dear wife waited. In the shadows at the turn of the stairs, Will Barrett accosted him, a cynical smile curving his wet lips, a warning light in his drowned eyes.

Years ago Charlie had taught himself to clean his mind of worry just as he brushed his teeth before going to bed. He was proud of his ability to banish business cares at night and often boasted that he slept most soundly during critical situations. Tonight, as he undressed, cleansed his mouth with an antiseptic solution, and made his round of the house, turning off radiators and switching out the lights, he had resolved to dismiss Barrett, Jacobs, and McKelvey with the same steely firmness.

Sleep was impossible. But Charlie would not admit that horror kept him awake nor allow the three ghosts to enter his bedroom. From somewhere inside the house came a clatter insidious because its rhythm was perfect three-four time. 'The cellar door,' Charlie whispered to the darkness. 'I forgot to fasten it. I remember that I forgot.' He was not at all certain of this, but his bed was warm, the halls drafty, and at the thought of a journey into the cellar, goose pimples came out on his arms and legs.

He decided to turn on the light, to dispel the illusions that thrive in darkness, to forget the clatter by giving his attention to reality. He was sleeping in his old bedroom, and it seemed, as his eyes became accustomed to the light, that he had never deserted this single brass bed to sleep in the cherrywood four-poster with a wife. On the opposite wall hung an etching he had bought during his junior year at Yale. A flock of wild ducks flew eternally to the left. 'It has movement,' Charlie had explained as his mother watched him hang it.

The cellar door kept up its clatter. Charlie's eyes roved from the flight of ducks to the books on the bed table. As he read the titles the sense of the past was shed, and Charlie knew his mother had been dead these eight months and that his wife, Bedelia, had chosen these books. Bedelia's taste was hideous. Charlie had tried to wean her away from Laura Jean Libbey by reading aloud to her from Carlyle's *French Revolution*. She had listened dutifully at the beginning, but, later, had confessed that good books put her to sleep.

Charlie opened the first book. It was just what he had expected. A beautiful heroine with windswept locks was caught in the jungle. In the distance, tomtoms. The black chieftan was just about to drag Lady Pamela from the compound when Cyril arrived to rescue her from worse than death. Single-handed, the hero fought and conquered the savage horde, love triumphed, and in Cyril's manly arms, Lady Pamela laughed away the memory of that quarrel which had separated them at the tennis party given by the false Rosamund.

Charlie was moved, not by their extraordinary virtues and tribulations, but by their Christian names, Pamela, Cyril, Rosamund. Never Mary nor Bill nor Pete nor Jane.

Maurine. Chloe. Annabel.

What about *Bedelia*?

The name of her father was *Courtney Vance*.

She had often entertained Charlie with amusing or dramatic accounts of her experiences. Now, as he tried to put her stories in chronological order, he realized that she had never told her life-story consecutively, but always in bits and pieces. His eyes fixed on the flight of wild ducks, he saw the child Bedelia, Bedelia Vance, with the dark curls down her back as sedately she followed her governess down the steps of the mansion in San Francisco. Her father had been an English gentleman, but his father had been a younger son without fortune and had come to California during the gold rush. Her mother's people were Irish, good blood, but ruined by their love of horses and the ingratitude of the peasantry. But the grandfather had struck gold, dinners for twenty-four had been set on gold plate in a dining-room with stained-glass windows, music had floated up to the nursery where the child, Bedelia, slept in a nightgown of the finest French flannel, hand-stitched by the family seamstress. The earthquake of 1906 cost them their fortune and the girls at the boarding-school, who had slavishly followed Bedelia's every whim, turned against her and made her so miserable that she had to run away. Orphaned, poverty-stricken, with only her pride to sustain her, Bedelia had found a situation as companion to a wealthy, irascible old lady who had treated her miserably at first, but later learned to love her like a daughter. At a fashionable resort in the East . . . Asbury Park, it was . . . the youthful companion had met and loved a young millionaire who had wanted to marry her and endow her with his fortune, but had been kept from happiness by his people who were against that girl because she was poor and had to work for her living. The young millionaire had died of tuberculosis and shortly afterward the no-longer irascible old lady had passed on, too, leaving Bedelia a legacy which had resulted in a lawsuit by the old lady's relations, who were greedy people and naturally against a girl who had won the love and affection which they had sought in vain. Rather than demean herself by fighting for money in a public court, she had fled to Chicago, where she had tried to earn an honest living in a shirtwaist factory, a sweatshop it really was, but she would have been content to work there humbly had not she been forced to flee the proprietor's evil advances. It was during this flight that she had met *Raoul Cochran.*

This was the first time Charlie had considered his wife's history as a whole and he saw it as unadulterated Laura Jean Libbey. The separate stories told at different times had seemed quite real to him. There had been no reason to distrust the warm voice nor to seek deceit in those dark eyes. Why should he, who had been captivated by her, doubt the passion of the consumptive millionaire, the gratitude of the irascible old lady, the advances of the shirtwaist manufacturer?

The three-four clatter continued. Charlie turned out the light, resolved that he would fall asleep immediately. The cellar door became the tomtoms that Lady Pamela had heard in the jungle, and Charlie felt himself turn cold all over, moistly cold as if the water were closing over him. He struggled in the dark, trying to extricate himself from the thick weeds and to find the posts of the pier.

McKelvey had died of ptomaine poisoning after a fish dinner. His wife had eaten a warmed-over chop that night because she disliked fish. 'Bedelia,' Charlie said as he stumbled through the dark to discover the source of the clatter, 'Bedelia is fond of fish. Particularly fresh-water fish like trout and perch. And also of shellfish, clams, oysters, crabs, and lobster.'

The cellar door was not guilty. It had been fastened with a sound new catch. Charlie, usually so keen at locating sounds in the night, was baffled by it. He was not even sure that it was real. His nerves were unsteady, his imagination working overtime. Just as he had made up his mind that there had never been a clatter, it started again.

He shuffled up the attic stairs in his loose slippers and stretched out his hand to find the light bulb hat hung from a twisted cord in the center of the bewildering blackness. His coming disturbed the mice who wintered there. He heard the swift, dainty scraping of their feet and felt something cold scratch across his bare instep.

Jacobs had been a Jew, one of those devoted husbands, probably the sort who brings his wife flowers on Saturday and takes out more life insurance than he can afford. How does one go about drowning a man in the bathtub? Had Jacobs been drugged, too, or was he taken by surprise, tickled and teased until two frail hands were ably, gently, to push him under. The water had been warm, sea green against the white tub, the bathroom had smelled of moisture and scented soap, and circles of water had formed about the dark head.

'Christ! I'm going crazy!'

He spoke aloud. His oath echoed in the dark attic. His hand found and lost the light. He groped for it and the dark was water closing over his head. Quite out of breath, he resolved to give up, but grew angry, stamped on the floor, and reached out again for the light. At length he found it, turned the switch, was assaulted by the sudden burst of brightness, saw the lean rafters and dense attic shadows, shuffled over to a window, opened it, shivered in the wind and felt for the hooks of the shutters. This he did four times until he made certain that every shutter was secure. As he started back and raised his hand to switch off the light, he hesitated, fearing the journey of a few feet to the attic stairs. He might have let the light burn, saved his nerves, and come upstairs in the morning to switch if off. But that was not Charlie Horst, who had been taught good sense and thrift when he was young and despised himself for knowing fear. He turned out the light and descended the stairs apprehensively while the three-four clatter pursued him.

Safe in bed again, he asked himself indignantly what sort of man would take a stranger's word before his wife's and allow his imagination to be inflamed by a cheap love-story. Tomorrow in honest daylight he would sift all the facts, separate truth from fantasy, weigh evidence, and face honestly whatever he came to believe. In the meantime he would forget the whole thing and refresh himself with a night's sleep.

Damn Ben Chaney! Charlie had been happy until he came along, had considered himself the luckiest man in the world. If Ben had never come to the gate that October afternoon, asking if they knew of a house that he might rent in the neighborhood! If Charlie had not been rash and profligate with his money, taking out more insurance than was reasonable for a man of his income! If his stomach had not gone back on him last week and brought about the situation that had caused all this trouble! If McKelvey had not sighed when the bedsprings creaked, if Jacobs had not groaned with every tick of the clock, if Barrett had not stood guard over his bed, blowing his cold breath on Charlie's face!

There was only one way to solve the problem. That was the straight way, the shortest distance between two points of view. Charlie must face his wife with it and say, 'Bedelia, my dearest love, Ben has told me an absurd story. Naturally I don't believe a word, the man must be mad, and I understand why feminine instinct has warned you against him, but since his story concerns you, it's better that you know it.' He heard his voice repeating Ben's story, telling her about Maurine Barrett and the man on the boat who had greeted her as Mrs. Jacobs. He saw Bedelia's face as she listened, courteously but without much concern.

The vision was comforting. Strengthened by good common sense, he resolved to speak of it frankly in the morning. The scene might cause her pain, but it would put an end to all doubts. Firm in the belief that the night's phantoms would be dissolved by honest daylight, Charlie fell asleep.

6

'Charlie, dear,' Bedelia said.

It was almost eleven o'clock and Charlie had not yet carried out his resolution to tell her Ben Chaney's story. He had not forgotten it nor changed his mind. His first thought on opening his eyes that morning had been of his vow. But Bedelia had slept late. Charlie had done all the housework while he waited for her to awaken. The tasks had become irksome. He had been fidgety, aware of every passing minute, every thought that entered his mind, every movement of his muscles. Yet he wanted the house clean before he faced her with his questions. He did not wish to create a disorder of the emotions before there was order in his house. For then there would never be any tidiness to steady him.

At half-past ten she had called him to say that she was awake and ready for her breakfast. Her fever was down, but she was coughing badly and Charlie thought it better that she remain in the bedroom that day. She wore a handsome gown of green serge with bell-shaped sleeves that were embroidered in gold, black, and red.

'Charlie, dear, I think I should like an egg this morning.'

'Yes, dear.'

When he returned with the breakfast tray, she had made up the bedroom. The rose-colored moiré spread lay smooth upon the bed, and the pillows were tucked into the bolster. The room was like a stage set for the big scene. Charlie decided that he would let her eat her breakfast before he began his inquisition. He set the tray upon a small table by the window and lined the upholstered chair with cushions for her. Bedelia ate slowly, looking out of the window and dreaming between sips of coffee.

Outside the window the world shone. Clean, unbroken snow stretched to the horizon. On each side of the river the dark rocks were bearded with icicles; and icicles, catching the sunlight and sending off rainbows, hung from the roof and window-frames.

At last her coffee cup was empty. Charlie moved his chair closer so that there was only the small table, set with empty dishes, between him and his wife. Bedelia had fallen into a reverie. The bones of her face were neatly modeled and her skin shone with a fine luster. Appreciating these qualities but looking beyond them for something deeper, Charlie willed her to return his glance.

'Why were you so upset when Ben mentioned Keene Barrett?'

Suddenly the whole thing seemed absurd to Charlie. McKelvey, Jacobs, and Barrett were merely specters and could not endure in the clear daylight. The blue fishermen on the willowware plates were more real.

'Ben is a liar. There's not a word of truth in anything he says.' Bedelia said this calmly as if Charlie's sudden and irrelevant question had not disturbed her. In the same level voice she asked, 'Do you love me?'

He did not answer. The specters, happily, were fading. So long as they remained ghosts, creatures of Ben Chaney's cruelty and Charlie's tormented imagination, they could never touch nor hurt the Horsts. But once Charlie heard his wife speak their names, McKelvey, Jacobs, and Barrett would not longer be phantoms but corpses of men who had once been happy husbands.

'You loved me yesterday. You loved me until he came and told you those lies.'

'How did you know he'd been here?'

'The doorbell woke me up. I heard him say the Keeley boys had taught him to use snowshoes.'

'Why didn't you mention it?'

'Why didn't you?'

'If you know what he told me, Bedelia, you know why.'

'You believed him. That's why you were afraid to tell me.'

'I didn't want to hurt you,' Charlie said.

'It hurts me more for you to believe lies about me. I don't see how you could. His lies! He's the most deceitful man I've ever met. He's never told a word of truth since we've know him.'

'Then you know what he said?' Charlie asked hesitantly.

'Do you remember what I told you last night? If I didn't love you so much I wouldn't be having the baby. I needn't have, you know.'

'Were you pregnant when you first told me about it? Or was it a trick to get me to increase my insurance?'

She went scarlet. The doll's mouth became a thin line.

'About this man from St. Paul, Bedelia? Barrett. What about him?'

'It's four months. Pretty soon I'll be feeling life.'

It was an obvious appeal for sympathy and Charlie had no

right to let himself be touched by it. But this was such a natural thing for a woman to say that it made everything seem right again, and he felt as a husband ought to feel when his wife talks to him of the growth of the child in her womb. The rocker groaned. Charlie caught himself thinking that he ought to speak to Bedelia about oiling the furniture.

She raised her head defiantly. 'It's just like Ben to believe the Barretts.'

Charlie gasped.

'They were always against me. You must believe me, Charlie. Do you?'

There it was, her confession, not in the words Charlie had expected but no less real. One phantom became a husband.

Although he had been steeling himself against this moment, Charlie cringed. His face was twisted and his body twitching. He closed his eyes, thinking that if he shut her out of his sight he would stand it better.

Bedelia watched intently. When at last she saw Charlie's eyes open, she threw him an appealing glance. He would not look at her, but she hurried on with her excuses, wooing him, hoping to win his sympathy. 'They were furious when Will married me. Keene's wife wanted him to marry an heiress, some girl whose father had a seat on the Stock Exchange. When they found out he'd married a penniless girl, they were horrid. Wait till you see Keene. He's got a mouth like a pocketbook.' Her mouth became shrewd and greedy in imitation of Keene's. 'He doesn't talk much. You'd think words cost money. When Keene and Hazel found out about Will's leaving me all of his insurance, they were horrid to me, just horrid.' Bedelia's eyes narrowed. She shuddered slightly. 'They're trying to make trouble for me now because they think they can scare me into giving them some of the money back.'

The irascible old lady's relations had been against her, too, and the family of the consumptive millionaire who had wanted her to inherit his fortune.

There was a long silence, and then Charlie said, 'Ben told me the Keene Barretts were fond of you. After your husband died they tried their best to comfort you.'

'Fond of me!' Her nostrils quivered. 'I wish you'd heard the insults. Hazel couldn't stand it when Will bought me my fur coat. The best Keene would give her was plush with a tiny little Persian lamb collar. Well, she's got my moleskin now and everything else that was mine.'

'That's right, you left it with her, didn't you? Why?'

'She'd have to add fifty skins to get it around her bust. This is all a plot to get my money away from me. It's like Keene to spend on detectives.'

'If there's no more to it than that,' Charlie said, 'why did you run away?'

'I told you. The Barretts made my life miserable.'

'Why did you change your name?'

'I was frightened.' She lowered her eyelids as if her enemies were confronting her, and she wished to avoid their faces. 'I knew they'd stop at nothing to find me and get my money away from me.'

'It wouldn't have been necessary to change your name. The insurance money was legally yours and they couldn't have got it away from you.'

'Is that so?' she asked gravely.

'Bedelia, please tell me the truth,' Charlie begged. 'I'm not against you, I'm . . .' he was reluctant to pledge love, and he said instead, 'and I want to help you.'

'Don't you believe me?'

'I'm afraid not.'

She looked hurt.

'You gave me a false name when we met. And when we married, you let them put that false name on our marriage certificate. I don't even know whether we're legally husband and wife.'

'Oh!' she cried. 'That's terrible.'

'Not so terrible as the other things,' Charlie said.

'But I *want* to be married to you.'

'Didn't you want to be married to the others?'

She rested against the back of the chair and looked down at her folded hands. Charlie had never before seen her sulky or ill-mannered.

'Didn't you *want* to be married to the others?'

'There were no others,' she said to her hands. 'No others except you and Will.'

'What about Raoul Cochran?'

She waited a minute and then she gave him such a heart-breaking glance that he forgot how wicked she was and regretted his harshness. Thirty seconds later he was sorry that he had offered the flash of sympathy and despised himself because he was not a strong man who could tussle with evil and conquer in fifteen minutes.

A cloud slid over the sun. The day's purity and sparkle died. The snow was a dirty grayness. Down the road moved a dozen men bundled to the ears, shoveling snow off the road, piling it in soiled heaps. Charlie saw the question in Bedelia's eyes and nodded. Their isolation would soon be over. The poor of the town were opening the road to their door.

At noon the men stopped work, climbed into wagons and were carried off.

'They've gone,' Bedelia said.

Apparently Charlie had not heard. He had lost all sense of time, of the things around him, and of his peculiar situation. The clock struck, but he did not count its notes. Bedelia watched nervously as he walked up and down, his eyes on the carpet.

'Charlie, I said they'd gone away.'

'Who?'

'The men who were clearing the road. They didn't get to the house.'

'They've gone to dinner. Probably down at Mitch's saloon. The town is paying for it.'

'Will they be back?'

'At one o'clock.'

'Oh, dear,' Bedelia said unhappily.

'Perhaps we'd better have a bite, too.'

'I'm not hungry.'

Charlie was glad. He was in no mood for small tasks.

'I do wish you wouldn't do that,' Bedelia complained.

'Do what?'

'Keep charging across the room like a caged lion. It makes me nervous.'

The conversation suggested a small domestic quarrel. There was neither drama in it nor the hint of tragedy. Charlie found his pipe on the mantel, but did not light it. He clenched his teeth on the stem, and held an unlighted match in his hand.

'I love you dearly, Charlie. If you'd only believe that.'

He took a long time to light his pipe, pull at it, and throw away the match. 'If you love me so much, why have you lied to me?'

'I've had an unhappy life.'

There was something ingenuous about Bedelia, and something sly. She waited for Charlie to show pity. He failed her, and she went to the mirror, smoothed her hair, and then found her lip salve and rubbed it on her mouth. Then she hurried to Charlie, confronted him, not in anger but in humility. 'You don't know how miserable I've been. You don't know.'

He looked down at the parting in her hair. 'I want to know the truth about your life, right from the beginning.'

Bedelia sighed.

At the parting her hair was paler in hue. Charlie did not like this and he moved away. He did not conclude as another woman would that she dyed her hair, but was faintly revolted without knowing why. Like Ellen he detested artificiality of any sort.

'Who were your people?' he asked sharply. 'Where were you born? What was you childhood like?'

'I've told you, dear.' Her manner had become casual. In a brisk, business-like way, she continued, 'I came from one of the best families in San Francisco. Before the earthquake we were very rich. We lived . . .'

Charlie seized her shoulders. He was on the point of shaking her. 'I know that story. I don't believe it. Tell me the truth.'

'Oh, darling,' she moaned.

His hands fell away. He walked off and then turned around and looked at her from a safe distance. 'Look here, Biddy, you can be honest with me. I'm not against you, I'm your husband, I'm trying to help you.' He kept his voice low, for he was trying to make her understand that he would not punish her for telling him the truth.

Tears welled up, flooding out of her eyes and rolling down her cheeks. She did not try to stem them nor to dry her face, but stood there helplessly, pressing her hands against her neck. Her wide stare was directed at nothing. For the moment her eyes had no function except to make tears. She did not sob. There was nothing Charlie could do but wait until she had finished crying.

At last she was finished. She rubbed her eyes with her fists and smiled ruefully. She took the handkerchief from Charlie and wiped her cheeks and eyes. 'I'm sorry I was such a baby.'

'Would you like a drink of water?'

'No thank you.'

'Brandy?'

'Nothing, thanks.'

She looked around the room. Her glance was inquisitive and stared as if Charlie were someone she had never seen before. Her grief had been like a trance, and now as she returned to consciousness she sought reassurance in familiar things. Soon she was smiling, calm, home again. She sat down in the chair beside the window.

Charlie took the seat opposite it and stretched his hand across the table. She took it shyly.

'I'm going to ask you a few questions. You must answer them honestly, Bedelia. Nothing will make me angry nor hurt my feelings. You can be as honest with me as you'd be with yourself. Promise?'

'Yes, Charlie, I promise.'

Thus she gave herself to Charlie and trusted him to protect her. Her hand quivered as it lay in his. The sense of responsibility increased his tension. He did not know what he would do after he had learned the truth.

'What's your name?' he said.

'Bedelia Horst.'

Charlie shook his head. 'No, that's not what I want. The truth. Were you christened?'

She nodded.

'What name did they give you?'

'Bedelia.'

'I thought you promised to tell me the truth.'

'My mother used to call me Annie.'

Charlie felt that he had made progress. 'Annie what?'

'Annie Torrey.'

'Annie Torrey, that was the name you were called by when you were a child, is it?'

'Torrey with a Y. T-o-double r-e-y.'

'What sort of name was it?'

'It was my mother's name.'

'Not your father's?'

She became pale and her cheeks seemed to sink in. Her hands clasped her throat again.

'I see,' Charlie said gently. 'Then you didn't know your father?'

She looked at him blankly.

'Didn't you know anything about him? How old he was, his nationality, what sort of people he came from, what he did for a living?'

'He came from an aristocratic English family. His father was a younger son and came to this country because . . .'

'Bedelia,' Charlie interrupted, 'we're not playing a game. You've promised me the truth; are you going to keep you promise?'

'Yes,' she said humbly.

'What about your father?'

'I told you. When they had a dinner party, he'd carry me downstairs from the nursery. There were gold plates on the table and hired musicians. My mother had diamond earrings and . . .'

Charlie went off on a tangent. He hoped to shock her into honesty. 'Do you remember McKelvey?'

'Who?'

'Wasn't he your first husband?'

'Herman Bender was my first husband.'

Charlie leaped. 'Who was Herman Bender?'

'I told you,' she said patiently. 'My first husband. We were married when I was seventeen. He kept the livery stable.'

Charlie was shaken. He had prepared himself for horror, but it was tidy horror that concerned facts he knew and had arranged in his mind.

'I promised to tell you the truth,' she said.

'Yes, yes, of course,' he sputtered. 'Go ahead, tell me about Herman Bender.'

'I never talk about him because I don't like to remember how horrid people were to me afterward. I had to leave town. They went around saying I'd known about the mushrooms. They were jealous when they found out about the thousand dollars.'

'Herman died after eating mushrooms?'

'I guess they weren't really mushrooms. But how was I to

know? He taught me to test them. He was always going to pick mushrooms. They made a good meal and didn't cost anything.'

'You gave him mushrooms and he died, and then you got some money?'

'We always cooked them in butter.'

'What are you talking about?'

'The mushrooms. He wouldn't eat them unless they were cooked in butter.'

'I want to hear about the thousand dollars.'

She spoke patiently. 'I didn't know about the thousand dollars, honestly. I'd heard about insurance, but I didn't know what it meant until they sent me the money.'

'Then why did you give him the mushrooms?'

'He liked them. And we could get them for nothing, all we had to do was go out and pick them.' The flesh tightened over her cheekbones. 'He was cheap. I didn't think he had any money the way he was always going on about ending in the poorhouse. He said the horses ate too much, ate up all the profits.'

'Where was this?'

'Just outside of San Francisco. I told you I was born in California.'

There were other things she had told him. He saw now that certain gems of truth shone among her falsehoods, and understood that when she tried to tell the truth it was tarnished by deceit. For Bedelia there was no clean line between honesty and fabrication.

'Did you love Herman Bender?'

Her laughter was harsh.

'Then why did you marry him?'

Bedelia looked out of the window. The wagons had brought the men back to work. Beside the road the mounds of snow were growing tall. And the men were working their way toward the gate.

'He had a good business and wasn't afraid of getting married,' Bedelia said, turning toward Charlie again.

'It must be hard to marry when you're seventeen and not in love with your husband.'

Her lips moved but no words came out. She was carrying on a debate with herself, arguing the reality of some image that had risen in her mind, pondering the wisdom of telling it.

'Speak up, Bedelia. I'll try to understand.'

The words tumbled out in a cascade. 'He was good to me sometimes and sometimes he was horrid. He'd hit me and knock me down. You don't know, Charlie! He was mean and he'd hit me if I asked for money. Maybe you don't believe that either.' Her hands protected her belly. 'I lost my baby. It was his fault.'

'And you got a thousand dollars for giving him the mushrooms.'

'No!' she cried. 'I didn't mean to, honestly, I was only trying to give him a cheap meal. It wasn't till afterward that I found out he'd gone and insured his life for a thousand dollars after I told him I was in the family way.'

'That's hard to believe,' Charlie said. 'His insuring his life showed consideration and tenderness, and looked as if he were glad that you were bearing him a child. It's hard to believe he hit you and made you lose it.'

Her face had become scarlet. She beat her fists against the table. 'You've got to believe that, Charlie. There are a lot of things you don't know because you don't know tough people. A husband's always glad when you tell him you're going to have your first; he thinks he's a wonderful fellow, he's going to be a father. That's the way Herman felt when I told him, only he had a terrible temper. When he got sore he forgot I was in the family way. He was sorrier when I lost it.'

'You might have had another.'

'If he'd lived,' she said piously.

'Or perhaps you'd have prevented it, since you seem to know how.'

'I didn't know that till later. I was green then, I didn't

know much of anything. It was later, a long time later, that I found out about those things.'

'Did you know them when you were married to McKelvey?'

Charlie was used to that look of blank inattentiveness. He spoke in a loud, authoritative voice. 'Bedelia! Look at me.' She turned her head as the subject might obey a hypnotist. Her eyes were still veiled. Charlie reached across the table, took her chin in his hand, tilting it and forcing her to keep her face turned toward him. Suddenly she smiled. The frost was out of her eyes, they were bright and alive again, her smile warm and loving.

He felt a brute for going on with his interrogation. 'What about McKelvey? Were you married to him or weren't you?'

'I don't remember.'

Charlie was not sure he blamed Herman Bender for his fits of temper. With the sense of impotence Charlie's fury swelled. 'It's impossible to forget a person you've been married to. Don't think I'm gullible enough to believe that sort of excuse.'

'Please don't shout at me, Charlie. I can't help it if I forget, can I?'

'Your memory serves you conveniently. This morning you told me there'd never been any other husbands but Will Barrett and me, and then suddenly you pull out this Bender.'

'Herman was so mean to me that I forget him a lot of the time.'

Charlie shook his head.

'I don't always remember unpleasant things,' Bedelia said plaintively, and when Charlie looked at her face he knew that this at least was the truth.

Still he tried patiently to get some order and logic into her story. 'What did you do after Bender died?'

'I went away.'

'Where?'

'Different places. I was companion to a rich old lady and we traveled a lot. We went to fashionable resorts, Nantucket, Bar Harbor, and Asbury Park.'

Charlie remembered that Ben had spoken of Asbury Park as the scene of her meeting with McKelvey. 'Did you meet anyone there?'

'That's where I met Harold De Graf. I've told you about him. He was a Southerner, awfully good-looking and immensely wealthy, but he had consumption. He fell in love with me . . .'

'Bedelia,' Charlie said wearily, 'I've heard that story. I want the truth. You promised to tell me the truth, you know.'

'Yes, dear.'

'Was there actually a rich old lady and a consumptive millionaire?'

'Of course, dear. I've told you about her. She wanted to leave me a lot of money, but her relations were against me, particularly her nephew; he was a terrible scoundrel and when I wouldn't let him make love to me . . .'

'What about Jacobs?' snapped Charlie.

Bedelia did not answer, but her left hand covered the right on which she wore the ring of gold and garnets that Charlie had given to her to replace the black pearl.

'Then you do remember Jacobs?'

A vein bisected her forehead. It stood out prominently, slanting from her hairline to the left eye. Charlie noticed that it was throbbing. Her teeth cut into her lower lip.

'You must remember Jacobs. You kept the black pearl.'

When she spoke, Charlie saw the mark of her teeth on the lower lip. 'It was mine. I had the right to keep it.'

'It must have been hard to leave everything else,' Charlie said coldly. 'All your clothes and the kitchen things and fur coats. But you kept the ring and it was the ring that trapped you.'

'You sound like you don't love me.'

Then men with snowshovels had reached the strip of road in front of their house. The vast silence which had surrounded the house was broken by the clatter of shovels and the men's coarse, good-natured laugh.

Charlie's legs were stiff. The back of his neck ached. Beyond the terrace the river rushed along as cheerfully as ever and in the western sky the clouds had become luminous islands on a pearly sea. The wagon had called for the snow-shovelers, who had been driven back to City Hall for their pay. It was five o'clock, and Charlie had been standing at the window for almost an hour.

He remembered with astonishment that he had not telephoned the office. Although his phone had been connected all day, he had not once thought to call the office. On the day of his mother's death he had telephoned his foreman three times.

Bedelia was sleeping. The quarrel had worn her out and she had been able to cast aside her worries and curl up on the bed like a kitten. For Charlie there was not such easy refuge.

When he made up his mind to ask his wife about Ben's accusations, Charlie had expected denial or confession. He had got neither, only evasions which fell between the two. She had owned neither to marriage nor acquaintance with Jacobs and McKelvey, but had given signs that both dwelt somewhere in the twisted avenues of her memory. He had mentioned Jacobs and she had made an involuntary gesture toward the hand on which she had worn the black pearl. And Asbury Park, which had been the meeting-place between romance with the tubercular millionaire. The fabric of her story was woven with threads of truth as well as with the colors of deceit. She had a strong enough memory for all her fancies; it was her sins that she forgot.

And there had been Herman Bender, the livery-stable proprietor, the husband she had forgotten in the morning and remembered in the afternoon. If his death had been, as she said, an accident, it had been a piece of remarkably good fortune for her. She had been freed of a disagreeable mate and endowed with one thousand dollars, which had seemed at that time a fortune. Her husband's death had come as a rare piece of luck and the tawdry accident became a pattern for crime. In one form or other she had repeated it remorselessly, always with greater cunning and new refinements. Charlie's flesh shrank as he recalled the emotions which had churned in him when she had first confided that she was pregnant.

She had never once admitted to murder. Nor had Charlie asked the direct question. Delicacy forbade it. He could no more speak to Bedelia of murder than he could mention deformity in the presence of the deformed. There had been pathos in her confession that she had married Herman Bender because the man was willing and he made a good living. No other answer could so clearly have shown that her early life had been sordid. Like the mansion in San Francisco, the aristocratic forebears, the gold plates, hired musicians, the diamonds in her mother's ears, it pointed to youthful poverty and shame.

Charlie pitied her because she had not been able to grow beyond these humiliations, but he was too honest to accept these as excuse for her crime. If everyone whose childhood has been sordid were to become a murderer, at least eighty per cent of the population would be homicidal. Early deprivations, unhappiness, hunger, may lead to a grudge against society, bitterness, protest, or the healthy attempt to make a better world for the new generation, but no sane judge would accept such excuse for deliberate, cruel, plotted murder.

There was no mystery about her motives. She had killed for money, planning her life like a business man who hopes to lay aside a tidy fortune for his old age. She had arranged her business affairs with acumen, had invested a part of her capital in each new venture. There was no mystery about it, no grandeur, but here was enigma, the enigma of the soul of a human being who is able to commit crime as normally and efficiently as the business man plans a deal. Why is one person incapable of crime, another able to kill in cold blood? Why, where, what is the cause of that delicate balance between good and evil? This is the mystery beyond all mysteries, the problem that neither detective, physician, nor psychologist has yet solved. Charlie remembered the newspaper story about the New Hampshire elder who had smothered his sister with a sofa pillow because, after seventeen years, he had believed she was interfering in his love affair. Why after seventeen years on that particular day?

Coral and lavender faded in the western sky. Twilight hung in the air like mist.

'Charlie!'

Charlie shuddered.

'I've come downstairs.'

His mother's white shawl over her shoulders, the green dress fading into the shadows, the white doorway framing the picture, she was like one of those dim portraits that hang in the old twilight galleries of Europe. As Charlie's eyes became used to the dusk, he saw the oval of her face pierced by dark eyes, and her hands holding the shawl.

'You shouldn't have come downstairs.'

'Charlie, I want to talk to you.'

'All right.' He led the way toward the living-room, which seemed safer than the den because it was larger. Bedelia chose the wing chair. Charlie turned on all of the lights and touched a match to the crumpled paper under the logs in the fireplace.

'The road's clear, Charlie, we could get to town.'

'Our drive hasn't been cleared yet.'

'You could clear it, couldn't you?'

'I intend to, first thing tomorrow morning.'

'How long will it take?'

'Two to three hours, I imagine.'

'Oh,' said Bedelia; and after a pause, 'then we could catch the ten-ten.'

'What for?'

'New York.'

Charlie did not answer. Bedelia looked at the what-not. There was a bare space which had once belonged to the Dresden marquis and his love. So much had happened since she had dropped the ornament that Bedelia had not had a chance to rearrange her shelves. She went to the what-not, tried a Sèvres vase in the bare space, but shook her head at it because the vase definitely belonged on the upper shelf.

'What do you want to go to New York for?' Charlie said at last.

Bedelia replaced the vase and stepped back to study the shelves. 'A holiday, dear. We could go to some Southern place in Europe. Italy, I'd like. The English always go to Italy for the winter.'

'I don't understand you.' That was a lie. Charlie knew precisely what she had chosen not to say.

'We've both been ill, Charlie. You've had a bad attack of indigestion and my cold may hang on for months. A vacation would do us good.'

She tried to make it sound as commonplace as it would sound to their friends if Charlie Horst and his wife should take a winter holiday.

Charlie cleared his throat. 'Is it because you want to avoid Barrett?'

Bedelia turned to the what-not again. She tried a set of silver furniture, minute and exquisitely wrought, in the place of the Dresden group.

'Have they any evidence against you?'

Her voice came to Charlie as from a great distance. 'I don't know what you mean.'

'If Barrett should identify you, would it prove anything?

Could they tell now, after all this time, whether Will Barrett was drugged before he fell into the water? And even if they should prove it, would they have any real evidence? Of course, your running off and changing your name doesn't help.'

Bedelia changed the positions of a carved ivory stork, a china dog, a carnelian elephant, and a pair of white jade cats. The motley menagerie pleased her. She stepped back and scrutinized it from a distance. 'They've got nothing against me, except the suspicion in their dirty rotten minds.' Her voice was not defiant, but merely contemptuous as if she were talking reluctantly about something unpleasant that had nothing to do with herself.

'Then why shouldn't we stay and fight it out? Why run away?'

'I'd rather go abroad.'

'Suppose he should identify you as his sister-in-law; he still has nothing definite against you. And besides, it happened in another state. All these cases were in different states, weren't they? Minnesota, Michigan, and Tennessee. There'd be the devil of a legal mess. And what proof have they of anything?' As he said this, Charlie saw triumph in the law courts, the judge leaning over to shake hands with the released prisoner while her loyal husband stood beside her, holding her other arm. 'First of all, they'd have to identify you as the Barrett Woman, as Annabel McKelvey and Zoe Jacobs.'

'Chloe,' she said.

Charlie stepped back so suddenly that he narrowly missed the fire.

Bedelia began to talk vivaciously of the trip to Europe. Winter seas might be rough, but the trip across would not take more than a week. Paris first, she thought, because she had longed all her life to see Paris and she'd like some new clothes. Afterward Italy, or, if Charlie preferred, the Riviera.

She had read a lot about the Riviera, knew about the grand hotels, seaside promenades, gambling casinos.

'We might even go to Monte Carlo,' Bedelia said. She was still unsatisfied with the arrangement of her shelves. On the palm of her right hand rested the three monkeys the Johnsons had given the Horsts for Christmas. To follow their advice, Charlie thought, to see no evil, hear no evil, speak no evil, was as weak as deliberately cultivating evil. The careful avoidance of all that was unpleasant and unsavory was not only Charlie's greatest fault, but the fault of his people and his class. By turning their eyes and ears from evil, they nourished evil, gave it sunlight, fresh air, and the space in which to flourish. The civilized man was not the man who shut himself away from evil, but who saw it clearly, heard its faintest rustlings, exposed it, shouted about it from the housetops.

A pinprick had destroyed his triumph. The trial that he had seen as easy victory became a nightmare. He saw his wife on the witness stand, being interrogated, cross-examined, bullied; he saw the flashlights exploding, the newspaper headlines, the lurid photographs and stories in the Sunday supplements. Reporters would pry into the secrets of the murderess's life with her last husband and nothing of their marriage would be too intimate for the sob sisters to search out and serve to the public in syrupy prose. They would pity her husband for having been taken in by this female Bluebeard and consider him lucky because he had escaped death at her hands.

Bedelia turned from the what-not and came toward him. The green gown was loose, but it clung to her body and he saw that he need not have asked Doctor Meyers about her pregnancy. It was all too apparent. Charlie counted the months on his fingers. A chill crept along his spine. Telegraph wires would flash the news from coast to coast when Charlie Horst's child was born; in the remotest villages the newspapers would print his name. And even if the courts should free Bedelia, the stigma would endure; she would be a marked woman, stared at and whispered about wherever she went, and her child would be marked, too, with the brand.

She chattered on about Europe. One would think Venice and Rome were no farther off than Georgetown and Redding. She had read all that romantic fiction and to her mind there was no place like Lake Como for fugitive lovers. They might find a house on a hill . . . 'a villa, you call it. They have terraced gardens with trellises and statues and olive trees and oranges and lemons. Lemon blossoms are sweeter than orange,' she told him gravely. 'We'd have four or five in help, you always do in foreign countries; they don't cost any more than one good servant here, especially with the wages they expect nowadays; they're really happy to go to work for you cheaply, and you always have your morning coffee in bed.'

'What do you mean?' Charlie asked, irritated by the completeness of her plans. 'We can't live abroad.'

'Why not?'

'My home's here, my business.'

'We could close the house. Bachman would run the business for you, or you could sell it. Judge Bennett would look after your affairs.'

'So you've settled my life for me?'

'Don't be angry, dear. It would be so pleasant, living in a warm climate, basking in the sun, swimming in the middle of winter. Wouldn't you like to swim in February, Charlie?' Deliberately avoiding the real motive for the journey, she made it sound as if she sought nothing but sunshine and lemon blossoms. Charlie looked at her face and saw that she was engrossed in this new reverie. He wondered if she had hypnotized herself into believing this lie, too.

'I intend to stay right here.'

She pouted prettily, still the saucy darling mildly irritated because her obstinate husband would not indulge her whim.

'My dear.' Charlie's voice sounded like his mother's in her

most righteous moments. 'We can't afford to live anywhere but here. When I asked you to marry me, I told you frankly that I wasn't a rich man. I've got no income except what I earn, and even my business means nothing without me. So it's no use arguing, we can't leave.'

She smiled graciously. 'I've got plenty of money.'

'You?'

Simultaneously he remembered that she had told him about an inheritance from Raoul Cochran's grandmother and that there had never been any such person as Raoul Cochran.

'I've got almost two hundred thousand dollars.'

'You!'

'Almost. Of course I've had to spend some of it.'

'Where did . . .' he began, but became silent in the middle of the question because he knew well enough where she had got the money.

'So it would be quite easy for us to live abroad. On the income, not the capital.'

'You don't think I'd live on that money!'

'The interest at four per cent is eight thousand a year. If we were very careful and invested only in three per cent securities, we'd have six thousand. You can live like a prince on that in Europe.'

'My God!' cried Charlie. 'Oh, my God!'

'Very well, if that's the way you feel.' The painted lips drooped cruelly. She turned abruptly and her taffeta petticoats echoed the movement. Charlie heard the silk rustle as she mounted the stairs and the sound which always seemed so feminine and fair to him was the whisper of evil.

The Danbury train whistled as it rounded the curve. Charlie took out his watch to see if it was on time. His habits had not been changed by shock and mental torment. He was still Charlie Horst, born and brought up in this fine house, a good architect and estimable citizen. His watch was always on time, his shoes were shined, his bills paid the first of the month. He looked around him at the pleasant room, at flames leaping in the fireplace, the love-seat in the bow window.

'Dearest,' Bedelia called.

'Where are you?'

'In the kitchen.'

'I thought you'd gone upstairs.'

'I came down the back way.'

She had taken off the white shawl and tied an apron over the green dress. Red-and-white checked gingham and her pose at the stove, with her head bent over the pot and a big spoon in her hand, comforted her husband.

The illusion of peace did not last. A spring snapped, metal screeched, a mouse squeaked thin shrill notes of pain. Bedelia clasped her throat with both hands and cast an anguished glance in Charlie's direction. He opened one of the lower cupboards and took out the trap that had been set there.

Bedelia turned away.

'Don't let it bother you,' Charlie said. As he carried the trap to the shed, he passed Bedelia. He held the trap behind him, his body concealing it from her. In the shed he finished the job, using a small hammer and killing the mouse with a single blow.

When he came back to the kitchen, he found Bedelia perched on the stool, her feet tucked under her, her arms wrapped around her body.

'Don't be frightened. It's dead.'

'I shouldn't have minded if she had died right away, but I suffer when creatures struggle for life. She was such a tiny mouse.'

'It might have been a male.'

'All helpless things seem female to me.'

She turned to her work. Charlie washed his hands and dried them on the roller towel. He was unsteady; his nerves twitched, his body was strung with live wires. For years he had been catching rats and mice in the house, had thought of them as pests and never been affected by their death. Bedelia's distress had been communicated to him.

The kitchen was silent except for the occasional tap of her high heels on the linoleum. Charlie could not endure the silence and he said, 'My mother was the same. She could never bear to see anything die.'

Bedelia turned from the stove to fetch some condiment from the spice shelf. He saw that her face was like the face of a deaf mute. Her eyes had a slight glaze and her mouth was a hard knot.

Charlie saw that the trance-like state was deliberate, Bedelia's method of wiping out an unpleasant scene. He became wildly angry. Cords thickened in his neck and his voice was harsh. 'No use working yourself up over the death of a pest. A mouse seems an inoffensive little thing, really quite touching, but it's destructive and dangerous, a menace. We've got to get rid of them for our own safety.'

Bedelia carried the spice shaker back to the stove, sprinkled the spice from it into the pot. 'I bet you can't guess what we're having for supper.'

Her voice was even, the look on her face bland. She smiled, her dimples deepened, and she gave a deep sigh of contentment as she stirred the soup in the pot. She looked so small and sweet, so feminine, so delightfully absorbed in her domestic task. 'There was practically nothing in the pantry, but I've managed to make a very good supper. You've no idea how ingenious I am.'

'She poured the soup into bowls and put them on a tray, which Charlie carried into the dining-room. She followed with another tray on which there was a covered dish.

'Guess what's in here,' she commanded as she set it on the table.

'What?'

'A surprise for you, dear. One of your very favorite dishes,' Bedelia said, and lifted the cover.

The French toast was done to perfection, its golden surface liberally sprinkled with powdered sugar.

7

Early the next morning a wagon, the first to pass since the snowstorm, rattled down the road. A little while later Mary trudged the mile from the streetcar terminal. She pushed through the drifts that surrounded the house, let herself in the back way, took off her mittens, and with her stiff fingers managed to light the stove. After she had warmed herself and put the kettle on, she wondered how late the Horsts would sleep. She had news for Hannah, but she could not use the telephone while her bosses were still in bed.

At half-past eight Mary went upstairs. Usually at this hour Mr. and Mrs. Horst had finished breakfast and Mary was almost through with her dishes. The house was deadly quiet. Mary tapped timidly at their bedroom door.

'Come in,' Mrs. Horst called. She was standing at the window in the blue dressing-gown with the rose-colored ribbons. Her hair hung in braids over her shoulder.

'I got back,' Mary announced.

'I'm glad, Mary.'

'I hope you're not mad at me, Mrs. Horst. I got snowed in.'

'So were we.'

Mary looked around the room. She felt vaguely that something was missing, but could not say what it was.

'I hope you got along all right without me.'

'Poor Mr. Horst had to do all the work. I've been in bed with a bad cold.'

Mary's eyes rested on the bed. Only one side had been slept in. She knew then what was missing. 'Where's Mr. Horst?'

'We were afraid that he'd catch my cold, so he's been sleeping in the other room.'

'Should I wake him up? I've got the coffee on and the oatmeal's made, you could have breakfast in five minutes.'

'No, let him sleep.'

'Won't he be late to work?'

'He'll have to clean the driveway. He can't get the machine out until he's got it cleared.'

'He could walk to the streetcar.'

'Never mind, Mary. Don't disturb him.'

'Will you have breakfast now?'

'No. I'll wait for him.'

Mary waited there, rubbing the toe of one foot against the other ankle. She had news of her own. With a broken giggle she told Bedelia that she had got herself engaged to Hen Blackman.

Bedelia beamed approval. 'Perhaps the blizzard was a blessing in disguise, Mary. I told Mr. Horst the other day that if you were half the girl I thought you were, you'd take advantage of this opportunity.'

Mary, flattered because Mrs. Horst had talked about her, could hardly get over her giggles. She told in full detail how Hen had popped the question. 'You know about it before Hannah,' she said, conferring honor upon her boss.

'As soon as Mr. Horst is up and you've given us breakfast, you can phone and tell her,' Bedelia said.

Mary was still giggling as she started for the kitchen. Her laughter ceased suddenly and she screamed. She had seen some disembodied white thing floating toward her on the back stairs.

'Did I frighten you, Mary? I'm sorry.' Charlie ascended out of the shadows. He had on dark trousers and a white shirt.

'I thought you were a ghost,' she said.

His felt carpet slippers slid across the floor soundlessly. Bedelia did not hear him as he entered the bedroom. At his

'Good morning, dear,' she jerked around.

'I seem to be scaring all the ladies this morning,' Charlie said.

'Martin's beer truck passed,' she told him.

'Yes, I heard it. But I was too lazy to get up. I didn't fall asleep until dawn.'

Bedelia looked around the room, letting her eyes rest for a second on this or that piece of furniture and then examining the next, and going on until she had studied everything carefully. Was she thinking of other rooms she had left, comparing this with them, wishing she might stay here with the drapes she had made on her sewing machine, the colors she had chosen, and the bed in which she had slept with Charlie? Did she mourn the husbands along with all the other things she had left behind, the furs and pretty dresses, the copper pots, the casseroles, the ingenious egg-beaters and can-openers?

The black pearl meant more to her than Jacobs. She would want to keep it to show off at the Casino in Monte Carlo. Would she keep the garnet ring that Charlie had given her for Christmas?

'Are you still thinking of Europe?' he asked.

She seemed not to have heard. Charlie wondered if he ought to repeat the question. He did not want to lose his temper, but he could not help resenting her indifference.

'It doesn't matter whether you're thinking about it or not. Because we're not leaving. We're going to stay here and fight it out.'

Bedelia smiled at her husband shyly. 'Oh, Charlie, dear, you're so good. I don't believe there's another man alive as good and sweet as you are.' She gave him her most enchanting smile.

'Did you hear what I said, Bedelia?' He tried to sound stern, but his voice was unsteady. 'We're going to stay here and fight it out.'

'I knew that.'

'How did you know?'

'You said so last night. You always mean what you say, don't you?' She offered this tranquilly, without bitterness. 'Don't worry, Charlie, dear. I'll do whatever you want. I love you so much, anything you do seems right to me.'

Her serenity bewildered Charlie. She had everything to lose, her reputation, her freedom, possibly her life. The simple faith with which she gave herself into his keeping struck him as false. She went about her tasks calmly, opened drawers, chose clean underclothing, examined ribbons and embroidery.

'This is serious . . .' he began.

Bedelia's cough interrupted. Her body shook and she staggered toward the bed, holding her hands over her mouth. Tears filled her eyes.

'I'm sorry,' she whispered in a husky voice.

'You're not well yet,' Charlie said. 'I should never have let you get up yesterday. Better stay in bed this morning.'

Weak, grateful for his solicitude, and as docile as a child, Bedelia crept into bed. The mood of humility continued. Mary brought her breakfast and, although Bedelia complained that she had no appetite, she obeyed Charlie and ate the good hot food.

'Are you going to clear the driveway now?' she asked, watching him over her cup of coffee as Charlie put on his hunting boots.

'Yes, but only to get it cleared. We're not leaving.'

'You said that before, dear.'

'I don't mean to be arbitrary, but we can't go on treating this as trivial. You may not realize the importance of my decision, Bedelia, but the future depends . . .'

'Why don't you call me Biddy any more?'

The triviality of the interruption angered him. He wondered whether she was purposely keeping him from talking about the future. A glance at her softened him. Sitting up against the cushions in that large, solid bed, Bedelia seemed far too frail, resigned, and patient to cause him the slightest anxiety. He wished that he, too, might thrust aside his fears and give his attention fully to toast and plum jam.

Bedelia was spreading her toast with jam carefully so that she should not soil her fingers. As Charlie watched her enjoy the jam, pour cream over her oatmeal, measure sugar into her coffee, she seemed so innocent, so sweet and sane that he was ready to discredit everything Ben had told him, and to forget the curious contradictions in her stories and behavior.

'You mustn't worry about anything, Charlie. Leave it to me. There's always a way.'

Charlie's hand was stayed on its journey with the boot-lace. Probably Annabel McKelvey had been as mild while she was planning to serve fish at dinner; Chloe had smiled gently upon Jacobs when she knew him to be against her; Maurine's sweet ways had lured Will Barrett toward the pier.

He hurried out of the room. His excuse was a journey to the attic to find his sealskin cap. It was kept in a cedar chest with folded travel blankets, his mother's Jaegers and her mink stole. The smell of mothballs brought back the past and, holding the stole in his hands, he could see it as his mother had worn it, thrown over a bony shoulder with her lean face between it and a velvet toque. 'Duty,' his mother had always told him, 'duty comes first, Charles.'

Laughter greeted his return to the bedroom. Mary had come upstairs for Bedelia's tray and was talking again about her engagement. It all had to be repeated for Charlie.

'You needn't worry about help in the house,' Mary said, 'I'm not getting married till June, so you needn't think about getting another girl for a while yet, and there's my little sister Sarah, she'll be looking for a place soon.'

'Before you do anything else, Mary, phone Montagnino. We've been cleaned out of everything. Bring me the pad and pencil, please.'

Charlie lingered in the bedroom. His spirit was soothed by the quality of Bedelia's voice as she said, 'I was thinking of pork roast, Mary. Mr. Horst is so fond of it and after the pot luck he's been having for the last few days and the pap we gave him while he was ill, he deserves something good. And don't forget apples . . .'

'We got plenty of apples in the cellar.'

'How often do I have to tell you, Mary, that I don't make apple sauce with Macintoshes? Order greenings.'

'Yes, ma'am.' Mary was sullen.

Charlie stayed on to hear Bedelia and Mary argue about the order. What could be wrong in a house where such passion went into a controversy over apples, where carrots and cabbage and kohlrabi were so earnestly compared? Let Barrett come! What better assurance had Charlie of the man's impotence than Bedelia's prodigal grocery order? Ten pounds of sugar, Mary, two of butter, six cans of tomatoes, five pounds of spaghetti—the narrow, mind you, not that broad macaroni—five pounds store cheese to be dried and grated, a peck of onions, two dozen eggs. A good housewife would never order so lavishly unless she was sure of the day after tomorrow.

In the midst of it Bedelia coughed again. Fierce tremors shook her. She lay back upon the pillows, utterly exhausted.

'You're not to get out of bed today,' Charlie said. 'Promise me you'll take care of that cough.'

'Yes, of course, Charlie, I'll do whatever you say.'

The telephone rang. Mary ran for it. Charlie tried not to listen, but he could not help overhearing her tell the news of her engagement.

'How happy she is!' Bedelia exclaimed, smiling with the complacence that women always show over a marriage or engagement. 'We must give her a nice present.'

'It was Hannah,' Mary said as she bounced back into the bedroom. 'They got their phone connected at last. They're almost out of food. They'd have starved if the Keeleys hadn't sent over some bread and eggs and bacon. Their road's blocked up, there's no way of them getting their groceries, only Hannah's thought of a way. Montagnino's sending their order out with ours, and the Keeley boys are coming down with their sled to get it. Hannah wanted to know if you'd mind us taking their order and I said it'd be all right.'

'Of course,' Bedelia said.

'Montagnino's sending the wagon out early, Hannah needs the stuff for lunch. They're having company.'

Bedelia coughed.

'It's that gentleman that didn't come last week. He's coming today.'

Charlie said, 'That's not possible, Mary. Their road's blocked, no one can get there.'

'Mr. Chaney's going on snowshoes to meet the gentleman up to the Wilton Station,' Mary explained. 'He's coming on the twelve-ten and going straight to Wilton. Mr. Chaney's taking a pair of snowshoes for him. They fixed it up on the phone, this gentleman; he called Mr. Chaney from New York on the long distance, Hannah told me.'

Charlie let down the flaps of his sealskin cap and tied them under his chin. He looked at the wallpaper, the furniture, Bedelia's silver toilet set, at everything except his wife.

Mary went on, panting with excitement. 'That's why Hannah's so set on getting her groceries on time. It's not a hard lunch to fix, but Mr. Chaney says it won't take no more than fifteen minutes on snowshoes from the Wilton Station and he wants lunch right away when they get back. Montagnino's sending up their order with ours and the Keeley boys are coming down . . .'

Given the chance Mary would repeat a fact five or six times. Bedelia cut her off. 'You'd better hurry and get our order in, Mary.'

'Yes, ma'am.'

Charlie hurried out of the bedroom. He did not want to be alone with Bedelia to talk about Ben Chaney's guest. He took the shovel off its nail in the shed and went out to clear the driveway. The air was like a tonic. He felt the way a prisoner must feel after years in a cell. The sky was a hard blue arch, the sun warm, and the snow had a crisp crust that broke under his feet.

He was not such a fool that he believed his troubles were over because the sun was bright, but he felt new strength in his body, clarity in his mind, and his nerves became steadier. He tried to consider his problem objectively, as if someone had said to him, 'See here, Charlie, a friend of mine's in trouble. You see, he got married recently and he's crazy about his wife, and now he doesn't know what to do . . .'

'What kind of trouble?' he would naturally ask.

'He's discovered his wife's a . . . a criminal.'

The word was not shocking. Criminal might mean petty thief or a woman who made herself a nuisance to the neighbors.

'What crime has she committed?'

'Murder.'

Murder. That gave a different complexion to his friend's troubles. But even murder had certain justifications. Self-defense, for instance.

'Who'd she murder?'

'Her husband.' But that was not the whole truth. 'Several husbands, in fact. Four, perhaps five.'

Objectively it was unbelievable, the sort of thing that could never happen to a friend of a friend of Charlie Horst's. He would have to ask why the wife had murdered hour or five husbands.

'For money. For their life insurance.'

There it was, the whole truth, so evil that there could be but one solution to the problem. No use arguing, 'But my friend loves his wife and she loves him. She doesn't want her husband to die, she loves him, she's bearing his child . . .'

He had to quit thinking. It was better to invest his energy in hard work. Each time he raised the shovel and straightened his body, he looked around and saw white hills, the charcoal black of trees and branches, their shadows purple on the snow, and his house, so sturdy and honest in its proportions, and so American and secure and right with its clapboards and its clean green shutters. With each shovel load he felt better and younger, almost as if he were tossing aside his problems with the snow. The events of the past few days seemed less real and his wife was as good and commonplace as any of the neighbors.

Montagnino's polished black delivery wagon set high on smart yellow wheels stopped on the highway. The boy jumped out. From the back of the wagon he took three bushel baskets, which he carried, one after another, to the shed. He was a handsome Italian boy with cheeks that glowed carmine on his clear dark skin. Although she was now Hen Blackman's fiancée, Mary did not mind stopping her work to chatter with him. He had plenty to tell her, of the customers who had been snowed in and unable to get groceries and of those who were still isolated. The snowstorm had made him important because some of the richest people in the neighborhood might have starved to death if he hadn't come out to the country this morning in his yellow-wheeled wagon.

Charlie worked for another hour. The exercise warmed him and underneath his heavy mackinaw he felt the sweat rising on his body. When Mary opened a window on the second floor, he ordered her to close it before a draft crept through the halls to his wife's bedroom. Suddenly he felt very weary. He stood like a lazy workman, leaning on his shovel and looking at the landscape. He had not done much physical work recently and his muscles had become soft. Enthusiasm was dying. But it was like his mother's son to push on, and he began again and kept at it in spite of weariness until he had cleared another six feet. Then he gave up and decided to finish after lunch.

Snow was caked on his boots. The soles were dripping. Charlie was too thoughtful ever to walk on the good rugs with wet boots. He went around the back way. The shed was dark, but he did not bother to switch on the light. Sitting on a three-legged stool he unlaced his boots. In a corner near the door he noticed the three baskets that Montagnino's boy had carried in. Two were empty and one was full. That would be Ben Chaney's order.

He heard a muffled cough and looked through the glass doorpane into the kitchen. Bedelia stood beside the table, her hand stifling the cough. She was bent over the kitchen table, working at something with a sort of surreptitious tension. She opened a package. Her body screened that part of the table upon which she had set the contents, but Charlie saw that she set the wrapping paper carefully aside and folded the string upon it. She thrust her right hand into the neck of her robe.

Mary thumped down the front stairs with the carpet-sweeper. Bedelia straightened quickly. Her glance slid slyly in the direction of the dining-room door, which was closed. Immediately she thrust into the neck of her robe whatever she had taken from it, and with a casual saunter, went toward the dining-room door. She opened it and called to Mary, bidding the girl hurry back upstairs.

'I want you to clean my bedroom while I'm out of it, Mary.'

'Oh, I didn't know you was downstairs, Mrs. Horst. Is there something I could do for you?' Mary called.

'Go upstairs and change my bed at once.'

Mary thumped up the stairs.

Before Bedelia returned to the table, Charlie had opportunity to see what she had taken from the wrapping paper. It was a wedge of Gorgonzola cheese, its surface green with mold. Bedelia reached into her robe again and Charlie saw that she had a small round box in her hand. It was the unlabeled pillbox he had found among her knickknacks the night she tried to escape. He had thought the powder in it was a polish for her fingernails.

Charlie was paralyzed. It was like a nightmare. He did not try to speak or move because he knew his voice was gone and his limbs were useless.

Bedelia had put the top back on the pillbox and returned it to her bosom. She wrapped the cheese in the paper and started to tie it up. But the string was knotted. She had to find the ball of twine that she kept in one of the drawers of her cabinet. It was not quite so thick as Montagnino's string, and Charlie saw that she was making a mistake, the stupid and trivial mistake which destroys the perfection of a crime. Evidently she did not notice, for she cut off a length of twine and tied it around the cheese. Then, walking on tiptoes, she carried the old knotted string to the stove, lifted one of the iron plates and dropped the string into the flames. She was not hurrying, but going about her preparations for murder as efficiently as if she were cooking a meal. A cautious glance around the kitchen assured her that she had left no trace of her work. With the parcel in her hand she moved toward the shed.

Charlie backed into a corner.

Bedelia entered the shed and blinked. It was dark and her eyes had become accustomed to the bright electric light of the kitchen. She had not the slightest idea that Charlie was there and passed close to him. Bending over the filled bushel basket, she rearranged boxes and parcels and placed the package under a cloth bag filled with salt. As she straightened, she sniffed at her fingertips.

Out, damned spot! out, I say.

Out, damned smell of cheese! Out, damned stink of murder!

Charlie had been stunned at first, had looked away

because he had not wanted his eyes to behold this fresh evil. As Bedelia bent over, arranging the parcels so that hers should not be too prominently placed in the basket, he knew that he could no longer close his eyes, deafen his ears, remain mute, or comfort himself with miracles. Cunningly, as she lay in the bed in which his mother had slept, his wife had planned the murder of two men. Charlie saw now why she had been so amiable in accepting his decision to stay and fight it out. She meant to stay, but to avoid the fight.

Circumstances had provided her with weapons for getting rid of troublesome enemies. Ben's fondness for cheese had served her like Herman Bender's taste for mushrooms, McKelvey's enjoyment of fish. The taste of Gorgonzola is so strong, so rotten, that the most delicate palate might not perceive the flavor of poison. Bedelia's enemies would not have died in her house after eating at her table. She would have no connection with their deaths, but would hear of the tragedy, like the rest of the town, through a telephone call or an item in the newspaper.

'Bedelia!'

She whirled around. Charlie came out of the corner. She saw him and stiffened.

'Oh, I didn't know you were here. You startled me.' Small spaces marked by heavy breathing separated the words. Hastily she added, 'That silly clerk of Montagnino's has made a mistake again. Putting some of Ben's groceries with ours. It's lucky I came down to check our order.'

The ease of her falsehood sickened Charlie. He had swallowed other lies because he loved her, but now that he had seen her cruel and deliberate preparations for a new crime, he abhorred the memory of that love.

'I'm sorry I broke my promise, Charlie, but you mustn't be angry. My cough is so much better it seemed silly to stay in bed.' A soft woman she was, yielding, gentle, shrinking before his male strength.

His fingers dug into her shoulders. He jerked her toward him. The neck of her robe was cut out like a V and above it her throat was like porcelain. His hand curled around it.

'Charlie—dear!'

That was all she could say. Charlie's hand had tightened on her throat. When she saw that he was not to be cajoled out of his anger, her eyes darkened and hardened. She fought back desperately, writhed in his arms, kicked at his legs. A kind of ecstasy seized Charlie. His knuckles bulged, knots rose in his hands as they felt the warm throbbing of Bedelia's throat. Her jetty restless eyes reminded Charlie of the mouse he had caught in the trap and he thought exultantly of the blow that had killed it.

Bedelia was the first to give up the struggle. She relaxed so suddenly that she fell back in Charlie's arms. Her face wore the curves of gentleness again. Slyness was erased. Whether for death or love she had yielded.

A mist rose, clouding his sight, dimming his mind. His hands loosened and fell away. His ecstasy passed and he felt weary. Both of them were worn out. Bedelia's eyes sought Charlie's. She tried to catch and hold his glance. Her hand groped forward, found his arm, lay heavy upon it.

'Charlie, Charlie dearest.'

He avoided her eyes.

'You don't understand,' she murmured.

'I'm afraid I do,' Charlie said coldly.

He pulled her toward him again as if her were going to kiss her, but instead he reached into the neck of her robe, took out the pillbox, and dropped it into his pocket. Then he went to the bushel basket and shuffled the packages until he found the one she had hidden under the bag of salt. This, too, went into the pocket of his mackinaw.

Bedelia leaned against the stool, watching him through her eyelashes. 'You wouldn't hurt me, Charlie. I know you wouldn't. I wouldn't hurt you either.' She had planted herself before him, barring his way to the door. 'I do love you, I'd rather die than see anything happen to you.'

He pushed her aside and left the shed. As he crossed the kitchen, he reached for the cord and snapped off the light.

In the hall he felt that she was behind him, but he did not turn. She caught hold of his arm.

'We haven't much time.'

Charlie jerked away. The whispered warning had made him her partner in crime. 'Go upstairs,' he said.

She was bent over, a suppliant, begging for mercy. She dared not look at Charlie, for his face was of metal, no more alive than the face of his ancestor, Colonel Nathaniel Philbrick, the bronze rider on the bronze horse in the square downtown. Bedelia spoke quickly as if she had only a short time and a great deal to say. 'We can get away now if we hurry.'

'Sh-sh!'

'We needn't take anything with us, we can buy whatever we want. I've got money, plenty of money, more than you know; it's in New York and I can get it without anybody finding out. Even you don't know the name.' Her voice reached a high note and cracked. 'I'll give it all to you, Charlie, every cent.'

'Sh-sh!' he said again. Mary was coming down the stairs slowly, squatting on each tread as she dusted the baseboard.

'You're all I've got,' Bedelia whispered. 'I haven't anyone else in the world. Who'll take care of me? Don't you love me, Charlie?'

The telephone rang. Charlie swept Bedelia off her feet and carried her up the stairs.

Mary saw them and her jaw dropped. The phone continued to ring.

'Answer it, Mary. Take the message. Say I can't come now,' Charlie barked at the gaping girl.

He carried Bedelia into the bedroom. After he had put her

on the bed, she would not let him go, but clung to him with tense, trembling hands. As he struggled to free himself, he noticed the garnet ring on the fourth finger of his wife's hand, and he remembered painfully his joy when he discovered the trinket in an antique shop.

'Let go!' he said.

'Don't be so mean to me, please, Charlie. Why don't you call me Biddy any more? You haven't called me Biddy for a long time now. Have you stopped loving me?'

The effrontery of it shocked him. He gave up the struggle and allowed her to cling while he sat at the edge of the bed. Her hands, gripping on his coat-sleeve, were no longer plump and seductive. The dimples had disappeared and there were blue veins running from wrists to fingers.

She tried, courageously, to smile at Charlie. 'You wouldn't let them take me away, would you? I'm your wife, you know, and I'm sick. I'm a very sick woman, your wife. I've never told you, dear, how sick I am. My heart, I might die at any moment. I must never be distressed about anything.' Her hands tightened on the rough wool of the mackinaw. 'I didn't ever tell you, Charlie, because I didn't want you to worry.' This she said with a sort of determined gallantry, both sweet and bitter.

Gently Charlie removed her hands. Bedelia submitted humbly, showing that she considered him superior, her lord and master. He was male and strong, she feminine and frail. His strength made him responsible for her; her life was in his hands.

He rose.

'Where are you going?' Bedelia demanded.

Charlie did not answer until he had reached the door. With his hand on the knob he turned and said, 'I want you to stay up here. You'd better lie there and rest.'

'I'll kill myself if you let them take me away.' She waited, watching the effect of her words. 'I'll kill myself and you'll be to blame.' She laughed harshly because she was frustrated. Charlie had shown no feeling.

He closed the door, locked it, and dropped the key in his pocket. He was no more moved by her threat of suicide than by her appeals and ruses. By getting away from Bedelia he had believed he could find clarity and think dispassionately. But his mind was a fog. He felt actually that his head was filled with thick gray clouds.

Mary came out of the living-room, the mop in one hand, the carpet sweeper in the mother. 'It was Miss Ellen Walker calling. She says she's got to see a man up Wilton way, and Mrs. Horst asked her for lunch. She's coming.'

Leaning the mop and carpet sweeper against the wall, she started up the stairs.

'Where are you going, Mary?'

'I got to ask Mrs. Horst about lunch.'

'Mrs. Horst has a headache. She's not to be disturbed.'

'What are we going to have for lunch?'

'What difference does it make?' he said querulously.

Mary's lip quivered. Mr. Horst was not usually rude. She sensed something queer about him and about the atmosphere of the house. 'Is Mrs. Horst very sick? Can I do something?'

He did not answer. Mary squeaked her hand along the varnished handle of the carpet sweeper. It sent shivers down Charlie's spine. Irritably he wondered if he was to be annoyed by Mary at this tragic and uncertain moment in his life, and a moment later, recovering, he rebuked himself for taking out his distress upon an innocent girl, a servant who was in an inferior position and unable to defend herself.

'Sorry,' he muttered. 'I was thinking of something else, Mary. Do what you like about lunch. I don't think either of us will want very much.'

'But Miss Walker's coming.'

'Of course.' He bowed his head. 'Whatever you do, Mary, will suit me.'

He went into the living-room. With his mackinaw on and the sealskin cap pushed back on his head, he sat down. For a long time he stayed in the same position, perched at the edge of the chair, legs apart, hands hanging between them. The hall clock ticked, Mary sang at her work, wagons rattled past on the cleared highway.

Charlie thought about his wife and his marriage and of the life they should lead if they escaped Barrett. He was no longer concerned with the past nor with moral issues nor his shattered pride. Within the half-hour he had caught his wife at a new crime. To save herself she had tried to kill two men. Her mind was a child's mind, her vision limited by her own needs and desires. If danger threatened again, she would try again to avert it, and probably with the same ruthlessness.

He rubbed his numb hands. Under the flannel shirt and the mackinaw his flesh was cold. He had had a glimpse of the future and what he had seen sickened him.

Shouts drew his attention to the world outside. The Keeley boys had pulled their sled down the hill and tumbled through the snow to the Horsts' back door. They chattered with Mary as they warmed themselves before the kitchen fire, and when they left they were eating apples. They had tied the basket of groceries to the sled, but it was not firm, and while one boy pulled the other held it. Halfway up the hill they switched jobs.

Charlie watched until the boys were out of sight. When this diversion was gone and he was obliged to face himself again, he felt guilty. Although the present crisis was not of his making, he could not absolve himself from blame. He had been weak with Bedelia. From the start he had blinded himself to her faults and indulged her caprices. He could not have known then that the little New Orleans widow was a murderess, but he had known that she told lies, played tricks, used her sex unfairly. He had cherished, even enjoyed, these little feminine faults because they had flattered him and swelled his male pride. By falling in love with weakness he had grown weak.

He became angry; angrier than he had been when he discovered his wife at the kitchen table with a wedge of cheese in one hand and poison in the other. This anger was more potent because it turned inward, upon himself. In the shed, when his fingers had tightened on Bedelia's throat, Charlie's fury had been aimed at her guilt. Now it was himself he hated. He knew that if he continued to live with Bedelia, he would go on indulging her, giving in, appeasing so that she would commit no more murders.

He rose and straightened his shoulders, walked up the stairs quickly and lightly. Bedelia did not hear him unlock the door or come into the bedroom. She had thrown herself across the bed, heedless of bolster and spread. Her hairpins lay in a pile upon the rose-colored silk and her hair flowed about her head, gleaming darkly.

Charlie stood above the bed and looked down at her. She was crying. Usually her tears affected him. He was not used to women who wept and asked for pity. His power to comfort her and dry her tears had always swelled his pride. As he stood above the bed, looking at her woeful, tear-streaked face, he pitied her, but in a different way, without the usual self-esteem. Without saying anything, he turned away and, after he had put on his felt bedroom slippers, left the room.

This time he did not lock the door. Bedelia lifted her head and looked after him. When he returned, however, she was lying in the same position, her eyes closed, her hands flat against the spread.

'Drink this,' Charlie said. He held out a glass of water.

Bedelia did not open her eyes.

He carried the glass to the bedside. 'Drink this, Bedelia.'

She opened her eyes and tried weakly to raise her head.

'Wait, I'll make you comfortable.' Charlie set the glass upon the bed table, lifted his wife's head from the uncomfortable wooden bolster, took out the pillows, arranged them and lifted his wife so that she was in an easier position. Then he offered the glass again.

'What is it?'

'Please drink it.'

'A bromide, dear? But I haven't a headache.'

'I want you to take it,' he said firmly.

Bedelia looked at Charlie's face and then at the glass. The water was clear and bubbling lightly as if it had just gushed out of the artesian well. Charlie had not known how much of the white powder to put in it, but he had guessed that a small amount would work as well if not better than too much.

She took the glass and held it in a pretty, childlike way with both hands. Miraculously her cheeks had filled out, the bloom returned, and her soft glances and dimples were much as they had been that day on the veranda at Colorado Springs. She looked at him expectantly as if she were about to propose some treat or holiday.

'Let's drink it together,' she said blandly.

Charlie staggered and groped for one of the bedposts. His heart beat swiftly and his face became purple.

Bedelia watched him, holding her head on one side and smiling gently. 'You drink first, dear, and then I will.' And in the same bland voice she used when she gave him the digestive powder, she added, 'Drink it fast and you won't mind the taste.'

Under his hand he felt the rough surface of the carved wood pineapple. That, at least, was real and familiar.

Bedelia patted the quilt to show how soft the bed was, and then turned her hand and made a little gesture of invitation. 'Come and lie beside me, Charlie. We'll be together.'

Maurine had asked so prettily that Will Barrett could not refuse to take her out for a midnight sail. Chloe had run the water for Jacobs's bath. Annabel McKelvey, when she set the fish before him, had been artlessly pleased to be able to serve one of her husband's favorite dishes. The happy husbands had walked into the trap without knowing a trap was there at all. But Charlie knew that the catch had been set.

He let go of the wooden pineapple and walked toward the head of the bed. His anger had grown cold. When he reached for the glass, his hand did not tremble. Bedelia leaned forward, looking up at him. Her face showed excitement and greediness. The tip of her tongue slid over her lips as if she were impatient to taste a spicy dish which she had not had for a long time.

With the glass in his hand, Charlie sat down beside her on the bed. 'Drink it,' he said, raising the glass until it was on a level with her mouth. 'There isn't much time.'

His face was stony. Bedelia knew that she was beaten. Her body stiffened, her back arched, and her eyes became hard and jetty. The cords of her neck stood out like pillars, and upon these two pillars her head trembled. 'I thought you were different, Charlie. I didn't think you were like the others.' She sighed, pitying herself, a woman wronged by a cruel man. Reproach shone out of her eyes and her lips were pulled into a hard knot that said, wordlessly, that Charlie was to blame for everything. She had married him with high hopes and he had betrayed her. He had changed for her, become like the other men she had known, *rotten, rotten, a beast.*

'I never thought you'd turn against me, too. Not you, Charlie.'

Charlie did not stir nor release her from the hard bitterness of his glance. Bedelia waited, her head trembling, her mouth pulled tight, her eyes glazed. There was no more greed in her, no more coquetry. Defeat had stripped away her charms and left a giant caricature of Charlie Horst's pretty wife.

'All right,' she cried at last, as if she could no longer endure the waiting, 'all right, but it'll be your fault, Charlie Horst, they'll blame you, you'll hang for it!'

The stone wall which Charlie had built around himself

collapsed. He felt sick with shame, guilty, as if he had been planning a crime for his own ends and had finally committed it. Looking down at his wife as she lay against the pillows, white and pitiful, he saw that she was thinking of herself as an innocent woman, suffering unjustly. She had planned a murder that morning, but the memory had fled along with the memory of her other crimes. The narcotic of self-pity had freed her of the sense of guilt. They were to blame, not she; they, the rotten men, the jealous women. This illness had enabled her to commit the cruelest of crimes and to forget them, to live almost normally, even to fall in love and to think of herself as a woman deserving a good husband, a home and a child.

Suddenly, as if she were this good wife and could not restrain her love for her husband, she reached for Charlie's hand and pulled it toward her, resting her cheek against it.

Charlie jerked his hand free. The pity which she felt for herself and which aroused his compassion was the spell she had woven around him, her charm and her madness. He had been caught in the net once and he did not intend to let it happen again.

'Drink it!'

'It'll be your fault, they'll blame you, you'll hang for it,' she repeated. And seizing the glass, she drank the mixture in one long swallow.

Charlie took the glass and put it back on the table. Then he left her and walked slowly down the stairs. The twelve-ten whistled as it rounded the curve. Charlie took out his watch to check its accuracy, counted the minutes until the train should arrive at the Wilton Station and Barrett shake hands with Ben Chaney.

Mary was at the telephone. 'That Montagnino!' She jerked down the receiver. 'Always forgetting stuff. Hannah wanted to know if they'd put the cheese with our order.'

When Mary had gone back to the kitchen, Charlie closed

the door that separated the rear of the house from the front hall and stairs. He went up as far as the turn, listened for a moment, then came down and got his overshoes out of the hall closet.

The great rock beside the river had been rounded by water and weather. Charlie stood in its shadow fumbling in his pocket for the paper parcel that contained the Gorgonzola. He opened it, crumbled the cheese into bits above the swiftly moving water, folded the paper and returned it to his pocket. He did not want any evidence left of the new crime Bedelia had planned. There was enough against her and no need to add another crime.

He returned to the house, put away his overshoes, hung up his cap and mackinaw. He lighted the living-room fire and, when the flames were high, burned the paper which had been around the cheese and the piece of twine. At the washstand in the first-floor bedroom he scrubbed his hands.

Mary was setting the table for lunch. Charlie did not want to be alone and he went into the dining-room to be with her. He pretended to be looking for his meerschaum pipe. Mary had set the table with the filet lace doilies and tried several centerpieces. None suited her until she thought of the white narcissus which Bedelia had planted in the blue pottery bowl. As Mary studied her table decorations, she narrowed her eyes and held her head on the side in exact imitation of Bedelia.

Charlie was at the window when Ellen turned in at the gate. He had the front door open before she reached the porch. The cold had painted red circles on her cheeks and her eyes were sparkling.

Charlie helped her take off the mannish coat. She raised her arms to remove her hatpins. This peculiarly feminine move-ment belied all her efforts to deny womanliness. Charlie's attentions pleased her. She spent more time than usual on her hair, which she had tried in a new fashion, parted in the center and drawn back to a figure 8 low on her neck.

'How are you, Charlie? Feeling better? Why aren't you at work?'

Charlie looked up the stairs. There was nothing to see except three photographs hanging on the wall at the turn. They were photographs of the Rocky Mountains which Charlie had taken before he lost his Kodak.

'Yes, much better,' he said, without turning his head.

'What are you looking for?' Ellen asked.

'Nothing.' He saw that he had been inattentive and hurriedly asked her the proper questions, about her health, her parents, her job. As they went into the living-room he had noticed Bedelia's workbasket on the small table beside the couch. And his eyes sought the what-not where the ornaments stood as Bedelia had arranged them. There, on the ebony board, crouched the three monkeys who neither saw, heard, nor spoke evil.

'How's Bedelia? Is her cold better? What a lot of illness you've had in the house this winter.'

'She's got a headache. I'm afraid she won't be down for lunch.'

'What a shame! Headaches are such a nuisance.'

'Are you cold, Nellie? What about a drop of sherry to warm you up?'

'At this hour!'

'I'm about to treat myself to a drink of cider brandy. Will you join me?'

'Charlie Horst, what's got into you?'

'I got a bit of a chill this morning shoveling snow.'

'Well, if you do,' Ellen said.

This was the first time since he married Bedelia that Ellen had been alone with Charlie. Every minute was precious to her. While he went off to get their drinks, she wandered about the living-room. She felt fiercely alive and impatient as if something tremendous were about to happen. When she was with Charlie and other people were present, she had always to defend her pride. The result was a certain brusqueness which was not attractive. Now this was gone. She was tender, girlish, even a bit flirtatious. When Charlie handed her the sherry, his fingers brushed against hers. She gave him a look of extraordinary boldness, raised her glass and smiled.

Yet they had nothing to say to each other. Charlie stared as if he were hypnotized by a commonplace piece on the what-not, those three monkeys that dwelt in every curio cabinet. Ellen gave up trying to interest him and played a game. She dressed all the furniture in dust covers, rolled up the rugs, hung muslin bags over the paintings that used to hang on the living-room walls. She saw the room as it had been the last time she was alone here with Charlie, just two hours before he boarded the train that was to take him to New York and Colorado. He was mourning his mother at that time and Ellen had thought this was what prevented him from saying anything definite. She had been certain that all the indefinite things he had said in the past meant that he was counting as much as she upon their marriage. The room had been somber then, the walls covered in grasscloth and hung with Japanese prints, and in the corner where Charlie and Bedelia had their precious what-not, there had been an inlaid curio cabinet. Ellen remembered that Charlie had told her his plans for doing the house over, and to show that he was in earnest had torn off a strip of grasscloth.

It had been a warm day, the windows had been open, and Ellen had worn a white linen skirt and shirtwaist with eyelet embroidery. She saw it now as she had seen it that morning, saw leaves upon bare trees and grass on the snow-covered earth.

Mary announced lunch. That pulled Charlie out of his reverie. He looked at Ellen as if he were surprised to find her in the wing chair. She kept up her game and, when they were seated across from each other at the dining-room table, her heart beat so crazily that she held both hands over it in order to guard its secret.

'Look what we got,' Mary boasted.

Ellen looked down at the half-grapefruit decorated with a cherry. 'How nice,' she said.

Mary had expected more. She thought grapefruit for lunch—and in January!—the ultimate luxury. 'Mrs. Horst thinks it's good for him. She thinks he ought to have fresh fruit every day.'

Charlie remembered what Ben had said about the happy husbands. Bedelia was good at her job as a wife, she knew all the tricks that make a home jolly and keep a husband comfortable. To her life with each husband she brought experience gained with his predecessor. Being a wife was her life's work and she was far more successful at it than those good women who think because they have husbands they are safe and can treat men like servants or household pets. To Bedelia each marriage was a pleasure cruise and she an amiable passenger, always amused and amusing, always happy to share the fun, uninhibited by the fear that any relationship would grow too important, because she knew the cruise would soon be over, the relationship severed, and she would be free to embark on a new journey.

'You're not listening,' Ellen said. She had started to tell him about her assignment in Winston. She was to interview a man who was celebrating his ninety-ninth birthday. 'Imagine, Charlie, living until you're that old and seeing your contemporaries all die and your family and friends, and even the people you didn't like, and then the next generation and the next, the babies you saw christened when you were middle-aged grow old and die.'

Charlie was still inattentive. Ellen blushed. She could understand his having ceased loving her more readily than she could accept his rudeness. The only excuse she could make for his lack of courtesy was illness. His color was not good, she noticed, and his eyes were dull. Perhaps the attack last week had been more serious than he had said.

'Charlie!'

There was nervous appeal in her voice. It caught his attention. 'What's the matter, Nellie?'

'You. Are you ill, Charlie?'

'I'm feeling splendid. What's on your mind?'

'You never did tell me exactly what was wrong with you last week.'

'Indigestion. I happened to faint, that's why everyone thought it was serious.'

'You're sure you're all right?'

'Are you worrying, Nellie?' he asked indulgently.

'I'm glad you're all right,' she said, and looked down at her plate so that he should not notice the color flooding her cheeks.

Mary came in with pancakes and sausage. She served them with unnecessary ritual, hovering over the table, waiting for praise. At last she left, saying 'Well, ring the bell if you want anything. I'll be right there,' as if they didn't know how to behave without Mrs. Horst.

They did not talk much. But their friendship was old and silence no burden. Ellen took out the packet of cigarettes, but Charlie had to be asked for a match before he noticed that she wanted to smoke.

She had to talk about it, to show off, as if the cheap cigarettes were compensation. 'Aren't you surprised?'

Charlie laughed. 'What's wrong about it if you enjoy it?'

Ellen laughed, too. 'I shall have to write Abbie and tell her you're not a prig after all.'

Two men were coming down the hill on snowshoes. Charlie's back was toward the window.

'If you think smoking makes you seem less feminine, you're wrong,' he said. 'You're always trying to make gestures, Nellie, and there's no reason for it. You're an independent woman because you go out and earn your living. And without acting as if you were bearing a cross.'

'I have no reason to complain. I enjoy it.' She watched a cloud of smoke drift toward the ceiling. 'But men don't like a girl to be to independent, do they? They don't feel that she's really female unless she needs a man to take care of her. Abbie and I talked it over quite a lot while she was here. The secret of Bedelia's charm, Abbie says . . .'

The doorbell rang. Charlie did not stop to hear Abbie's opinion of Bedelia. He was in the hall and opening the front door before Mary came out of the kitchen.

'Something's got into 'em today. Her, too,' Mary told Ellen.

Charlie opened the door to Ben Chaney and a stout man.

'Mr. Barrett, Mr. Horst.'

Charlie nodded jerkily.

'Glad to know you,' muttered Barrett. His sagging cheeks were like deflated balloons, his mouth the mouth Bedelia had imitated, a pocketbook with a strong clasp. Barrett's eyes took in all the fittings of the house as he estimated the income of the owner.

Charlie said that he was having lunch and asked if they would join him.

'Thanks, but we've had ours.'

They followed Charlie into the hall. He noticed that Ben glanced toward the dining-room, saw Bedelia's narcissus on the table and Ellen at Bedelia's place.

'Perhaps you'd like a cup of coffee. You must be cold after that walk.'

'Not me,' Barrett said. 'Where I come from it's a lot colder than this. Matter of fact, I'm all heated up from the exercise.'

At the hall mirror Ben straightened his tie and smoothed his hair. 'Barrett isn't staying long. He's got to leave again this afternoon, but he's an old friend of Mrs. Horst's and thought he'd like to say hello.'

'My wife has a headache. She's lying down.'

Just then Ellen took it into her head to greet Ben. Remembering Abbie's news, she stared boldly, trying to penetrate his disguise and find something of the detective in him.

'Won't you go upstairs and see if Mrs. Horst will come down? Mr. Barrett is anxious to see her again.'

'What about your interview?' Charlie asked Ellen. 'Aren't you afraid you'll be late?'

She looked at the big round watch strapped to her wrist, sighed and finished her coffee.

'Perhaps she'd prefer to have Barrett come up,' Ben suggested, glancing sideways at Ellen.

'I'll go and see,' Charlie said. 'Good-bye, Nellie. Don't wait for me.'

He walked up the stairs lightly, his shoulders thrown back, his head high.

'That's Charlie all over,' Ellen said as she came out of the dining-room. 'Worries about my appointment for me. Never missed a train in his life, not even a streetcar. Will you excuse me?' She was annoyed because Ben had interrupted her conversation with Charlie and disappointed because Charlie had dismissed her so curtly. She went to the first-floor bedroom, washed her hands and put on her hat.

Mary was in the dining-room, clearing the table. She called a greeting to Ben, too, hoping that he would start a conversation and that she could tell him about her engagement. He said, 'Hello, Mary,' and closed the dining-room door.

Charlie hurried down the stairs.

Ellen was coming out of the dining-room, pulling on her gloves. She stopped and watched while he joined the two men in the living-room.

Ben hurried toward him. Barrett shoved his bulk out of a low chair. Sunlight poured in through all the windows. It lay in gold patches on the rugs. In that clear light Charlie's face was like damp clay.

He tried to say something, but his voice died in his throat. He swallowed painfully and stood there, a pitiful figure with his arms hanging limp, his shoulders sagging, his Adam's apple working up and down.

'How is your wife?'

Charlie turned to Ben. A flush rose about his collar and the clayey hue of his face gradually changed to a strange purple-red. A network of blue and red veins stood out against the glazed white of his protruding eyeballs. When at last he spoke, his voice was a steel file.

'My wife's dead.'

His anger mounted. He raised both fists as if to strike Ben, and then he let them fall again and his hands dangled impotently from his sleeves. The moment was silent and frozen as if everything would stay as it was then, the furniture fixed forever in the same positions, the colors never fading, dust never gathering, the sunshine never quite falling in oblique panels from the windows, the curtains never to be drawn, Charlie and Ben, Barrett and Ellen, to keep these postures always, like figures carved out of marble or metal. The house rang with a silence that had more life to it than any sound. It was as if the clock had stopped and the river ceased flowing over the rocks.

Charlie's shoulders drooped, the lids fell over his eyes, and he took a couple of stops forward, moving cautiously like a blind man. He held out his hand to Ben Chaney. As if that had been a signal, the others began to breathe again. Barrett's head rolled on his wide collar like a joint rolling in a socket. Ben took something from Charlie's hand and looked down at it.

Ellen said, 'But she wasn't ill. She had a headache.'

Charlie stumbled to the love-seat. His body caved into it. Ben followed and stood in an erect and vigilant position beside him.

'Suicide?' Ben asked, looking down at the pillbox which Charlie had given him.

Ellen seized the word and threw it back at Ben indignantly. 'Suicide! How can you say such a thing? What makes you think it?'

Barrett started to speak, but Ben shook his head and raised his hand for silence.

'You must be crazy!' Ellen shouted at Ben.

'I'm not surprised,' was all he had to say. He went into the hall and closed the door before he used the telephone.

In the kitchen Mary sang as she washed the dishes. Barrett took a cigar out of his pocket, looked at it, looked at Charlie, and put it back. Ellen went to Charlie, crossing the room softly, stopping only on the rugs and avoiding the spaces between them. She did not speak nor touch him, but stood there with her head bent and her right hand in the fur-lined glove resting on the printed linen that Bedelia had chosen for the love-seat when she came from Colorado as Mrs. Charles Horst.

THE END

In November of 1899 Vera Caspary was, as she liked to say, "born in the nineteenth century by accident." Her mother was in her forties, and Vera was eighteen years younger than her oldest sibling. A simultaneously spoiled and intimidated "baby," she grew up on the south side of Chicago in a family of Portuguese-descended Jews. Her father, who was a buyer in women's hats, wanted her to attend the University of Chicago, but shy and bookish Caspary thought she lacked the feminine wiles for co-ed life. Eager to write and be independent, Caspary got her foot in the door as an ad-agency stenographer. She pestered her bosses for writing assignments and answered job openings for writers with her initials, only to be turned down when she appeared. The year American women got the right to vote, Caspary began writing ads. Caspary wrote her first headline—"Rat Bites Sleeping Child"—for an exterminator. In the early twenties she left full-time copywriting to freelance and begin her first novel draft (Caspary 1979, 3, 6, 26–27, 51, 71–74).

Caspary's nineteen books, including the Edgar award-winning autobiography, *The Secrets of Grown-Ups*, sold well and were widely reviewed. Twenty-four movies were made from Caspary's scripts, screen stories, and novels. The directors of these movies included Dorothy Arzner (*Working Girls*, 1931), Joseph Mankiewicz (*Letter to Three Wives*, 1949, which won two Academy Awards), Fritz Lang (*The Blue Gardenia*, 1953), and George Cukor, whose film, *Les Girls* (1957) earned Caspary a Screen Writers Guild award. Nominally single, in 1949 Caspary married a man of whom her family would have approved, though they would not have sanctioned her long affair with him. The Viennese-born producer Isadore Goldsmith, or "Igee," became the love of

Caspary's life until his death in 1964. This was the life Caspary dramatized in her fiction, centered in women characters' struggles to exercise the freedom of choice that jobs provided.

In many of her novels, Caspary effectively merged women's quest for identity and love with murder plots. She declared openly that she was not a "real" mystery writer, meaning she didn't like crime fiction, and had no interest in private eyes and police procedures. She preferred character studies more than intricate plots that finally reveal "the sweet old aunt or a birdwatcher who ruthlessly kills half a dozen people to get hold of the cigarette case with a false bottom that conceals a hundred-thousand-dollar postage stamp" (1979, 104). After completing a trio of forties murder mysteries—*Laura* (1942), *Bedelia* (1945), and *Stranger Than Truth* (1946)—she declared herself "on holiday from murder. The fact is," she said, "I'm not nearly as interested in writing about crime as I am in the actions of normal people under high tension" (Caspary, 1950). Her novels revolve around women who are menaced, but who turn out to be neither merely victimized dames nor rescued damsels. Independence is the key to the survival of such protagonists as Laura; lack of choice engineers the downfall of her villains, among whom Bedelia is paramount.

Since Caspary wrote her mysteries from the forties to the seventies, before the widespread development of female detectives, her reading of "detective" throughout her writing career was gendered as unattractively male. She wasn't impressed by the tough private eyes of the thirties or by the male protagonists emerging in forties noir fiction and film— cynical loners manipulated by women and/or manipulators *of* women. Caspary pointed out that Mark McPherson, her police detective in *Laura*, was not hard-boiled, but sensitive and imaginative. When Otto Penzler asked for an essay on McPherson for *The Great Detectives*, Caspary chose to discuss Laura's condemnation of detectives as the moment Mark came alive. Shortly after her reappearance in the novel, Laura tells Mark that detective stories contain two types of characters, "the hard-boiled ones who are always drunk and talk out of the corners of their mouths and do it all by instinct; and the cold, dry, scientific kind who split hairs under a microscope"(77). In her article for Penzler Caspary echoes Laura that both types are "detestable," which was why, until *Laura*, she "had never glorified a detective" (Caspary, 1978, 144-45).[1]

Yet murder, as Caspary said in a 1970s working draft of her autobiography, was "another matter." "I see now," she mused, "that my [screen] stories were the extension of a long series of murder fantasies, not that I've ever pulled a trigger or wielded a knife, nor identified myself with the detective. Like Laura I hate detectives." But she liked to make up plots as an "observer" and "witness" ("Discards," 577), a stance she would later apply to creating multiple narrators and viewpoints in many of her novels and scripts. Caspary made murder a context in which both male and female characters resolve their own mysterious lives, as though the crime itself were a metaphor for the conundrum of relationships versus independence.

"A FLAMING THING" IN THE 1920s

Jane S. Bakerman discusses at length the lives of Caspary's working girls in Chicago rent districts, offices, and speakeasy settings. She notes, "Much of the frustration [of Caspary's characters] arises from the duality of their concept of the American dream, for while struggling to establish identities for themselves as wage earners, they believe, simultaneously, that they will have no identity at all unless they are indispensably desirable to *the* man" (1984, 83). Caspary similarly recalls the heady mix of wage-earning and flirting she experienced. "Working among men," she says candidly in *Secrets*, "I had discovered that a girl need not be beautiful, not even particularly pretty. She had only to be a girl." Caspary had grown up seeing herself as clever but unattractive. She quotes her somewhat competitive mother as having frequently said, "You wouldn't be so bad looking if it weren't for your nose." Vera herself called this the "harsh Caspary bone structure." Though she turned out to be a striking woman, it was a revelation to her that "The compliments of accountants and macaroni salesmen assured me that I had feminine power" (1979, 27, 44).

At the start of the twenties she still lived with her parents, taking advantage of their evenings out to neck on the sofa and inventing out-of-town interviews for her job in order to lose her virginity. This was a turbulent time, particularly in 1924, during which her father died on the same day Bobbie Franks vanished. Vera not only observed the Leopold and Loeb murder from inside her community, but she spent weekends with her lovers at the Loebs' cottage in return for handling its rental while the family avoided public contact (1979, 81–88). The "baby" became the support of her traditional mother, who was impressed that her daughter could "pound" money out of her typewriter. Vera had already left full-time advertising to freelance and begin writing fiction. Later in 1924 she moved to New York to edit *Dance Magazine*, achieving her goal of living a Bohemian life in Greenwich village as she had on Chicago's near north side. As she put it, life as a "flaming thing" meant that "Sexual inhibition was to be avoided like pregnancy and a repressed libido shunned like a dose of clap" (1979, 96).

Caspary's chief fictional portrait of her twenty-something-at-work-and-in-love self was *Evvie* (1960), for which she merged Chicago and New York settings. In *Evvie*, Louise, who works for her living, tries to shore up her lovely roommate, Evvie, who lives on an annuity from her stepfather and who pursues an obsessive love affair that leads to her murder.

The novel is more an account of the era than a murder mystery, however, and its frank references to abortion and free love—as well as a scene in which, as Caspary put it, "two naked girls discuss sex"—was still shocking enough to be banned in Ireland (1979, 265; "Correspondence 1957–58").

The climactic, wild party in *Evvie* was modeled on a birthday celebration given for Caspary in 1926 by her pal Connie Moran at her Rush Street studio in Chicago that "smelled of paint and cats, spicy foods and French perfumes." Caspary describes vividly in the 1970s draft of *Secrets* how at the real-life party the "bootlegger came with a gallon of pure alcohol which we mixed with distilled water," the Dartmouth football team crashed the party, an admirer threw Vera into Connie's china cabinet, and Caspary learned that another good friend had taken up with her own former lover ("Working Draft," 42, 134). All these details were applied in *Evvie* to illustrate the mix of liberty and vulnerability of women's coming of age in the twenties.

Her writing and editing projects during these years are stories in themselves. They included the Rodent Extermination League's copy for war-produced live anti-rat virus that died in the mail, a correspondence course to learn ballet whose impresario was entirely fictional, an ad campaign for a book on sex and love, and another mail-order course on playwriting whose lessons Caspary absorbed as she wrote them. Caspary called these her "fraudulent years" (1979, 68). Some particular oddities of these years are portrayed in *Stranger than Truth*. This satire was one Caspary had long wanted to write as retribution for the death of her editorial assistant on *Dance Magazine*, Bryne Macfadden. Bernarr Macfadden, the magazine's publisher and Bryne's father, was a man much odder than fiction. As a health fetishist who promoted his lifestyle in his publishing, Macfadden allowed no deviations from his routines. He forced his daughter to exercise vigorously to strengthen her heart problems and discouraged her from seeking medical treatment for a chronic cough that turned out to be tuberculosis, as this could damage his lucrative "cures." When Bryne grew weaker and at last began to hemorrhage, Caspary was asked to tell her father. He responded by cutting off Bryne's income so that she could not pay for a doctor. He did not attend her funeral, and her sisters could not forgive him (1979, 97–103).

In *Stranger than Truth* Caspary transformed the Macfadden story into that of a plagiarist publisher of a series of "True" magazines—Crime, Romance, etc. This lying purveyor of truth dominates his daughter, Eleanor, who accurately suspects him of murder. Comic relief is provided by a fanatically devoted secretary's testimonial, and the father's secret is uncovered by an alcoholic Greenwich Village poet and an editor. Lola, the poet, has a white-painted milk bottle full of gin that Caspary lifted straight from the Macfadden offices, where the editor-in-chief even had to take off his "eye crutches" when the publisher was present (1979, 91–92). When the novel came out, Mary Macfadden, Bryne's stepmother, wrote Caspary a letter of approval ("General Correspondence").

BETWEEN THE HAMMER AND THE SICKLE: CASPARY IN THE 1930s

In the 1930s, and somewhat in contrast to her first years in Hollywood, Caspary was attracted to Communism. During this time, Caspary supported herself with movie "originals," or screen stories, which were summaries of action and character from which screenplays could be written by others. Women were admitted easily into screenwriting during this period because writers weren't highly valued or highly paid, whether male or female (Warren 1988, 9). During the same period, Caspary met many Communists, some of whom introduced her to socialist politics. Her mentor and early collaborator Sam Ornitz explained the apple-sellers Caspary had seen in New York to her as capitalist victims. Even while selling screen stories, having a house built in Connecticut, writing radio dramas for a season in New Orleans, and bringing her mother triumphantly to Hollywood shortly before her death, Caspary secretly joined the party, attended "cell" meetings, helped to raise money for organizations associated with Communism, and wrote socialist plays and scripts with George Sklar, who would later co-author the play version of *Laura*. In the 1950s Caspary was "gray-listed," and provided technically truthful but unrevealing testimony in response to California investigations of un-American activities (1979, 192–97). In 1968 she wrote a novel, *The Rosecrest Cell* (1968), based on this period in her life, admitting that "The skeleton in my closet carries a hammer and sickle" (1979, 169).

Her involvement with Communism was sincere, if ultimately limited. In 1939, on the money from an "original" sale, Caspary planned a visit to Russia to view Communism first hand, but then derailed her trip in Paris in order to marry an anti-Nazi Communist spy whose sister had put them in touch. Though she detested the man, who talked only of American film stars, Caspary had promised to save him. Eventually she had either to use or lose her own visa for Russia. When her new fiancé's papers did not arrive in time, Caspary left with relief. She later heard that he had succeeded in reaching the United States. During her travels in Russia, personal encounters impressed her most while she was chilled by "the sense of constant surveillance" and tension she found in the Russians she met (1979, 182–87). By the end of the thirties, Caspary had begun to part company with Communism and to return to themes of independent women at work.

Laura was the novel Caspary published ten years after her autobiographical 1932 family saga, *Thicker than Water*. In drafting *The Secrets of Grown-Ups* in the mid-1970s, Caspary discusses at length how she wrote and rewrote a never-published novel during the thirties, which became a sounding board for her evolving politics and eventual dissatisfaction with them. In the much-reworked and finally abandoned political manuscript, she recalls, "Four hundred pages, or five hundred or six, were not enough to contain my rage." Part of what she was unable to express was "the pie in the sky hopes instilled by the Cinderella legend," which Caspary, having just read Marx, saw as "the opiate of the bourgeois woman" ("Working Draft," 255–57). Caspary thought she ought to write a "proletarian novel," while in real life, "In bed, wearing a lace-trimmed jacket and eating breakfast off a tray, I read *New Masses* and *Daily Worker*." But sexual politics ultimately were more her theme than socialist doctrine; in the end "Poor hapless Cinderella—special target of my rage" and "the illusory prince" became her focus (1979, 170–71).

CASPARY'S TURNING POINT NOVEL: LAURA

To escape politics and war news in the early forties, Caspary began *Laura* as a "mystery and a love story." The original idea had come from reading about a girl killed in a gas blowup that had destroyed her face ("Working Draft," 428). *Laura* already existed as an unfinished play and as a movie original, neither of which Caspary was able to sell in those forms (Caspary 1941). This time she would change her narrative strategy, finish the novel to her satisfaction, and, though she did not know it, forever after become known as "the author of *Laura*."

Caspary's life among women in business and the arts generated both the heroines and villains of her "psycho-thrillers," as publishers and reviewers called her psychological mysteries. Of these, Laura Hunt and Bedelia Horst are the pole stars, demonstrating balance of feeling and reason on the one end of the continuum, and the abandonment of balance altogether at the other. These women are not, as they have sometimes been categorized, sheer femmes fatales. In *Laura* Caspary gave urban noir a Gothic fillip in which women negotiate the mean streets of a male world.

Laura is Caspary's manifesto, applying her experience both in advertising and as a woman professional with a private life. Laura makes it on her own in the big city, enduring many Caspary-like rejections from prospective employers. Laura acquires in Waldo a godfather who shows her around town and boosts her career, but she must also reject the illusory Shelby, who exudes charm but has the heart of a competitive stepsister. The soft-boiled Mark has no clues except Laura's discarded possessions, including her painted image, all symbols of her self-reliance. There are no photographs of family or lovers in Laura's apartment, only her own portrait, a startling illustration of the individual as the social unit.

Caspary's fairy tale for working women takes place in a world of men who use women for advancement and self-reflection. The potential darkness of this world places *Laura* into the noir category and shadows even Caspary's non-crime fiction with related suspense. "Who can you trust" was a game working women had to play frequently, and *Laura* makes evident that women might be labeled femmes fatales simply because they worked in the male-dominated business world. Liahna Babener calls the novel rightly "a proto-feminist commentary on the state of sexual politics in America at mid-century." She further argues, "The underside of achievement for women is often emotional alienation and punitive retaliation and as Caspary demonstrates, Laura's plight is that her public stature and sexual autonomy have ignited the envy and anger of the men who surround her, now culminating in a killer's wrath" (1994, 84–85).

In *Laura* Caspary hit her stride as a novelist. She was already an experienced plotter of screen story synopses and the author of several plays and scripts. Her earlier novels use third-person narration, and parts of them read a bit like movie-scenario summary. In *Laura* Caspary's characters speak directly, and the effectiveness of their witnessing monologues influenced the style of Caspary's later work.

To display Laura and her suitors Caspary applied what she called "the Wilkie Collins method" of multiple narrators, each of whom tells us about the others as well as revealing their own selves. Waldo Lydecker, Mark, and Laura herself are writers in their own ways (of a newspaper column, police reports, and advertising copy). After her friend, play and screenwriter Ellis St. Joseph, drew her attention to dramatic monologues in Collins' novels, Caspary allowed Laura, Mark, and especially Waldo to "write" their own accounts. Waldo even allows himself to narrate scenes in which he was not present, assuming an authorial role. Caspary based her fastidious, fascinating, and fat villain on Collins' Count Fosco (in *The Woman in White*, which Caspary outlined to study its structure), though lean Clifton Webb is the image that now comes to mind for Waldo Lydecker (Emrys 2005, 9–10).

Mark, the second narrator, who later admits he has written and collated this informal account, dryly recounts Laura's return and the unfolding investigation, in which she is now a suspect. Shelby's viewpoint appears in a brief section of interrogation, but the novel's third narration goes to Laura herself as she reaches conclusions about the obsessed Waldo, who loves her too much, the cheating Shelby, who doesn't love her enough, and the detective whose independence she trusts as a reflection of her own. Mark then recounts the conclusion. The lively voices of these three narrators, including the contrasts between them and each character's assessment of the others, are important ingredients. When the book appeared, reviewers consistently cited this structure as fresh and enjoyable.

LAURA *ON SCREEN*

Seeing Laura as a traditional femme fatale stems largely from the Otto Preminger film, which appeared in 1944 and was, from the start, classified as noir, thus enhancing the association of Laura with deadly females. *Laura*, in fact, was one of four films discussed in the first recorded use of the term "film noir" in 1946 (Jackson 1998, 94). With its rainy urban nights, black-and-white contrasts, and Waldo's opening voiceover, Preminger's film seems unmistakably part of the noir canon of harshly-lit urban crime.[2] But in other ways, particularly those most faithful to Caspary's characters, the adaptation does not fit noir parameters for cynical, tough loners driven to murder by earthy fatal women on mean streets. In *Laura*, the chief criminal and its most world-weary character is a highbrow aesthete, its settings are upper-middle-class apartments and upscale restaurants, the romantic lead is a policeman, and the heroine holds down a good job and keeps rooms of her own. If there is a femme fatale in *Laura*, it is surely the model, Diane Redfern, who entangles Shelby, pawns the expensive cigarette case he gave her, and dies as Laura's stand-in.

The film obscures this doubling through the portrait of Laura, which dominates her apartment and appears in the most crucial scenes. In Caspary's version of the portrait as Waldo describes it, Laura sits "perched on the arm of a chair, a pair of yellow gloves in one hand, a green hunter's hat in the other." In the film, the glamorous "portrait," actually a photo of Tierney touched up to look like a painting (Preminger 1977, 76), embodies the male gaze of the infatuated artist rather than the living woman. In the novel, Waldo finds the painting too "studied, too much Jacoby and not enough Laura" (Caspary 2000, 39). The same can be said of the film, and of commentaries focused on the ethereal and seductive picture of Laura posed in an evening gown. We never actually see Tierney dressed or posing as in the painting, but most often in a suit or casual clothes.[3]

The contrast between painting and woman illustrates the gap between Caspary's Laura Hunt and Preminger's revision of her character. Caspary saw Laura as a thirtyish, successful woman who had lovers as well as colleagues and friends, rather than the young temptress of the film's portrait. In her synopsis of the novel, which made the rounds of film producers, Caspary stated plainly that "He [Mark] finds the living Laura more fascinating than the image of the dead woman" (1942, 2). When Preminger showed Caspary the screenplay for the film, Caspary recalled—in both a 1971 article, "My 'Laura' and Otto's," written just before the film's thirtieth anniversary, and in her autobiography—that she argued with him about Waldo's symbolic gun and Laura's character. She was more successful about the character than the weapon.

In her autobiography, Caspary praised the film warmly for its nuanced direction, which created the world she had in mind for Laura, with its "gossip and phony charm." But she was appalled by the Laura of Preminger's script, calling her "the Hollywood version of a cute career girl." She quoted Preminger as saying Laura was " a nothing, a nonentity," and that Laura "has no sex. She has to keep a gigolo." His conclusions caused Caspary to "rage like a shrew" in defense of her strong yet feminine protagonist (1979, 209). Her reply to Preminger, first restated in *The Saturday Review* a few years before she began writing her life story, bridged the span from Bedelia to Laura. Caspary demanded, "Do you mean she never got money out of men or mink or diamonds? That doesn't mean a girl's sexy, Mr. Preminger, it just means she's shrewd. Laura's just the opposite. She gives everything with her love" (1971, 27).

Caspary lost the battle to retain Waldo's walking stick/gun. Even though she had researched its feasibility, Preminger used a shotgun hidden in a clock instead. But Caspary became convinced that Laura's "romantic short-sightedness" came across as well as it did in the film because she had "shouted" about it. She still thought Laura "would have been an even greater picture if the melodrama in the end had been equal to the mood of the beginning" (1971, 27). After the film appeared Caspary was paid by *Good Housekeeping* to research *Murder at the Stork Club* on location in New York. One evening Preminger appeared at the next table. Caspary still felt strongly enough about the film to get into another shouting match with him over whether or not she had influenced the script. "I accused him of a faulty memory," Caspary recalled. "He retorted that I was telling lies" (1979, 211).

In the film Caspary wanted to see the intersection of class, crime, and sexual politics that she had created in the novel. Laura's criteria for romantic partners are personal attraction and shared interests. She doesn't need a man to support her or to be a life-long Pygmalion, and she soon outgrows mothering her babyish lovers. She can choose across class lines, rejecting the aristocratic Shelby for the low-brow policeman. Waldo obliquely critiques and ultimately tries to obliterate Laura's freedom to choose.

Preminger's gigolo reference apparently came from his misreading of Laura's narration in the novel, in which she pictures Shelby rebelliously giving Diane the cigarette case Laura had bought him because "he hated himself for clinging to me, and hated me because I let him cling" (*Laura*, 145). Laura has decided not to marry Shelby, understanding that their marriage would have been "shoddy and deceitful, taut emotion woven with slack threads of pretense." Some of that pretense would have been hers, for she faults herself for "wearing" Shelby to show off having a man. She says she bought him the cigarette case "as a man might buy his wife an orchid or a diamond to expiate infidelity" (*Laura*, 148).

Laura's independence makes her both vulnerable—to being pitied for not having a husband at almost thirty—and free enough to play some of the same relationship games men play: using objects in place of feeling. However, Laura imagines Shelby feeling like a gigolo, not only because of their financial inequality but also because of his genteel Southern heritage in which men are supposed to support and dominate women (*Laura*, 145–149). Her complex analysis in these passages is considerably different from Preminger's conclusion. Like Caspary herself, Laura was neither the most promiscuous nor the most chaste of women. In her drafts of "My 'Laura,'" Caspary emphasized that Laura "knew how to love," "had enjoyed more than one lover," and had "enjoyed her lovers lustily" (Draft Article, 9). She considered being this explicit almost thirty years later to rebut Preminger's misinterpretation of Laura's sex life.

LAURA *ON STAGE*

The play version of *Laura* that Caspary wrote with George Sklar in 1945 revolves more centrally around Laura's relationships than either previous version. Waldo's character is intensified in each act so that he appears more clearly as a suspect than in the novel or film, not only because of additional scenes with Mark McPherson, but also because of two added characters, Laura's landlady and her son. Laura's point of view is preserved in the play through her speeches summing up her past affairs. Of most interest perhaps are Laura's additional scenes alone with Waldo, which bring their early relationship, including a disastrous sexual encounter, to life. After Laura tells Waldo to "Stop pretending you're in love with me," we learn that at one point in the past Waldo apparently made a pass at Laura and felt painfully rejected, though her version of that evening is that "You called me wanton. You said I was throwing myself at you. You stood in the hall and shouted at me to get out" (1945, 62–63).

The addition of the immigrant janitor's wife, Mrs. Dorgan, and her jazz-mad son, Danny, who also is in love with Laura, may be due in part to Caspary's collaboration with George Sklar. Mrs. Dorgan's presence adds immigrant and working class issues, as when she upbraids Laura for influencing her son. After declaring that "I've sacrificed my whole life for that boy," she goes on: "I gave up my own career—I was a natural born coloratura—We have a musical tradition in our family. You see me as a janitor's wife, someone who cleans the halls and scrubs the steps" (1945, 38). But as she has also revealed herself as the sort of controlling wife and mother Caspary had written about in *Thicker than Water* and would later address at length in *Thelma*, Mrs. Dorgan is also Caspary's creation. Mrs. Dorgan even threatens to evict Laura to control her son further. She functions principally in the play as a parallel to Waldo's possessiveness of Laura, positioning Waldo himself as a male version of Caspary's typically controlling villains who seek to manipulate their nearest and dearest.

BEDELIA: *"THE WICKEDEST WOMAN WHO EVER LOVED"*

If *Laura* is new woman noir, then *Bedelia* is its prequel, set in 1913, the era in which Caspary grew up and a time she viewed as closer to Victorian mores than the following decades of her working life. *Bedelia* was written during the last years of Caspary's affair with the still-married Igee. After she discussed the novel with and dedicated the book to him, Igee produced the British film version. Though Caspary consulted on the script, she was exasperated by Igee's decision to reset the plot as contemporary, which she felt missed the point that Bedelia had few options for independence. Caspary felt so strongly about this that she later wrote a screenplay of *Bedelia*, hoping for an American production (1979, 225–26).[4]

Bedelia's character inherits her deadly illusions from several villainous female protagonists in earlier novels, including the title characters of Gustave Flaubert's *Madame Bovary* (1856–57) and Mary Elizabeth Braddon's *Lady Audley's Secret* (1861–63). Like them, Bedelia comes across as perversely sympathetic, partly because the men in her drama aren't exactly heroes, and partly because she embodies the dilemma of women who have few, if any, opportunities—

except for marriage—to improve their financial position and live well. Bakerman accurately calls Bedelia "a professional wife" (1984, 48).

In Flaubert's novel, Emma Bovary marries for security, but her Romantic dissatisfaction with the life of a provincial doctor's wife leads her to lies, bankruptcy, and adultery. Deserted by her husband, Lady Audley abandons her child, takes on a new identity as a governess, and marries into status. When her legal husband returns and recognizes her portrait, she kills him, and is exposed by Robert Audley, nephew of her second husband and friend to her first. *Bedelia* is also a narrative of unmasking. Bedelia resists having her portrait made, yet clings to her black pearl ring as fatally as Lady Audley preserves her child's shoe.

Because of Caspary's explicit interest in Wilkie Collins' novels, Bedelia may also be cousin to Collins' poisoner, Lydia Gwilt, whose revenge drives the sensational plot of *Armadale* (1864). Lydia, on her own in a sexist and class-ridden England, murders her abusive first husband and manages to escape legal punishment by manipulating the pity of men. Unlike Bedelia, Lydia's viewpoint comes across vividly in her diary and letters, but the two women ultimately drink their own poison, undone by fatal husbands whom they can neither reject nor dispatch.

In *Bedelia*, Charlie Horst's most horrifying revelation is not that his wife may be trying to poison him, but that his sexy, submissive, perfect wife is playing a deliberately dramatic role. Having scorned Bedelia's favorite reading—novels of women's adventures in love—Charlie finds himself living in one. He is shocked to discover that her name, tragic past, and cloying present are all fictions: she has learned to manipulate men's expectations of women with deadly efficiency. Bedelia is a complex killer protagonist; instead of driving men to crime and destruction, Bedelia is a hard-boiled murderer herself, though stewed in women's fiction rather than crime novels. As a female criminal who seeks to elevate her position, Bedelia evokes commentary on the ways in which women may get ahead. Bedelia may be, as an early cover had put it, "The Wickedest Woman Who Ever Loved," yet money cannot be her motivation, since in her sequential wifely roles she can't use it openly. As a serial bride Bedelia seeks again and again the thrill of seduction, of being chosen, of exercising the power granted to females.

Caspary wrote several stinging portraits of women who marry for security and live for illusion with disastrous results, notably *Thelma* (1952), narrated by a Caspary-like friend of the title character who has more to occupy her than love affairs. As Caspary put it when drafting her autobiography, "My protagonist is always a career girl unless, as in *Thelma*, she is the anti-heroine who believes that a woman achieves success only as the wife of a man who supports her in style." She went on to identify Thelma as a composite of her fault-finding and eventually mentally ill sister and another relation, who "lamented the failure of her daughter happily married to an artist who hadn't a lot of money." Caspary admitted she understood this type from the inside as a woman she could have been ("Discards," 576). Thelma marries a man she doesn't love in order to be given material wealth and security, though she remains romantically attached to a footloose former lover. Thelma's long-suffering husband and daughter turn on her in the end, rather than fall victim to her machinations permanently.

Through the character of Ellen in *Bedelia*, Caspary explores a self-supporting woman. The novel's omniscient narrator notes that in another era Ellen would have been considered attractive, but "fashions in women change as drastically as in clothes" so that "nowadays Ellen's face was considered too long, her head too narrow, the pale brown coronet of braids absurdly out of style"(*Bedelia*, 8). Ellen thinks of herself as "the Tailored Girl and enjoyed wearing suits and shirtwaists" at her job, but she suffers the candor of her stylish friend, Abbie, who tells her, "There's nothing so abhorrent to the masculine eye as a plaid silk shirtwaist. It simply shrieks old maid" (*Bedelia*, 14).

Caspary's fiction pivots on the trade-offs women face. Ellen, though pitied by Abbie and unloved by Charlie, dresses as she pleases and also smokes defiantly. Bedelia gets the man, but she must play the expected role, at least until she kills her latest husband. It is Bedelia who is bitter, who sees men as "rotten" and "beasts" (*Bedelia*, 94), not the disappointed Ellen who still has a life because she has a job. As Charlie tells her (while Bedelia is dying upstairs), "You're an independent woman because you go out and earn your living." Ellen retorts, while smoking a cigarette, that she enjoys her life, and comments pointedly, "But men don't like a girl to be too independent, do they?" Charlie, who is thinking about how he will have to discover his charmingly dependent wife's body, doesn't respond (*Bedelia*, 185).

In *Bedelia* Caspary manipulates point of view far differently than in *Laura*, yet to equal effect. Whereas *Laura*'s narrators reveal their information, much of it incorrect, in *Bedelia*, the narration reveals the thoughts and feelings of Charlie and Ellen, but not those of Bedelia or her nemesis, detective Ben Chaney. Like Charlie and the others, we never know exactly what Bedelia thinks or feels, only what she chooses or can be pressured to reveal. While this limits the portrait, the strategy allows for much of the novel's suspense as we wonder how she will respond in the end to the growing charges against her. But whether she is trying to flee from exposure, attempting to seduce Charlie into believing her, or taking poison at his command, the mask never completely slips. Similarly, Ben's disguise as a painter stays in place until he reveals himself.

WRITING HER OWN LIFE

Caspary herself was as complex as any of her characters. She was moved by ideals affecting workers and women, but was much more inclined to start a social group than to recruit, organize, or protest. In the thirties she created the "Conversation Club," a group of Communist wives who put on social events (1979, 181). Caspary was aware that she was not going to portray World War II Rosie the Riveters, but her own trajectory as a professional. Yet she remained conscious of working women in all contexts. In her seventies Caspary visited and taught writing workshops to prisoners in the New York Women's House of Detention. When she proposed a nonfiction book on the lives of inmates, she also proposed to portray the lives of the staff and administration working there as well ("Women in Crime," 17–18).

Kathi Maio, in her review of *The Secrets of Grown-Ups* for *Sojourner*, called Caspary a "Rebel with a Cause," and accurately assessed her "mild-mannered radicalism." As she put it, "Caspary is not primarily a feminist. But, rather, a natural and unabashed female rebel" whose stances therefore can be "contradictory" (12). Perhaps it is more precise to say that Caspary's rebellious spirit enabled her to enjoy her professional and private lives. For example, early on she chose to break into business writing to support herself so that she might write fiction. In 1910, a generation of Jewish women educated in the United States began to enter colleges and the business world. Caspary might have done either. Her choice of stenography placed her in the business category chosen by about 15 percent of Jewish women her age, a perfectly acceptable one to her family (Schloff 2003, 97).

But Caspary had no intention of launching a business career. She used her father's age and her own lack of confidence as excuses for not attending college (1979, 37). She may have realized that the University of Chicago was likely to steer her toward such domestic careers as teaching, nursing, and the new profession of social work, rather than writing. She must have recognized that Jewish professionals often worked in their own communities. Caspary had a larger scope in mind. Caspary used stenography to break into copy writing and then creative authorship. It is no accident that her first novel, *The White Girl*, is about an ambitious black woman who passes as white, or that Caspary places this protagonist in a shop much like her father's workplaces, with an owner who is to some extent a portrait of her father.[5] Vera herself "passed" as a good-girl office worker until she could pass on to a more Bohemian artist's life in the wider worlds of Chicago, New York, Hollywood, and Europe.

Caspary considered herself a non-practicing Jew. In reply to a query for a display on "The Jewish Woman Writer" in 1977, Caspary said, "I am quite without religion but definitely feel that I am Jewish" ("General Correspondence"). However she was conscious that prejudice operated within and without Jewish circles, and rejected both contexts. Her family saga, *Thicker than Water*, as autobiographical as many of her other novels, examines hierarchies of race and class within a Jewish community over several generations. She was quick to rebuke anti-Semitism. Early in her writing career Caspary rented a room in which to work temporarily. When the landlady revealed she had told the other boarders that Caspary was "only half Jewish," Caspary snapped back, "'What a pity,' I said, 'that it was the front half'" ("Working Draft," 41).

Caspary's core identity was as a writer. Many of her characters beyond Laura and Waldo also write, including Sara Collins' radio mysteries in *Murder at the Stork Club*, a false diary by the title character of *The Man Who Loved His Wife*, and the overall chroniclers of *Stranger than Truth* and *The Mystery of Elizabeth*. Even Bedelia constructs her own romance plots. The power of imaginative shaping ultimately allowed Caspary to focus her own life on a writing career in which she drew heavily from that life for fiction.

In her autobiography Caspary frames herself as the ultimate fictional character. At the beginning of her life story she describes a "specter" that she has tried to bury "in a closet smelling of old women's dresses." This is who she might have been, a "skinny girl shivering as the Chicago wind sweeps across the Wells Street station of the South Side El." This failed self is one whose life has been eaten up by family duty and dull subsistence though she longs for better things. "Saddest of all," Caspary writes, "She is a writer among those secretly writing in locked bedrooms the poem, the story, the novel that will never be published" (1979, 1–2).

At the end of her autobiography, Caspary again evokes this ghostly double who jeers at the successful writer. She concludes, "Everything good in my adult life has come through work: variety and fun, beautiful homes, travel, good friends, interesting acquaintances, the fun of flirtations and affairs, and best of all, the profound love that made me a full woman." Here Caspary may be bowing to her upbringing as well as thumbing her nose at those who thought she couldn't have both career and marriage. She closes by saying, "Those who come after us may find it easier to assert independence, but will miss the grand adventure of having been born a woman in this century of change" (1979, 281). Caspary was, to paraphrase Ida Cox, a woman wild enough not to live the blues. Because of her independent spirit, her fiction and self-portrait continue to champion self-supporting women even into the twenty-first century.

A.B. Emrys
Kearney, Nebraska
October 2005

Notes

I would like to thank the Friends of the Library, University of Wisconsin-Madison, for a grant-in-aid and the Research Services Council at the University of Nebraska-Kearney for their additional support, all of which enabled me to use the extensive library resources at the University of Wisconsin and thoroughly explore the Vera Caspary Papers archived at the Wisconsin Historical Society. I am also grateful to the Authors Guild for permission to quote from Caspary's works and unpublished manuscripts. The archive includes the drafts and revisions of *The Secrets of Grown-Ups*, which is far longer in manuscript than in its published version, as well as working drafts of Caspary's published works, business and fan correspondence, and unpublished scripts and other writing.

Except for the present Feminist Press editions, all of Caspary's books are out of print. Assorted editions of some are available from online booksellers, and some large libraries still have copies. *Laura* has been released on DVD, and the adaptation of *The Blue Gardenia*, Caspary's screen story of a lonely telephone company worker who may or may not have killed the company masher, is available on DVD, as is Caspary's screen adaptation of *A Letter to Three Wives*.

1. Caspary created three professional detectives: policeman Mark McPherson in *Laura*, insurance investigator Ben Cheney in *Bedelia*, and Joe Collins in the novella *Murder in the Stork Club* (also published as *The Lady in Mink*), who must clear his radio mystery-writer wife of suspicion. Caspary also read some mystery writers she liked, such as Cornell Woolrich and Frances Iles. She had met Dorothy B. Hughes, whom Caspary admired as "a blithe spirit, a hard-woking [sic] woman who wrote her books, kept house, raised three children and never complained of anything!" ("From Readers," 1981).

2. In a script not used, both Mark and Laura had voiceover narrations, paralleling Waldo's voice that still introduces the film (Preminger 1978, 77).

3. Some odd criticism has resulted from admiration for the glamorous picture of Tierney. The only book chiefly about Caspary's work, *"Laura" as Novel, Film, and Myth*, by Eugene McNamara, does contain insightful comments, especially on the film's production, but also dwells heavily on "myth." It is sometimes unclear whether the author has in mind the character of Laura in either novel or film, or Tierney, the picture of her, or the theme song.

4. I have seen the American script and read Ann Warren's comments on the British script. In both scripts Bedelia apparently is not pregnant, and takes poison left for her but not actually pressed upon her by Charlie.

5. The suicidal ending of *The White Girl* was the publisher's choice. Caspary's manuscript describes the protagonist picking up the pieces and getting on with her life ("Discards" 117–18).

Works Cited

Babener, Liahna. "De-feminizing *Laura*," in *It's a Print!: Detective Fiction from Page to Screen*, edited by William Reynolds and Elizabeth Trembley. Bowling Green, OH: Popular Press, 1994.

Bakerman, Jane S. "Vera Caspary's Chicago, Symbol and Setting." In *MidAmerica XI: TheYearbook of the Society for the Study of Midwestern Literature*, edited by David D. Anderson. East Lansing, MI: Midwestern Press, 1984.

———. "Vera Caspary's Fascinating Females: Laura, Evvie and Bedelia." *Clues*. 1.1: 46–52, 1980.

Caspary, Vera. "Laura." [catalogued as "Untitled Murder Story"]. Box 11. The Vera Caspary Papers. Film and Manuscript Archive, Wisconsin Center for Film and Theater Research, Wisconsin Historical Society, Madison, 1941.

———. "Laura, 1942, Synopsis." Box 5. The Vera Caspary Papers. Film and Manuscript Archive, Wisconsin Center for Film and Theater Research, Wisconsin Historical Society, Madison, 1942.

———. *Bedelia*. Philadelphia: Blakiston, 1945; New York: Feminist Press at the City University of New York, 2006.

———. "General Correspondence January 1946–June 1962–March 1980." Box 2. Folder 1. The Vera Caspary Papers. Film and Manuscript Archive, Wisconsin Center for Film and Theater Research, Wisconsin Historical Society, Madison, n.d.

———. Script of Recorded Interview [later used in *The Boston Herald*] by Dudley Fraser for Little, Brown & Company, 15 July 1950. Box 13. The Vera Caspary Papers. Film and Manuscript Archive, Wisconsin Center for Film and Theatre Research, Wisconsin Historical Society, Madison.

———. Letter to Joan Khan, December 31. "Correspondence from Readers 1957–58," The Vera Caspary Papers. Film and Manuscript Archive, Wisconsin Center for Film and Theater Research, Wisconsin Historical Society, Madison, 1960.

——. "My 'Laura' and Otto's." *Saturday Review*. 26 June 1971: 36–37.

——."Mark McPherson." In *The Great Detectives*, edited by Otto Penzler. Boston: Little, Brown, 1978.

——. *The Secrets of Grown-Ups*. New York: McGraw-Hill, 1979.

——. "Correspondence from Readers 1979–1981." Box 28. Folder 5. The Vera Caspary Papers. Film and Manuscript Archive, Wisconsin Center for Film and Theater Research, Wisconsin Historical Society, Madison.

——. *Laura*. Boston: Houghton Mifflin Co., 1943; New York: Feminist Press at the City University of New York, 2006.

——. "Discards and Rewritten Pages." *The Secrets of Grown-Ups*. Box 29. Folders 4, 12. The Vera Caspary Papers. Film and Manuscript Archive, Wisconsin Center for Film and Theater Research, Wisconsin Historical Society, Madison, n.d.

——. "Draft Article." Box 28. Folder 17. The Vera Caspary Papers. Film and Manuscript Archive, Wisconsin Center for Film and Theater Research, Wisconsin Historical Society, Madison, n.d.

——. "Screen Stories." Box 9. The Vera Caspary Papers. Film and Manuscript Archive, Wisconsin Center for Film and Theater Research, Wisconsin Historical Society, Madison, n.d.

——. "Women in Crime." Box 29. The Vera Caspary Papers. Film and Manuscript Archive, Wisconsin Center for Film and Theater Research, Wisconsin Historical Society, Madison, n.d..

——. "Working Draft 1927–1954." *The Secrets of Grown-Ups*. Box 29. Folders 3. The Vera Caspary Papers. Film and Manuscript Archive, Wisconsin Center for Film and Theater Research, Wisconsin Historical Society, Madison, n.d.

Caspary, Vera and George Sklar. "The Exiles." Box 10. The Vera Caspary Papers. Film and Manuscript Archive, Wisconsin Center for Film and Theater Research, Wisconsin Historical Society, Madison, n.d.

Caspary, Vera and George Sklar. *Laura: A Play in Three Acts*. New York: Houghton Mifflin, 1945.

Emrys, A.B. "*Laura*, Vera and Wilkie: Deep Sensation Roots of a Noir Novel." *Clues*. 23.3: 5–13, 2005.

Jackson, Kevin. *The Language of Cinema*. New York: Routledge, 1998.

Maio, Kathi. "Rebel With A Cause." Books. *Sojourner*. 12 January 1980.

McNamara, Eugene. *Laura as Novel, Film, and Myth*. Lewiston: Mellen, 1996.

Preminger, Otto. *Preminger: An Autobiography. Garden City, NY*: Doubleday, 1977.

Schloff, Linda Mack. "We Dug More Rocks: Women and Work." In *American Jewish Women's History: A Reader*, edited by Pamela S. Nadell. New York: New York University Press, 2003.

Warren, Ann L. *Word Play: The Lives and Work of Four Women Writers in Hollywood's Golden Age*. Ph.D. dissertation., University of Southern California, 1988.